The Pill

© 2021 by Caryn Hines, dba Whisphire
All rights reserved. Published 2021

Printed in the United States of America

www.thepilltrilogy.com

ISBN 978-0-9996748-0-2

Cover Design by BA Advertising Graphics, LLC
www.BAadgraphics.com

Graphic Design by Pique Publishing, Inc.
www.PiquePublishing.com

Library of Congress Control Number: 2020922397

To: Guy

Wishing you all the best,

The Pill

Caryn Hines

Caryn

Dedicated and grateful to:

The Lord, my husband Darryl Wyles, my brother Gary Hines, and sister-in-law, Annette Fearce

Special thanks to Evita Leonard, Willette Moch, Sonia Salmon-Gayle, Alexis Adams Brown, Charlene Brown, Robin Sullivan, Jill Collins, Todd Larson, Aime Alonzo-Serrano, Nadia Geagea Pupa, and Bernadette August—it truly takes a village

With special love and immense appreciation to my father William T. Hines

and my mother Bettye J. Hines—everything always is for you

Table of Contents

PROLOGUE

"This looks like a nice spot."

The top of the urn squeaked as Charles Henry Morninglory slowly unscrewed it. "Do you want to do it, or shall I?"

"Why don't you do a little, and I'll do the rest." Naomi shoved her hands further in her pockets and sank into her coat to avoid the freezing rain that spat ice at her.

The pair stood in silence on the curved pavement of the Tidal Basin. Chunks of ice and slush floated atop the furious ripples of the Potomac River. The threatening gray clouds hung low, mirroring Naomi's mood. Her dear father had once been a handsome man, but now his walnut-brown face was as deeply creased as the nut itself. Daddy had aged ten years in the three weeks since Mama died.

She lifted the burnished copper urn from her father's deeply veined, shaky hands and scattered the rest of her mother's remains into the Potomac River. They wordlessly watched the brownish-gray clumps fall onto the ice. Naomi bristled as the ashes darkened while moistening and seeping into the water. *Mama was so much more than this.*

"Well that does it." Mr. Morninglory gripped his daughter's arm and led her away from the walkway that hugged the reservoir. "It's too slippery around here. I don't want you to fall."

"Should we have some words or something?" Naomi resisted moving.

"I said mine. You can if you want to." He stood stoically, holding his daughter's arm tightly. "Your mama never believed that I loved her. Wasn't like it is now. All that mushy-gushy. Like the movies. I came home every day. That should have proved to her that I loved her."

"It did. She knows you loved her." Her father's wet wool coat scratched her skin as she nestled against him, shielding her face from the pricks of ice shards raining from the sky.

Mr. Morninglory smiled wanly at his daughter. "You look just like your mama when she was your age. Spitting image of her. Like I didn't have nothing to do with you at all. Like you got nothing but her genes." He stroked her face. His eyes widened as he focused on his daughter's beautiful countenance, bursting with blooming youth. "I wish I was young again. Young like you. The world...this world is for the young."

"You're just feeling blue, Daddy. This weather isn't helping."

"I'd do so many things differently. So many regrets. Too many. About the only thing I don't regret is you." He tapped his foot against the edge of the walkway, his eyes fixed on the wet, dark clumps of ash sinking further into the river. "I'd have told her 'I love you' at least one more time."

"She knew, Daddy. She knows."

"The house...is paid off. You'll find all of my papers in the upstairs closet."

"Come spring and the sun is shining, it's warmer, you'll feel better. Feel more like yourself." Naomi hugged him tighter. "Don't forget, we have a lot to look forward to this spring. My graduation...you'll be there, cheering loud enough for both you and Mama. I can see you now, just hollering out my name. Then, in a few years, after Haron and I finish our programs, we'll be getting married. You'll be walking me down the aisle. See, so many things for us to look forward to."

"No matter what, you finish your medical school. Keep pushing through. Be a good doctor. We love you." He stared through his daughter. "All right, then, let's get out of this weather. Let's get you back so you can finish studying."

"I already told you, most of the work now is just clinic. I have my notes to write up, but that won't take too long. I'd rather make sure you're all right."

She walked arm in arm with her father to the parking lot. He read her worried expression. "I'm all right, honey. Just old. Just tired and old." He lightly kissed his daughter on her cheek and leaned against the car door to close it.

"I'll call you later. Go home and get some rest." Naomi waved to her father. His face was gaunt. His vacant bluish-gray eyes sank into the folds that had once been his eyelids. His gait was frail and unsteady in a way she had not noticed before.

Daddy had always been quick to laugh and inspire laughter. A lightweight boxer in his youth, he had prided himself on controlling his physicality and demanding that his body respond as he wanted. The discipline of a boxer served him quite well after he met Mama and settled into a lifetime of working behind the counter at the post office on 17th Street.

Now, Daddy succumbed to his overcoat, allowing it to swallow him whole like a hungry gray wool python. Naomi fought the image of her father as a fading, frail man. She willed her vibrant Daddy back. She hated seeing him steeped and stooped in regret. If only she could bring back his youth.

It was a busy time for Naomi, but as she backed out of her parking spot, she vowed to spend more time with Daddy. She had just a few assignments left to finish before graduating from Howard University College of Medicine. After graduation, after she packed Haron for Boston, after she herself packed for Baltimore to start an advanced program in dermatology at the university there, then, yes, then there would be ample time for Daddy.

As her father stood in the parking lot, his gray plaid fedora low over his eyes, Naomi steered her car away and watched him shrink to the size of a frozen toy soldier. Daddy would be fine once she gave him more attention. Yes, all he needed was a little more care.

The doctors at Providence Hospital were wrong. Naomi recognized the intern with the shaggy, bushy hair as a student who graduated from Howard last year. The shaggy intern and the intake doctor tried to convince her that Daddy did not slip. The pathway along the tidal basin was icy. Daddy said so himself. What was he doing back there anyway? He didn't need to go back there, where they had scattered Mama's ashes. Naomi swore she thought she saw her father walk to his car and get in. The shaggy intern told her that there were no bruises on her father's body, that it was unlikely he had slipped and fallen.

Daddy knew she needed him. He would never leave her alone like that.

CHAPTER ONE

"Those damned greedy doctors." Naomi flipped the light switch of the lab of the Renew Your Youth Center, ignoring the black dark of the morning. "I could still be in bed if they weren't constantly trying to undermine me."

She thought about Dr. Ava Ellington, Director of New Patient Cultivation, and Dr. Lloyd Overbrook, Director of Regeneration Stabilization, the instigators of the coup. It had become the mantra she used to propel her from bed at four-thirty a.m. every day this week to lumber into the Center before everyone else so she could activate the start of the manufacture of the day's pills. She concocted a reason for Marlon, her driver, to stop picking her up in the morning to drive her to the Center, but instead requested that he meet her later at the Center to take her to off-site meetings and other errands. It was a lame reason, but it would have to suffice. It was a necessary protocol, since Naomi kept secret that she had installed in her right palm a chip that activated the dosage delivery machines.

Naomi held her palm firmly against one of the machines, aligning her chip with the magnetic strip. She glanced at the timer above each machine as it counted down the sixty seconds needed for the machines to start operating. They had underestimated her. Ellington and Overbrook. There was always a workaround, and Naomi had found it: install a mechanism for the dosage delivery machines so that she controls access to both the manufacture and the release of the medication for all of the patients.

Fifty-five seconds.

All they care about is more money. More patients meant more money for them. It didn't matter to them if the patients got the proper care. But it was her name, her invention, and she'd make damned sure to keep it that way. All they wanted were more patients in the Center. It wasn't about healing anymore.

Dermatologists were not true inventors, Naomi fumed remembering what *The New York Times* had written about her: *"Her talents were better suited at developing creams, serums, and lotions like the rest of her profession."* Just as Louis Pasteur had invented a vaccine to prevent polio, she invented a pill to reverse aging. People always said what she couldn't do and what she couldn't be. Just like in med school, the faculty overlooked anyone who wasn't on the surgical track. At Howard, the faculty had told her, "Black people didn't go to dermatologists and white people didn't go to black dermatologists." As a woman, they told her, podiatry was more family friendly. If she wanted to make a living as a doctor, pursue podiatry. Everyone had feet.

Forty-nine seconds.

Then there was Haron Fitzgerald—Harry. He made med school bearable. But even he wasn't enough when Mama died. When Daddy died. *If only they had lived to see me graduate. If Daddy could have held on just two more months. Daddy's sudden death on the heels of Mama's sudden death.* Naomi thought her grief would kill her, too. Harry loved her then. His stress with finishing school and trying to get his residency program squared away meant he couldn't cope with her grief. Somehow it strangled the joy out of their relationship. Harry needed—wanted—a dutiful, happy wife, beautiful and pliant to the crests of his career, not someone so somber, groping around in the depths of grief.

Forty seconds.

Just when Naomi had felt the fog of her grief was lifting, and it was safe to come up for air, Harry had accepted a residency at Harvard. He failed to mention Quinn—that Quinn pressured her mother's family of doctors to pull the strings. The triple blow—losing Mama, Daddy, and Harry one right after another—shattered her conviction to become a doctor. What was the point of studying advanced dermatology at the

University of Baltimore? What was the point of anything at all?

Naomi blinked away the past, hoping to send the memories flying, but they just alighted onto something else.

Thirty-two seconds.

Curtis Washington looked like the answer. He cloaked himself in kindness. Twenty-twenty is hindsight, but who knew you could divorce him but he wouldn't go away? A cocoa-brown albatross in a custom-made Italian suit. He was just like the recurring nightmare Naomi fought frequently where she is in med school and can't find her classroom, or the one in which she learned she had a class she never attended and she is short of the credits needed to graduate.

Just when life starts surging like Rock Creek after a heavy rainfall, the dream and Curtis pop up. Cunning and clever. So helpful in the beginning. Offered his willing arms of comfort after the death of Mama and Daddy, after Harry. When Naomi left medicine, Curtis knew she didn't know anything about the insurance business. But there he was at her desk every day with helpful suggestions. Older, knowledgeable, and confident, he righted her capsized ship and piloted it while she worked beside him. He didn't care that she was glum and didn't notice she was numb. Curtis mistook her grief as personality and delighted that he had someone to mold, to tell what to do. Naomi was just grateful and relieved that Curtis wanted to do all the thinking for her.

But eventually Naomi woke up—as if Mama and Daddy had shaken her from heaven, made her remember her promise to Daddy. They had invested too much time and money in their only child for her to throw medicine all away. Curtis was astute in discerning her winds of change, so he became indispensable. Paid off her medical school loans.

Twenty-five seconds.

Yes, he forecasted like a premonition that she was on to something. Sure, he had sold his mother's house to give her seed money to experiment with the regeneration therapy, but Naomi returned it all back to him in the divorce. It was a lot of money, and he would be sitting pretty, except that he used it to pay off his debts to everyone in the world. Curtis was better with other people's money than his own. He had many miserable traits but he one she admired—persistence. Since the courts had dismissed both suits he had filed to grab equity in the Return Your Youth Center, Curtis tried another tactic. He had perfected the art of guilt.

Guilt that he had taught her the insurance business. Guilt that he had sold his mother's house for her to start her business. Guilt that she had left him for Harry. Guilt that Curtis had taken her back, only for her to leave him again when he had an affair. Guilt that she had hit the stratosphere after they divorced. Guilt that she had been living her wildest dreams without him. But she was done with that. She was done with all that guilt. *Thank God that Harry is nothing like Curtis.*

Eighteen seconds.

So successful. Still so fine. Fifteen years had aged him to perfection. Harry's detour to Quinn, and hers to Curtis, were a minor hiccup in their path to reconciliation. Her secret supplications conjured Harry to his rightful place beside her. If she could wait just a few more hours...just a few more hours.

Three, two, one second...done.

Naomi wiped her sweaty palm across the pocket of her lab coat and watched the blue light course like blood through the body's veins, inching across the panels of the dosage delivery machines, signaling they were synchronized and fully operational. She clicked the light switch off and walked down the hall into the break room. She stood on the step stool as she reached in the cabinet for a box of Keurig coffee pods.

"Morning, Dr. Morninglory," a technician passed by the open door. "How're you doing today?"

"Good morning, Raoul. Fine. Everything's just fine."

*　　*　　*　　*

"Imagine that this little thing did all of this. It looks like a dot."
Raina Kastori, age seventy-two, held up the tiny blue pill. Her five-carat, cushion-cut flawless diamond ring sparkled in the stark light
of the examination room. She stared in amazement at her twenty-five-year-old reflection in the mirror. Her translucent honey-colored
skin glowed just as it had forty-seven years ago. The crow's feet at the
corner of her eyes had vanished. Her hair was voluminous and as dark
as coffee beans. She shed the thirty-five pounds she had gained from a
lifetime of raising her children. Her perfect eyesight restored.

Naomi nodded. "Yes, it's small, but very powerful." She moved to
the door. "Will you excuse me? I'll be right back." She darted down
the hall and rapped on Ava's open door. "Please take over for me in
Examination Room Three."

"I have an appointment in twenty minutes," Ava implored after
checking her schedule on her computer.

"Don't worry about that. Technically, since she's actually a patient
for New Patient Cultivation, she should be on your schedule. I'm sure
you'll find a way to wrap her up in time for your next appointment.
Oh, she also needs a reminder that her bill is overdue. The file is
loaded on the computer and she's waiting for you in Examination
Room Three."

Naomi walked away and disappeared into her office down the hall.

It was always like this with Naomi. Ava seethed, grabbing a pen
from the cup on her desk. Despite carefully organizing her daily
schedule to the minute, Naomi often deliberately wrecked it at a
moment's notice just to prove that she was in charge. Sure, she owned
the stupid Center, but she didn't own Ava.

"Mrs. Kastori? Dr. Ava Ellington." Ava shook the woman's
small, soft hand. "Dr. Morninglory had asked me to take over for
her. Another matter came up...suddenly." Ava tabbed to Raina's
computerized file and quickly perused it. Sure enough, Finance
flagged Raina's account.

"Oh, that's fine. I was just telling Dr. Morninglory that this little pill
is just a miracle." Raina swallowed and handed Ava an empty paper

cup. "Just look." Raina, transfixed in the mirror, rubbed her smooth, even honey-colored skin.

Ava crushed the paper cup in her fist and tossed it into the waste-can. "I take it that you are pleased with the results of the regeneration therapy."

"Oh, my goodness, yes. I really didn't believe it at first. But when I saw the gradual changes over these three months..." Raina spun in the mirror. "You know what? My period even returned. I can even have a baby?"

"Yes, if you were able to at twenty-five, you are able to now. Many of our patients opt to start families again."

"You know, my granddaughter is expecting. We could be pregnant together. Just amazing what this pill has done. And I can't believe that I'll stay this way. Forever."

"You will as long as you keep up your treatments—speaking of which, Mrs. Kastori, next week you'd be moving on to Dr. Overbrook for stabilization, except that..." Ava hated it when Naomi put her in this position. She was New Patient Cultivation, not Finance. And she had to tread lightly, because Naomi heralded Raina Kastori on the Renew Your Youth Center website and displayed her on the cover of the Center's latest brochure. If Raina caused a dust up withdrawing permission to use her likeness, Scobey in Communications would blame Ava, not Naomi. Nobody ever blamed Naomi. "When we tried to access the funds from your account, it denied the transaction."

"Oh, that. Yes, of course, I know. Just extend me for another week. You know, when they forced us out of our country, Switzerland tied our money up. My husband—the prime minister is there, working it out. You know, the prime minister and I are having...money troubles." Raina whispered *sotto voce*. "I'm sure the funds will be available soon."

"I'm afraid we did extend your services last week and again this week. Your last week's payment of $80,000 wasn't received, either. Combined with this week's payment, you're in arrears of $160,000. As much as we'd like to, we won't be able to schedule your next appointment until that's paid. Payment is due when services are rendered." Ava punctuated the statement with a well-practiced smile. "And if stabilization is not ongoing, as Dr. Morninglory no doubt explained during your initial consultation, you will experience a complete reversion to your present age—seventy-two, between twenty-four and forty-eight hours. It is of major concern because reversion can be very painful. For some, the shock to the body can lead to death."

"I remember that all too well." Raina twisted the large gold beads around her neck between her fingers. "If *you* can't extend me the courtesy of another week, then I must talk to someone who can. Where is Dr. Morninglory? I want to speak with her at once."

Ava wheeled her stool to the counter and paged through the staff schedules on the laptop. "It says here Dr. Morninglory is out."

"Out? Well, where is she?"

"It doesn't say." Ava smirked. *It figures, every two weeks or so, Naomi Morninglory disappears.* "It just says she's out."

CHAPTER TWO

Just before, Naomi always tingled. Being with Harry was the only time life did not revolve around her patients. Would she be able to calibrate Mrs. Hueng's regeneration therapy so that the sixty-four-year-old, first-time mother delivered healthy twins? Whether eighty-five-year-old Enrique Velasquez would be disciplined enough to return to the Center in time for his regeneration pill each week while on his worldwide comeback tour? Not to mention how regeneration affected the vocal quality of his voice. Would the rigors of touring lure him into the old habits, like the drugs that ended his career so many years ago?

Still haunted by Patria Wilson, the singer who had regained her gorgeous looks but that drugs had reduced her seven-octave voice to a croak, Naomi knew the limits of regeneration. And when her demanding patients didn't receive the miracle of their dreams, the desperation that gripped them often resulted in death. She sighed, thinking about how Mr. Velasquez's undiminished glee resisted her warning to manage his expectations. The idea of reliving his heyday outweighed her caution. Regenerating was not a panacea for everything.

But these and all of Naomi's other worries evaporated when Harry moved his strong caramel hands across her body, instantly transporting her from their lives into his.

"How long are you going to be, Dr. Morninglory?" Marlon sliced through her thoughts when he halted the car in front of the Mandarin Oriental Hotel.

Naomi wished Marlon understood that being her bodyguard and driver did not entitle him to also run her life. "A few hours." She grabbed her white alligator Birkin bag.

Marlon opened the door. "Doctor, it is two-forty-three now. You know rush hour is starting, and I can't get you back to the meeting on the other side of town in a half an hour. It's going to take longer than that. I need at least an hour to get through the traffic."

Naomi waved dismissively at Marlon.

"Angenois yells at me when you're late for the five-thirty senior staff meeting," Marlon admonished, seeking to avoid another upbraiding from Bertrand Angenois, Chief Operating Officer at the Renew Your Youth Center, like the one he received the last time he had delivered Naomi back to the Center behind schedule.

"Don't worry. If we're late, I'll handle Bertrand Angenois."

Marlon frowned and furrowed his brow, pressing the door closed.

Naomi briskly walked away from the car, stopped at the revolving door of the Mandarin Oriental Hotel, and turned back to her bodyguard. "Okay, okay. I'll be down at four-thirty. Good enough?"

Marlon nodded from the driver's seat and drove off.

Naomi's Gucci stilettos clicked against the russet, mustard, and cream-colored patterned marbled floor as she darted through the orange-blossom-fragranced lobby. Once she reached the elevator banks, she pushed the 'up' arrow button and dialed her phone with a single push of her French-manicured finger.

"Hey, I'm downstairs in the lobby."

"Hey, baby. I'm on the seventh floor. Room 7211."

Naomi loved the Mandarin, as its sumptuousness appealed to her senses. The hotel staff, well-rewarded by both her and Harry for their discretion, devised ways to divert the paparazzi whenever Naomi was expected. The staff who were acquainted with her and Harry's mid-afternoon trysts always welcomed and guarded her like an old friend. But she still preferred her own house, where she cooked for Harry, plying him with his favorite dishes or introducing her favorites to him, enjoying his satisfaction, pretending he was all hers.

Then, after a gratifying meal, their souls entwined in earthly passion. She loved to watch Harry dress, imagining it was the start of their day together and would end just as it began—in each other's arms. Instead, Naomi luxuriated in Harry's vapor—the musk he left on her sheets that lingered for days.

At home, Harry ran Naomi's comb through his salt-and-pepper curls and rubbed her lotion into his blemish-free skin, returning to Quinn, thoroughly imprinted with Naomi's aroma. While Harry was here, he starred in her inside life. Being one of the most famous and wealthiest women on earth caused a duality in Naomi—her inside and outside life. Harry stood as buffer between her and the public, where hordes of people angled to reach her for something: for the wealthy, to get moved up on the list to undergo her regenerative therapy; for the applicants, jockeying to become one of her well-paid employees; for the business person, to learn the secrets of what was in "the pill"; or for the lucky, to be a lottery winner and receive her therapy at no cost.

Harry quieted her inside life and calmed her. She trusted him. He firmly planted his strength at her gate, preventing access by the endless distant relatives and long-forgotten acquaintances who insisted she invest in their latest invention or rescue them with a financial infusion. That's not what Harry wanted. Harry wanted *her*. Naomi relaxed with Harry, her lab partner from Howard University School of Medicine, some eighteen years ago. True, Harry had married his mother's choice, Quinn, and moved with her to Boston, where he had finished an anesthesiology residency program and earned a Harvard law degree. But that was a long time ago.

It took only four minutes for Harry to walk down the aisle of the auditorium after Naomi presented a TED Talk that changed her life. Over dinner that night, four years ago, Harry had confessed and professed he had never stopped loving her. His marriage to Quinn had been an orchestrated performance he no longer wished to star in. After his youngest son went off to college, he would leave Quinn. Would she leave Curtis?

Traveling so frequently for his businesses as an anesthesiologist, attorney, expert witness, author, and lecturer, Harry spent too much of his time in hotels. Naomi, too, traveled frequently as a much-sought-after conference speaker, but she rocketed back to D.C. Now, with the pressure of daily activating the dosage delivery machines, she could never be away from the Renew Your Youth Center for more than twenty-four hours. Their hectic paces meant that she rarely had Harry all to herself. When she did, she wanted their time together to feel special—not like an antiseptic extension of work. No, meeting in a hotel wasn't ideal, but at least it was something.

Harry straddled between the threshold of the hotel room and the corridor, waiting for Naomi to disembark from the elevator. The doors opened. "Didn't take you very long." He didn't look up from texting.

"I was very motivated." She gently pushed him inside the room and closed the door behind them.

"So was I." He thrust his phone into his shorts pocket. He scooped her up in his arms and buried his nose in the large dark-brown curls that tumbled over her shoulders. He inhaled deeply. "You can't believe how glad I am to see you. How much I missed you." He slowly kissed her on her temples and traversed his mouth gently across her face to her waiting lips. He lightly wet them with his tongue, while his fingers busily unbuttoned her emerald-green silk shirt. Like a leaf, it wafted to the ground.

"You knew I was coming back early. I like this." Harry admired Naomi's intricately laced black bra. "But I like it better this way." He unhooked it, releasing her flesh. Her nipples stiffened. "*They* like it better this way, too." He covered one breast with his mouth and flicked his tongue against the point.

She uttered a soft moan. "What they like, what I like is this..." Her hand brushed against the bulge in his khaki shorts. "I can see we are all in agreement." She unzipped her metallic navy linen Prada skirt and stepped out of it.

"I got a little something for you." He leaned over the king-size bed and retrieved a bottle of warming massage oil. "Roll over." He squirted the liquid on her back, and his thumb and fingers found muscles she didn't even know she had. As the heating sensation intensified, he parted her buttocks with his tongue and fingers. Jolted, she tried to move beneath him, but he held her firmly, timing his rhythmic tongue and finger pulsations to her labored breaths.

"Ah, shit!" Naomi shouted several times, escalating her voice to a feral scream. Barely able to recover, she turned and lay on Harry's glistening chest. "Your turn."

"I only want to pleasure you."

"Bullshit." She grinned widely, holding his growing penis in her hand. She angled herself on top of him and sat on it. It glided easily in the moistness between them. She squeezed him, undulating, as he breathed heavily and reached for the headboard. His hazel eyes squinted as his tears mixed with the sweat on his face. In one final thrust, his explosion saturated the bed.

Naomi dropped beside him. Both were unable to move.

"That's worth coming home early for." Harry laughed and kissed her cheek.

"How is Yale?"

"The boys like it. I don't think they see very much of each other, between Langston's freshman summer prep class and Dubois juggling his summer job in New Haven with his varsity football practice. They have very busy lives. I felt like they had to squeeze me in." He absently kissed her breasts.

"How is Quinn?" She tugged hard on his salt-and-pepper curls.

Harry rolled away from her and hugged a pillow. "Good. She's good."

The intimate delight that undulated through the air in the room diffused into staleness appropriate for visiting strangers. On cue, Harry's cellphone rang, and he leaned from the bed to retrieve his shorts on the floor, quickly finding his phone. "What time is your flight?" He glanced at his watch. "Delta 3756. Five-forty-seven p.m. No, no problem. I...I was just finishing up. I'll meet you at the gate. Okay. Bye."

Naomi kicked Harry under the covers.

"Don't be upset. Hey, listen, this was nice, wasn't it?" He gripped her leg between his.

"Early, my ass. This is the reason why you didn't want to meet at my house? Because we're closer to Reagan National here."

"She changed her flight. Quinn was supposed to come home tomorrow, but I had a feeling she would do this. I think she suspects that things aren't quite over between us." He threaded his arms through the brightly colored madras shirt and hurriedly buttoned it.

"Well, she's right. When are you going to tell her that you're moving out?" She tucked her emerald silk blouse into the navy linen skirt.

"Baby, give me a little bit more time." He playfully pulled the blouse out of her skirt, bent down, and kissed her flat cinnamon stomach. "I'll tell her in my own way, in my own time. Be patient. Please." His dazzling white smile, revealing deeply dimpled cheeks, never ceased to conquer her defenses.

"I've been patient. Four years is patient enough."

"I will tell her."

"I kept my end."

"I know you did, baby. It's just that my end is a little bit more complicated than yours."

"Now, Harry. Don't put it off any longer."

"I'm going to tell her. How could I not? I love you too much." He embraced her, kissed her ear, and then closed the door behind him.

*   *   *   *

"Like this..." Bertrand Angenois gently gripped the child's shoulder and turned her toward him as he kicked the soccer ball. Angeliqua shook her head, her braids swatted against her face.

"Kick it toward that side of the field. With the side of your foot." Bertrand demonstrated, and the ball gently rolled past Angeliqua. "Why not?" he continued. "Keep your legs loose. Don't lock your knees. You gotta to be ready to run." He rocked back and forth, lifting his feet up. He wiped the beads of sweat from his face with a hand towel.

"Look, Mr. Bertrand—this way?" Dekka gave the ball a powerful kick, and it flew past Angeliqua and Relia.

"Good, Dekka. Practice together." Bertrand drew an invisible circle in the air between Angeliqua, Dekka, and Relia. All at once, the fourth-graders swarmed to the left side of the field.

"Oh, shit," Bertrand muttered under his breath as he sprinted to the swarm. He pushed into their midst and found two tumbling girls in the grass. He grabbed the flailing brown arms and pulled one girl off of the other. "Stop it, stop it! We didn't come here for this! What's going on?" His large dark-chocolate hands held each girl firmly by their necks.

"She tore my shirt!" N'dreishia screamed as tears streamed down her smooth ebony cheeks.

"She called me a bitch!" Shequillah countered. "I ain't no bitch!"

"She said I eat pussy." N'dreishia was unable to wrestle from Bertrand's strong arm to get to Shequillah.

"Okay, okay. That's enough. What's this beef about? It must be more than some silly name-calling."

The girls went silent. N'dreishia fidgeted with the threads hanging from the hem of her torn purple shirt. Shequillah stared angrily at Bertrand. Her chest was heaving, and her light-brown face was bruised and red.

"Quickly, I don't have all day," Bertrand's voice boomed between them.

Silence hung in the air as the crowd of girls stood still and stared. Bertrand's brow furled. "What's this standing around for? We're not watching the tele—we're at practice. There's no standing in practice. Laps with high knees around the field. Get moving. Now." He loosened his grip on N'dreishia and Shequillah. "Hey, I thought you two were friends. Last year, every time I saw you, you two were inseparable. Now, you're trying to kill each other. What's this all about?"

N'dreishia looked down and mashed her neon green-clad toe in the grass. "I *was* her friend but now all she want to do is be with Chrysanthemum. She act like she don't want to be my friend no more since Chrysanthemum moved into the neighborhood."

"Is she here, Chrysanthemum?" Bertrand quizzed the girls looking toward the other girls who were lapping around the field. Ever since he started the Lady Bobcats Soccer Club for girls in Congress Heights, the players were constantly joining and departing the team. With this revolving door of members, Bertrand was never really sure who was in the club or on the field.

Shequillah's braids flew across her face as she shook her head. "That's because Chrysanthemum is *my* friend. She more of a friend than you ever been."

"Enough!" Bertrand wiped his towel across his face and turned toward the gawking runners. "Never mind what's happening here, you concentrate on your laps. I said high knees and I meant it! Pick those knees up!" He turned back to the two girls, put his arms around them and pushed them into a huddle. "Listen, on this field, you are on the same team. You can't be fighting each other, because you got to use your energy to fight *them*." He pointed toward the other side of the field. "Teammates are sisters. Teammates are blood. It doesn't matter what went on before you came onto the field, because the only thing that matters is, you have to work together to win. You gotta have her back. And *you* gotta have *her* back. Together."

The girls squirmed to get out of his grip. Shequillah hunched her shoulders and refused to look at N'dreishia. Bertrand released them and stepped back. "Tell me something. Is it possible for you to have more than one friend?"

Shequillah looked down. Her hands were firmly on her hips, her arms akimbo.

"I'm speaking to you," Bertrand snapped. "Look at me when I'm talking."

The child raised her dark brown eyes to meet Bertrand's. "Yes, I guess so."

He turned to N'dreishia. "And you, maybe you need to widen your circle a bit. Are there other girls you have something in common with?"

N'dreishia pressed her lips out in defiance.

"Look, you have a whole field full of girls who just might like to get to know you better. But this...this gotta stop. We are all counting on each other. We're a team. Feel me?" He held out his fist.

After what felt like an eternity, N'dreishia hit his fist with hers. Bertrand's stare bored holes into Shequillah's unrelenting cinnamon-colored skin. Finally, Shequillah hit N'dreishia's fist, and then Bertrand's.

"All right, since you like to fight so much, fight this ball." He threw the ball in the air, and it landed at N'dreishia's feet. He pointed toward a corner of the field. "Drills. The two of you over there for the rest of practice." He shifted his gaze toward the lappers. "Come on, Lady Bobcats, enough playing around! This ain't no shopping trip! We got a game to play on Saturday, so get to work!" He clapped his hands loudly as he ran toward the girls.

A curvaceous woman the color of hot griddlecakes dripping with butter sauntered slowly onto the field. "Hi, Mr. Bertrand. I guess I'm a little early in picking up Shequi. I mean Shequillah."

"Hi, Sheila, I call her Shequi, too. Otherwise she reads me the riot act."

Sheila laughed. "Yeah, she's been known to do that."

"You've got yourself quite a little athlete there. I'm going to make her goalie for the next game."

"I'm sure it's all thanks to your good coaching."

Sheila stood close to Bertrand, who stepped back. "Well, we're not done yet. So why don't you come back in an hour?" He turned his back to her and headed toward a cluster of girls.

"Oh, is it okay if I just sit right here and wait for practice to be over?" Sheila called to him. "I like to watch." She removed the six-pack of bottled water from the folded chair and placed it on the grass.

"Sure. Make yourself comfortable. But we might be a while. We still got some drills to do."

"Take your time, I don't mind. I like the view."

CHAPTER THREE

"I think it's a dumb idea." Naomi walked in front of Bertrand, cutting him off in the hallway as he attempted to step in tandem with her.

"You think any idea that doesn't originate with you is dumb." Bertrand checked the time on his watch. "I just think that going on patient rounds each week with a doctor keeps me informed from a ground-up perspective. My way of being able to respond from a well-rounded point of view. It also allows me to see how each doctor conducts the patient appointments. It may help me streamline the operation. Shave a few minutes off of these appointments. Make things more efficient."

"That's what makes us a premier facility. Attention to patients." Naomi snorted.

"That's what makes us unable to handle more patients. We can all be more concerned about efficiency. Don't you think?"

"Then can't you make me last? After you've had a chance to observe all the other doctors?"

"Stop trying to get rid of me, Dr. Morninglory. This week, for better or worse, you're it. Shall we?" He held the door open for her, revealing an obviously gleeful Caprice Deveaux in the examination room.

"Good morning, Ms. Deveaux. I'm Naomi Morninglory." The doctor held out her French-manicured hand for Caprice to shake. Bertrand followed her and closed the door behind them.

"Oh, Dr. Morninglory, I've waited so long. It is an honor to finally be here. To meet you." Caprice squirmed excitedly in her seat.

"This is Bertrand Angenois, our Chief Operating Officer," Naomi motioned toward Bertrand. "This is his week to do rounds with me so that he can stay current with the needs of our patients. You don't mind if he sits in during our visit, do you?"

"I promise you won't even notice that I'm here." Bertrand smiled, nodded, and sat in the seat beside the door.

"Not at all. In fact, I think today is my lucky day." Caprice eyed Bertrand as if he could renew her youth all by himself.

"Mine, too." He smiled widely.

"Mine, three." Naomi glanced at Bertrand and turned back to Caprice. "Now, just relax. In your first appointment, we are just going to talk. Did you bring anyone with you? Is there someone in the waiting room? I ask because we generally advise patients to have a loved one, or someone they trust, sit in the first session. It is hard to remember everything we discuss, and, although the disclosures in your contract, and on our website, spell things out pretty clearly, people often miss things or forget things. Having a trusted loved one present during the visit can help you remember things as they come up."

Caprice listened patiently to Naomi and then fixed her gaze on Bertrand.

Bertrand smiled. "Don't worry. I'm also a medical professional, a nurse, so feel free to share your medical information. Your health concerns." He leaned back in the chair and crossed his arms.

Caprice turned her attention to Naomi. "No, I'm alone. I mean, my husband didn't travel with me. It's all hogwash to him. But he indulges me. We can proceed. Honestly, I don't need anyone else. I read the disclosures. I think I understand everything. I'm ready to begin, Doctor."

"Okay." Naomi touched the computer screen on the wall. "Well, from our initial screening, it looks like you are an excellent candidate for the regenerative therapy."

"Regenerative therapy? It's the same as 'Renew Your Youth'?"

"Exactly. 'Renew Your Youth' is the brand name; 'regenerative therapy' is what it is. Much like 'Advil' is ibuprofen."

"Gotcha. So, you really think I'm a good candidate?"

Naomi nodded and slid her thumb across the screen of the wall, displaying an array of pictures of patients before and after their therapy. "In addition to maintaining HIPAA guidelines, we keep the names of our patients confidential, so you don't have to worry that we will expose you to the public. These are a few of our patients who have undergone the therapy and granted us permission to display their pictures.

"Let me explain how regenerative therapy works. First, you decide on an optimal age. For example, this person is sixty-eight, and she selected twenty-seven as her optimal age. For three months, we work on regenerating you back to that age, and then, once you have reached it, every week for the rest of your life you come into the Center for the pill. During the transition period you will experience tremendous pain, such as stomachaches, headaches, and joint pain. Bear in mind, everyone is different. That pain does eventually subside. We discourage the use of painkillers, because it may change the effectiveness of the pill. If the pain gets too bad, an occasional ibuprofen, aspirin, or some other over-the-counter pain reliever may be taken."

"However," Bertrand interjected, "we caution that you use even these pain relievers sparingly. Our studies have shown that even over-the-counter pain relievers may dilute the pill's effectiveness."

Naomi pursed her lips. "Then, at the end of the three-month period, you will be your optimal age. See, this person looks like she did at twenty-seven."

"Incredible." Caprice clasped her hands together.

"Yes, it is pretty amazing." Naomi touched the wall again, and the screen disappeared. "I would be happy to answer any questions you may have."

"What kind of pill is it? I mean, what's in it?"

"The ingredients are a trade secret. But it is a combination of synthetic and natural compounds that cause cells to rapidly divide, to the point that they mimic a certain desired age between twenty-one and forty-nine. We do a comprehensive examination of you from extracting samples of all of your bodily fluids, skin samples. We review pictures of you at your optimal age and reconstruct your body so that we can regenerate you to that time by replenishing deficiencies that caused aging. These deficiencies are synthesized into a customized pill form."

"Gobbledygook! I'm just glad it works! Why do I have to come into the office to take the pills? Can't I just get a prescription and take them at home?"

Naomi stood leaning against the cabinets in the examination room. "Well, it is a two-pronged answer. One, we want to monitor you closely during the regenerating process to make sure you are doing all right. Obviously, something this powerful may affect you in unpredictable ways, so we want to stay on top of that. Every week at the Center, we take your vitals and samples of your bodily fluids, and, depending on the severity of your side effects, we can offer some solutions. Make adjustments, as needed."

Bertrand interrupted. "In fact, we have a whole department dedicated to alleviating the side effects. Dr. Van Stritton is the department head, and it's called the 'Collaborative Treatment and Severe Reaction Department.'"

Naomi shot Bertrand a silencing glance and continued. "As I was saying, the second reason is, quite frankly, to prevent our competitors from reverse-engineering the drug to see what our ingredients are."

"But, Doctor, they already know. I've seen your competitors' advertisements on late-night television. I've seen 'Young Again' and 'Always Young.'"

Bertrand rose, walked toward the computer screen, and touched it lightly. "I'd like to answer that...if I may, Dr. Morninglory. Legally they have no authority to do those advertisements. We are the only legitimate age-reversing company that exists in the market today. You may notice that we don't advertise, because we don't have to. Between the publicity and word of mouth, we are filled to capacity. As your experience tells you, it can take between three to five years to even get an appointment. There is a reason why you didn't choose them, isn't it? We can boast that our results are 100% effective, and no other regenerative therapy company can come close to that. I believe our closest competitor, 'Always Young,' has a success rate of thirty-eight percent. We have the most effective regenerative therapy service and offer a comprehensive maintenance program to ensure that you get and maintain your optimal age. We offer a premium service for a premium clientele. Our patients never go through this alone. Each patient is given 'round-the-clock access to a doctor who can assist them in the regenerative process. We know it can be scary and want you to know you have nothing to fear." He took Caprice's hand and held it.

"I-I-I'm n-n-not afraid," Caprice stammered.

"But you don't have to take our word for it. I'm sure while you were waiting for your appointment you did your homework."

"Yes, I did. I suspect that a few friends underwent this therapy, but they're not saying. You know how Hollywood is. One woman who looked sixty-one now looks like she's twenty-two. I read all the information I could get on it. The anonymous reviews were highly complimentary. But, I do have a question."

Bertrand cocked his head. "Shoot."

Naomi cleared her throat and cut her eyes at him.

"What if I decide, say, after ten years or so, that I no longer want to continue with the therapy?"

Naomi exited the computer, and the screen vanished from the wall. "We ascribe a maturation phase program to you, where you are given another pill to ease your return to the age you actually are. It takes a shorter period of time—about six weeks. But, of course, everyone is different. Without the maturation medication, and, say, you reverse cold turkey to your actual age, it can be quite painful, and we don't recommend it. "

"Is there an extra cost to enter into the maturation phase program?"

Bertrand leaned forward in his seat. "Presently, it's included in the cost of your treatment. But we are reorganizing our payment structure, so it is good possibility that that may change."

"The pamphlet—the website list some side effects. Can you give me more information about that?"

Naomi pulled her white lab coat closed to cover her cobalt blue St. John suit and crossed her feet so that her black patent Ferragamo flats touched. "Of course. This is why I like to have a loved one present during the consultation. People often are so excited that they don't actually hear the information about the side effects. It helps to have an interested party with you listening. First, let me say that every day we are making inroads in eliminating, or at least alleviating, the side effects associated with the regenerative therapy.

"Second, regeneration is not an exact science, and it is evolving every day. As I said before, everybody is different, and, consequently, so are the side effects. After years of study, what we have gleaned is, it seems to affect some aspect of your core makeup. Let me explain. It can be as simple as affecting your sense of humor, and the things that you found funny before are not what you find funny during the therapy. Now, that may seem small, but that can have a disastrous effect on your social relationships, friendships, marriages.

"I've also seen it affect singers' voices, changing the quality, tone, range. Doctors, lawyers, business professionals, actors…I've seen it impair their cognitive function, their memory. I emphasize this because you may regenerate to your optimal age but lose your earning capacity because you are unable to remember. I know you were an actress in the movies years ago. I remember some of your pictures. What are your plans after you regenerate?"

Caprice tucked a curl behind her ear. "Well, now I work with my husband in real estate. But once I regenerate, I want to return to my acting career. I worked with all the big names from the time I was twenty-three to about thirty-nine. After thirty-nine, all my offers dried up. The only offers I received were as someone's mother. Some of the men playing my sons were older than I was. I'm fifty-eight, and they say now I'm too old to even play a grandmother. Can you imagine? I haven't been able to get a decent role in years. It's so depressing.

If I regenerate to twenty-two, I can return to acting in the kind of roles I do best. But this time, I'm wiser and have so much more life experiences to pour into my roles. It's funny, I still feel young on the inside. I don't feel any different than I did when I was twenty-two. Now, I want to be young on the outside...again."

"I see. Well, I'm glad that regenerative therapy is available to you to help you fulfill your dream. As mentioned in the disclosures, other side effects may include heart conditions, chronic diarrhea, organ fatigue, such as kidney and/or liver malfunctions. And I have to stress that there is no way of knowing how you will be affected. You, of course, may be one of the lucky ones and only experience something like blurred night vision or accelerated growth of your fingers and toenails."

"Doc, I know it's a roll of the dice, but I'll do anything to get my life back."

"Any other questions?"

"No, I don't think so. I'm convinced. Doc, can I ask you a personal question?"

"Sure."

"Do you 'regenerate'? You look too young to be so accomplished. I was expecting a much older woman."

"You're too kind. I thank my parents for their good genes. But no, I am not undergoing regenerative therapy. I'm often asked that. Because I'm so busy concentrating on my patients' health, I can't risk experiencing any of the side effects. I want to make sure that I am able to give you the best care possible." Naomi smiled.

"Okay, Doc, I'm ready to take the plunge. What's next?"

"That's what we like to hear. Sounds like you are ready to sign up. If you go out of the hall to the left, a nurse will escort you to the Finance Department so that you can get started. Thank you for choosing us to go on this exciting age-reversing journey with you."

She shook Caprice's hand. Bertrand opened the door and followed Naomi out.

"I hope to see *you* again." Caprice shook Bertrand's hand and held it.

"There's a good chance of that."

Naomi and Bertrand watched Caprice sashay down the white linoleum floor. Her pale-pink silk gossamer pants flowed with each movement of her hips. Her matching Manolo Blahniks treaded lightly on each tile.

Naomi elbowed Bertrand sharply in the ribs. "Stop flirting with the patients. One of these days, one of them is going to take you seriously."

"I hope they do."

Astrid met Naomi in the hallway with a printout of her schedule. "Dr. Morninglory, the make-up artist is in your office. Lesley Stahl is due at one p.m. Mr. Steinberg is also working in your office until *60 Minutes* arrives. He said he wanted to go over a few things before your interview, and also has some documents for you to sign. Oh, Doctor, Mr. Polk demands to see you, but you don't have time before your *60 Minutes* interview."

"That's all right. I'll see him. Please put him in Examination Room 4."

The bespectacled face of the elderly man's skin folded like a Shar-Pei. He sat fully clothed on the examination table, nervously dangling his feet.

"Hi Mr. Polk. Are you feeling okay? Is there something wrong?"

"Yes, yes, there is. Dr. Morninglory, I am eighty-four years old, and I earned all of these years. I am a God-fearing man, and I don't like to be mistreated," he huffed.

"Sir, has someone mistreated you? I will speak to them at once."

"I worked for many years as a clerk for the Federal Government. I should have been made a supervisor, but it never happened. They passed me over for a promotion for forty-three years. I couldn't even get a promotion when I transferred to the janitorial staff. They said then I was overqualified. All because I'm a black man. I ended up training my supervisors time and time again. Smarter than all of them, and I still got passed over."

"Yes. I'm sure that was very difficult. Mr. Polk, what can I help you with?" Naomi patiently sat down across from the examination table.

The thin man hunched forward. Tears welled in his eyes. "I don't know if I should regenerate to thirty-three years old. I don't have any family. All my friends are dead. I'll just be young and alone. I was only doing it because I thought I could take care of myself better if I was younger. It would make it easier to go up and down the steps, to go to the grocery store, if I was younger. I sold everything I own, including my house, in order to get this therapy. The way I figure it, I have enough money for two years of this stuff, maybe three. This is the last day I can decide under my contract to get this price. Tomorrow is my birthday and the price goes up when I turn eighty-five. What do you think I should do, Doctor?"

Naomi laid her hand on Mr. Polk's gnarled knuckled hand. The elderly man reminded her of her father who now would have been around Mr. Polk's age, if he had lived. "Mr. Polk, you're the only one who can make that decision. This may be a chance for you to start something new. If you regenerate, you can get out more and meet new people, learn new things, perhaps do some things you weren't able to do during those forty-three years that you were working. Do you like to travel? Maybe join a travel club? "

"Oh, I don't know. Not with these aching knees, and I move so slow, I could never keep up."

"Mr. Polk, did your knees ache when you were thirty-three?"

"No, no, ma'am, they didn't."

"Mr. Polk, then, after you regenerate, they won't hurt anymore."

"They won't?"

"No, sir, they won't. I tell you what. Why don't you take some more time to decide? I will contact the Finance Department and tell them we are extending your decisional period for thirty more days. Who is the doctor assigned to your case?"

Mr. Polk rummaged through a brief case full of crumpled papers. He pulled one out and smoothed it. He read the paper out loud: "A Dr. Ava Ellington."

"Have you had a chance to talk to her?"

"Yeah, but I...I don't think she understands what I was saying."

Dr. Morninglory pulled a business card from the pocket of her smock. She scribbled her number on it. "Okay, here is my cell number. If you have any more concerns about the therapy, we can talk about it. Just give me a call, okay?"

"Okay."

"Happy birthday, Mr. Polk."

"Thank you, Dr. Morninglory."

CHAPTER FOUR

Mortena Schminsky was always beautiful. As a baby, her peaches-and-cream complexion, her hazel eyes flecked with turquoise, her frothy strawberry-blonde curls, and her easy smile melted all of the hearts in her small farming town seventy-five miles outside of Kansas City, Missouri. In fact, one of her earliest memories was toddling down an aisle of Sears & Roebuck, clinging tightly to her mother's pant leg, because every few feet strangers stopped and smiled at the beautiful baby. Rottredge and Aurora Schminsky, as all parents do, believed their baby was special but didn't quite see what all of the hullabaloo was about.

Aurora, a bookkeeper, concentrated on stretching the dollars she and Rottredge earned at their gas station and convenience store, so they could cover the needs of her husband, their two daughters Monika and Mortena, and finally herself. Aurora owned five acres of land on which Rottredge planted corn after he finished working as a mechanic at the gas station. She didn't understand or couldn't be bothered with the attention Mortena received. More and more, Aurora found herself asking everyone to stop telling the child that she was beautiful. "It's going to her head and making her think she's more than she is." Aurora thought out loud often within Mortena's young earshot.

More so, Aurora hated the ways Mortena preened and posed at the compliments of strangers. "Being beautiful ain't going to put no food on the table or money in the bank," she drilled into both of her daughters. "Just make sure you're clean, be polite, and study hard, so that you can earn enough to stand on your own two feet. Besides, beauty is nothing you can count on, because it fades."

From the time she entered kindergarten, Mortena received much attention. Attention from boys who liked her and pulled her strawberry-blonde curls and pushed her on the playground. Attention from girls who either wanted her in their group to attract attention from boys or did not want her in their group because she detracted attention from them. Attention from the teachers who thought anyone this beautiful deserved good grades, and attention from the other teachers who doubted anyone this beautiful had a brain so she deserved bad ones.

Mortena basked in the adulation of her admirers and believed their praise was well placed. Aurora had hoped her lessons would anchor her daughter, but instead they buoyed her daughter, as she floated to the waiting arms of her constant stream of admirers.

But Aurora was not the only family member that wished Mortena would get over herself. Monika, eight years older than her sister, had the same flawless clear complexion, hazel eyes flecked with turquoise, and strawberry-blonde curls, but somehow, they were arranged in a way that didn't inspire. Indeed, she was lovely, but standing next to Mortena, her beauty vanished. Monika seethed silently around Aurora and Rottredge, who hoisted Mortena's care upon Monika's small shoulders as they concentrated on juggling their multiple businesses. Monika despised the attention Mortena received and hated that it had become her responsibility to field the onslaught of questions from Mortena's onlookers:

"Who really cares what she likes to eat?"

"No, she didn't get her hair from her mother, but did you notice we have the same hair?"

"No, our parents don't have those color eyes."

"Yes, our eyes are beautiful, and I think so every time I look in the mirror."

Monika's envy metastasized, torturing Mortena in tangible and intangible ways: glass in her food, hair remover in her shampoo, glue on her bed pillow, all the while teasing Mortena that she was stupid and insignificant. Mortena learned how to fight because her older, stronger sister tried to smother her in her sleep with a pillow. Mortena learned how to take a punch from the times her sister threw her off the bed, and how to give a punch from the times her sister refused her admittance in the bathroom. As Mortena matured, she learned many things from her sister's envy: one, to distrust girls, in general; and two, to distrust Monika, in particular.

So, at thirteen, Mortena decided that beauty was a currency she could leverage. She could sing and dance a little, but mostly her gift was a love affair with the camera. She daily pestered her parents until finally, when she was fifteen, Aurora and Rottredge relented and signed the consent form for her to compete in the Junior Miss Maize pageant. "Can't hurt," Rottredge reasoned, "and it might even help me sell this year's entire corn crop."

Mortena finished second.

Undeterred, for the next two years Mortena cajoled local business owners to contribute to the pageant expenses Aurora refused to cover. This time, Mortena entered into the Junior Miss Missouri pageant, and, among a sea of corn-fed beauties, she won, receiving a trophy, a $500 scholarship, and a year of lessons with the famed pageant coach, Linda Montague.

Mortena and Ms. Montague worked for a year on Mortena's walk, her oratory skills, and her talent-interpretive dance. Aurora did not hide her disgust but was resigned that she could do nothing to dissuade her strong-willed daughter. When the year was up, Mortena entered into the Miss Missouri pageant and won first runner-up: $12,000 and a round-trip airline ticket to anywhere in the continental USA. That was enough for Mortena to ignore her mother's advice to put the money in a certificate of deposit at the bank for twenty-four months, and enroll in the fall at the local community college. It was also enough for her to ignore her father's demand that she listen to her mother. Instead, Mortena packed her bags for Hollywood.

When she walked off the plane at LAX, Mortena did two things: cashed in her return airline ticket, and changed her name to Caprice Deveaux. In Hollywood, she blended in with all of the other tall, thin, young blonde girls at every audition she managed to wrangle. Boudoin Shelby, her agent, convinced her to try the casting couch a couple of times, but that only yielded two-bit parts in movies no one even saw. Her sporadic work in commercials, coupled with temp work, kept her fed, gave her a roof over her head, and allowed her to pay for acting lessons. But Aurora was her contingency plan when she came up short, which was often.

Aurora never let her daughter forget how much this was costing during their weekly Sunday night phone calls. So, after six years in L.A., Aurora demanded that her twenty-four-year-old daughter return home and marry locally. Besides, Mortena, now Caprice, was needed to help run the businesses, since Monika had married Roy and had three children, and Rottredge was getting older and slower, making it increasingly harder to juggle the corn farm, the mechanic shop, and the convenience store. "Enough of this nonsense," Aurora opined during their Sunday night calls. "You're pretty, but you're no movie star. Doris Day, Debbie Reynolds, Ursula Andress, Bo Derek, Suzanne Somers, Farrah Fawcett you're not. Now, *those* girls are pretty. Besides, I ain't seen you in anything since you got there, and I ain't sending you no more money."

One day at the laundromat, while reading a biography of Marilyn Monroe, Caprice eavesdropped on a conversation between two women she recognized as regulars at the audition circuit. They whispered that Stanley Donen was casting for an intriguing blonde to star in a mystery in a sequel of sorts to *Charade*. Stanley was seeking America's answer to Brigitte Bardot.

Caprice threw her wet clothes into her laundry bin, ran home, and called Boudoin Shelby, the agent who had unceremoniously dumped her because the numerous auditions he had sent her on were fruitless. Shelby told her that she was too young to play a spy. No one would believe it. He told her that she had no experience and the commercials and bit parts in the B movies did not count. He told her that Stanley was looking for an established actress that could carry a picture. Stanley would not even consider an unknown. Shelby told her, finally, that Caprice should forget about it because the part had been cast. All of which fueled her excitement and determination, even though she had $64 left in her checking account, and even less in her savings.

She finger-combed her strawberry blonde tresses, dressed in the Chanel suit she had procured at a Beverly Hills Goodwill thrift store, and hastened to Stanley's office. Stanley's secretary refused to alert him that Caprice was waiting in the reception area and refused to give her an appointment. The woman icily told her that the role was cast but if she left her CV and headshot they would call her if something else came up.

"This is *my* part!" Caprice screamed at the woman, elbowing her away as the woman blocked Stanley's office door. The receptionist called security. Minutes later, a burly security guard rushed in. The guard, Caprice, and the woman tussled, circling in a manic dance, in a tangle of arms and legs. Hearing all the noise, Stanley ran out to see what was happening and witnessed Caprice in the throes of the fight. The three looked up as Stanley yelled for them to stop the commotion.

"I just wanted to meet you, Mr. Donen," Caprice offered as she unwrapped her arm from the guard and peeled her other hand from the receptionist's neck. "I am perfect for Catherine Hartman in *Second Guessing*." She straightened her white boucle jacket, adjusted her matching skirt, and looked down at her legs, seeing no hope in hiding the massive tear that ran the length of her left pantyhose.

"Well, come in then," Stanley told her. "I've never seen anyone so beautiful throw punches like that." He tested Caprice for the part of Catherine Hartman, a government spy in love with a thief who risks her own life to save him from imprisonment. Stanley complimented her on her natural ability to deftly inject humor into drama. But he also told her that the Academy Award-winning actress, Citrine Blair, had been offered the part and accepted it. She was to star opposite Harrison Ford.

Three weeks later, Caprice sat in her empty apartment, having sold all of her possessions to buy a return ticket home because Aurora refused to send her any more money. Her packed suitcase sat beside the door, ready for her flight in the morning. She was about to call the phone company to discontinue service when the phone rang. It was Boudoin Shelby:

"Citrine insisted on hiring her own make-up artist, special lighting, a Christian Dior wardrobe, a caravan of trailers with interiors painted robin's egg blue, and her food freshly cooked and flown daily from France. Stanley Donen wants to know are you still interested in playing Catherine?"

Caprice won a Golden Globe award and garnered an Academy Award nomination. Though she lost out to Jodie Foster in *Silence of the Lambs,* producers dropped scripts at Caprice's feet and filled her mailbox for the next fifteen years. Boudoin Shelby vetted Caprice's offers as a tennis pro volleys balls across the net, finessing movie deals with tie-ins to luxury cosmetic, handbag, and jewelry companies. Editors courted her, because a magazine cover with Caprice Deveaux guaranteed a boost in circulation. Her screen idols, Richard Gere, Robert Downey, Jr., Tom Cruise, and Rob Lowe vied for romantic interludes. Her dalliance with Tupac Shakur made the evening news. She bought a beachfront home in Malibu and called Sophia Loren, Cher, and Demi Moore "neighbors." She went shopping for a flat in Paris with Naomi Campbell. Never one for the party scene, Caprice visited the homes of her friends Diana Ross and Ryan O'Neal, who admonished her that keeping a low profile could cost her roles.

Aurora insisted Caprice save her money and cautioned that this "Hollywood stuff" was frou-frou and she had better marry stability. Walking down Rodeo Drive, Caprice bumped into a man as he hopped out of a dark metallic-gray Jaguar. The older pudgy man had a receding hairline and wisps of salt-and-pepper hair. He apologized and smiled the sweetest, gentlest smile she had ever seen. Recognizing Caprice, he asked for her autograph, and as they chatted, he introduced himself as Findlay Fourchette. When they parted, Caprice watched Findlay enter a building with an engraved brass plate affixed to the concrete façade that read, THE FOURCHETTE CORPORATION.

Utterly smitten, Findlay called everyone he knew in Hollywood to find out the name of Caprice Deveaux's agent. Never having a sister, Boudoin Shelby relished his role of blocking the male population's attempts to get to Caprice. Not even an Egyptian businessman's gift of a $70,000 Rolex watch wrenched Boudoin Shelby's grip on Caprice's phone number.

Being from New York City and living in Hollywood for twenty-five years, Boudoin honed his ability to read people quickly. He suspiciously accepted Findlay's courtship of him as an avenue to Caprice. Slowly, Boudoin's heart thawed—not merely because Findlay's net worth was upwards of $45 million, or that Findlay took him to the Beverly Hills Four Seasons for a $350 lunch, or because Findlay's voice cracked when he spoke to Boudoin so giddily about Caprice.

Ice began to drip from Boudoin's heart when Findlay told him that his mother's recent death left a void in his life. A puddle of water formed when Findlay said he missed taking his mother to church every Sunday and cooking her sunny-side eggs for breakfast afterwards. The puddle grew when Boudoin learned that Findlay still loved his ninety-two-year-old former mother-in-law and looked forward to taking her to their monthly bingo dates, despite that his ex-wife dumped him. The ice totally melted when Boudoin and Findlay left the restaurant and Findlay handed the homeless lady huddled in the corner of the parking lot two $20 bills.

Boudoin gave Findlay Caprice's phone number. The next day, Findlay invited her to dinner. Two months later, he flew her on his private plane to Kansas City, and they drove over an hour to the Warrensburg farm to meet Aurora and Ruttredge. The next morning, Caprice and Findlay went to the courthouse and married.

The week of her forty-seventh birthday, Caprice noticed that the only mail in her mailbox was a coupon for Elizabeth Arden and a few bills. She also noticed there were no paparazzi when she went to get a tofu shake and the barista failed to tell her how pretty she was. She handled the wrinkles around her eyes, the fleshiness under her eyes and jaw, and the creases in her neck each time she saw in her reflection in the mirror. She dealt with the laugh-lines around her mouth and her graying eyelashes. She even dealt with the gray hairs that sprang in her pubic hair and constantly depilated the loud gray hairs from her chin. Long ago, she came to terms with her weekly salon appointment that kept her flowing curls strawberry blonde. But Caprice had never known life without the compliments of strangers. Obscurity and invisibility caused a depression so deep that Findlay's love could not hoist her out of it.

For his part, Findlay baited his rod with a floor-length red fox coat, a brand-new Jaguar to match his own, and two trips to Greece to lift Caprice from the lake of depression. Her sullenness, like a fever, finally broke, and she admitted to him what was bothering her; getting older made her invisible.

Findlay stroked his wife's increasingly frail ego: "You're not invisible, honey." But it was not enough to coax her from the fetal position on their couch. Bewildered, but desperate to make her happy, he promised that the profit from his two upcoming real estate deals would be used for her regenerative therapy. "We'll try this Hollywood thing again," he guaranteed.

Delayed a bit by the soft real estate market, Findlay made good on his promise nine years later: "At fifty-eight, Caprice will be a twenty-four-year-old movie star."

*   *   *   *

"Hi, Ms. Deveaux. This is your contract." Melody Proctor pushed a three-inch-thick volume toward Caprice. Her rainbow nail embellishments sparkled as her index finger moved up and down each page.

"Hello, would you like my autograph? Do you have a blank sheet of paper?" Caprice smiled genially.

Melody stared at Caprice blankly.

"You know, *Warm Spies, An Afternoon in London, Dinosaurs*

in Space..." Caprice ticked off her most well-known movies. "I was nominated for an Academy Award for *Second Guessing*."

"Second *what*?"

"Guessing. *Second Guessing* with Harrison Ford. You know Han Solo from *Star Wars*."

Melody blinked at Caprice. "I did see *Dinosaurs in Space* when I was in elementary school. Were you in that? Hmmm, you look different. I'm not allowed to get any memorabilia from the clients. Thanks anyway." She turned the contract so it was right-side-up in front of Caprice. "Ma'am, depending on the age you select, that determines your price. At fifty-eight, if you select an age between eighteen and twenty-nine, it's $400,000; thirty to thirty-nine, it's $300,000; and forty to forty-nine, it's $200,000, annually. These prices are in effect for a full year. Then, each category goes up $50,000. The only payment we accept is payment in full each year, or a weekly automatic debit. I need your initials right here."

Caprice printed "CD" in the blank. Melody continued. "If you select the weekly automatic debit option, then finance charges and an installment fee will apply. Also, if you select the weekly automatic debit option and your payment is rejected, you have a five-day grace period. You have to notify us as to when the payment will be made during that five-day period. If the payment is not made during this time, then you will be denied treatment. I need for you to initial this."

Caprice applied her initials again.

"Regenerative therapy is inherently dangerous. You are undergoing changes to your body that affect every area of your life. Because it is an inherently dangerous activity, you assume the risk. The Renew Your Youth Center is not responsible for any injuries to your body because of the side effects. The Renew Your Youth Center is not responsible for side effects that occur because of the cessation of the therapy. We call that 'user error.' We are not responsible for any side effects that occur because of discontinued treatment for non-payment. I need for you to initial this page here."

Caprice initialed the page.

"You have thirty days to review the contract. Your next appointment will be with a regenerative doctor and a financial counselor. They will be available to answer any other questions you may have. If you want a psychotherapist to assist you with the regenerative process, one will be assigned to you. At the appointment with the regenerative doctor, you will need to provide the optimal year you wish to regenerate to. Have you thought about that, Ms. Deveaux?" Melody again smiled her practiced smile.

Caprice bounced up and down in her chair. "Yes, looking back, I think twenty-four was my optimal year."

"Then, at that appointment, either your payment in full will be due, or, if you select the automatic payment weekly option, your first payment of $7,692.31, plus a $45 finance charge and a $50 installment fee, will be due." Melody scribbled "$7,787.31" in one of the blank lines. "I need for you to initial this, Ms. Deveaux."

She did, and Melody heaved the contract up to her. "Congratulations on starting your therapy. I hope you will be thrilled with the results." Melody fought sounding rehearsed. "We will see you in a month, Ms. Deveaux."

"Oh no, I intend to start tomorrow."

CHAPTER FIVE

Astrid's amber-tinged dreadlocks cascaded down her back, swinging mightily as she ushered Lesley Stahl to Naomi Morninglory's bookcase-lined office. Framed pictures of Naomi with Bill and Hillary Clinton, George W. and Laura Bush, and Barack and Michelle Obama were interspersed with a framed copy of her Person of the Year *TIME* magazine cover, a plaque of her MacArthur Fellow award, her NAACP Image Award, several patent grants, and numerous awards from various medical organizations.

"Can I offer you something to drink, Ms. Stahl? We have orange blossom or green tea, decaffeinated coffee, water." Astrid assisted Lesley in removing her jacket and hooked it on the coat rack.

"Your hair is beautiful. That light brown-blonde color is quite unusual. Gives you a glow." Lesley placed her notes on Naomi's desk.

"Thank you." Astrid blushed and brushed a few errant locs from her shoulder.

"I'll just take some water, thank you."

"The production team can set up beside Dr. Morninglory's desk. She will be here in a minute. She is tending to a patient right now and apologizes to you for the wait. This is Oliver Steinberg, Dr. Morninglory's lawyer. He will be on hand during the interview."

"Yes, our legal department and Mr. Steinberg are well acquainted."

"Ms. Stahl, good to meet you in person." Steinberg shook Lesley's hand.

"Likewise, Mr. Steinberg."

Dr. Morninglory hurriedly strode in, removed her doctor's smock and handed it to Astrid, and pulled her cobalt blue St. John skirt down while the make-up artist quickly dotted blush across her cheeks.

"Please forgive me Ms. Stahl, I had a minor emergency, but things are well under control now. Please, please have a seat."

"We can reschedule if you need to?"

"No, today is fine."

"So, you're ready to start the interview?"

"Yes, yes, please, let's begin."

"You look like you are on your own little blue pill. You look so young to be thirty-eight and have accomplished all of this."

"Thank you. Yes, my patients often remark about that. But no, I owe it all to genes."

"I read somewhere that you made this discovery while trying to come up with a way to treat bruises and other skin conditions from inside the body instead of topical. Is that correct?

"Yes, that's correct."

"But that's not the full story, is it?"

Naomi's eyes narrowed, and she uncrossed and re-crossed her legs. "What do you mean, Lesley?"

"I mean it's widely believed that your father committed suicide after your mother's death. I read somewhere that after your mother's death, your father aged so quickly that you wanted to come up with a way to make him young again. And that was the impetus for you to assist people with their aging."

"My father did not commit suicide. He slipped on some ice...fell into the Potomac river." Naomi sputtered. "People say all sorts of unkind things, and that is just one of them. He fell."

"I see, but that is what made you come up with the pill?"

"No, not initially." Naomi slowed her breathing. "Initially, as a dermatologist by training, I wanted to heal people who had skin disfigurements from burns or other accidents. I wanted to help people even out their skin tones. You know, Lesley, that the skin is the largest organ. I thought that if I could help heal the largest organ, then well-being would follow. Instead of a topical cream, I wanted to heal from the inside, and so I discovered—quite by accident, actually—ingredients that came to be known as 'Renew Your Youth' or regenerative therapy. But seeing my dad age so fast, in a matter of weeks, from grief, I wanted to do something to restore his vitality."

"I see. How long did it take you to invent this?"

"Through trial and error, and clinical trials, it took about sixteen years."

"You were determined."

"Each time I wanted to quit, something happened to let me know that I was close."

"Can you explain to us how it works?"

"It is a form of cell therapy."

"I understand that the therapy itself is excruciating."

"Yes, unfortunately, the process is painful. I try to never underestimate that for my patients. It is not for those with a low pain threshold."

"And they are not supposed to take painkillers."

"Yes, it could dilute the cell therapy. They can take low dosages of aspirin or ibuprofen, but even that sparingly."

"We talked to Carl Murphy, one of your patients going through the process now. He could only talk for a few hours at a time. He was in so much pain."

"Mr. Murphy is in the beginning stages. Often, the beginning stage is the worst part, but bear in mind it is different for everyone. But, yes, it can be quite painful."

"How long does this stage last?"

"Well, for each person, regeneration is different. It depends on the age of the person, the age they want to regenerate to, what we call their 'optimal age,' their general health condition. But for most people it takes approximately three months."

"Three months of pain to shave twenty or thirty years off. Not a bad deal. What is in this 'cell therapy'? How does it work?"

"It is a patented process, and the actual ingredients are a trade secret. But what I can tell you is, the ingredients are a synthetic and natural compound that causes cells to rapidly divide so that they can restore a patient to any age between twenty-one and forty-nine."

"How is it that a patient can actually pick the age—the optimal age, as you call it—that they want to be restored to?"

"As part of the treatment, we study the patient's body and molecular structure to detect what the condition of the body was at, say, twenty-two years of age, and we can duplicate that molecular structure gradually by providing it in a customized pill. Each dosage is customized to contain a series of ingredients that will treat the cell structure of the patient until we reach their optimal age. At that point, we continue with the dosage for the rest of the patient's life. We monitor the patient, and at times, make adjustments, either because the body has grown used to the dosage and a stronger one is needed, or the patient is experiencing some external factor that is affecting their internal condition, such as, if they move to a warmer climate, wetter or dryer climate, higher elevation, etc."

"Really? You mean climate affects the molecular structure of our bodies?"

"In our research, we've found that everything affects the aging process. So, yes, we need to know where they live and will be living so that we can recalibrate their pills, if necessary."

"And you can stay 22 forever? What if you decide that you've had enough? Can you go back to your real age?"

"Yes, patients can opt for discontinuation. We have a whole department—our Maturation and Reversion Department is devoted to assisting patients with what we call 'reversion.' Again, that is a customized process entailing a customized pill."

"That's why it costs so much, because each pill is customized?"

"That contributes to the cost."

"What if, say, a person decides that they don't want to be twenty-six anymore but also don't want to return to being seventy-seven? Can they pick another age and revert to fifty-two?"

"Not at the present moment. But we are working on a way to offer that advancement service to our patients."

Lesley narrates: *The woman behind the fountain of youth revolution is Naomi Morninglory. A diminutive African-American*

woman, only thirty-eight years old, who looks more like a high-
school student than a doctor running her own revolutionary clinic. A
dermatologist by training, Dr. Morninglory grew up in Washington,
D.C., the only daughter of an accountant and a housewife. She was
educated in Catholic schools and decided at age twelve that she
wanted to be a doctor. While in medical school, her mother, a two-
pack-a-day smoker, contracted lung cancer, but it went undetected
until it was too late. She died two months before Naomi's graduation
from Howard University College of Medicine, and her father died
from drowning in the Potomac River, three weeks after her mother's
death. In the midst of profound grief, Naomi decided to give up
medicine altogether and went to work, at all places, an insurance
company.

"Your parents died."

"Yes."

"And you gave up medicine. Why?"

"I felt that the practice of medicine gave doctors the ability to heal. And both my parents needed treatment that they never received. I was hurt and felt I couldn't give to others what my parents needed."

"What treatment did your mother need that she didn't receive?"

"She died of lung cancer. It's difficult to treat, but I always felt if it had been detected early enough, she may have lived."

"And your father—what treatment did he not receive?"

"I think he was so sad when my mother died. If...if there was grief counseling...if his doctor had given him a physical, maybe they could have prescribed something that would have helped him regain his balance. He would not have fallen."

"And then, after some time, you decided to return to medicine. What was it that made you want to come back to practice medicine?"

"I was working at the insurance company, and the majority of the women that I worked with were complaining about their looks: I'm too this, or too that, my skin has this issue or that issue. They were spending so much money on creams and potions but not getting the results they sought. I felt a nagging to return to medicine and treat the skin. It was an inescapable feeling."

"Couldn't escape it?"

"No. I tried for two years, but it followed me there. To the insurance company."

"Then what?"

"Then I reapplied for an advanced dermatology program at the University of Baltimore. And was accepted."

By day, Dr. Morninglory treated keloids and pigmentation problems and performed laser surgery, cosmetic fillers, and injections. By night, Dr. Morninglory spent sixteen years of trial and error trying to find ingredients to heal bruises and even out skin imperfections. Then, one day, Dr. Morninglory stumbled upon the makings of "Renew Your Youth," the Regenerative Therapy, a bright greenish-blue pill half an inch wide that turns back the clock to what Dr. Morninglory has coined as your "optimal year." It allows a patient to pick the year that they feel they were at their best. Yes, you heard me right—it gives people the ability, through hindsight, to pick a year they believe they looked and felt their best.

As a result, Dr. Morninglory has been able to allow women in their fifties, sixties, or even nineties, well past childbearing years, to return to fertility; allow men who have lost their hair to return to a time where their hair was plentiful; allow people who have cancer pick a year when they were cancer-free; give people who have invested years in a career and essentially want a do-over in life; give actors and actresses the possibility to stay young in front of the camera forever. It even allows people who have been paralyzed in catastrophic accidents to regain the use of their limbs, fuses broken spines. The possibilities are limitless.

"You give people a 'do-over'?"

"People have said that. Some choose to use this time of being young again as a 'do-over'."

"Tell me about how this allows paralyzed people to walk again."

"Well, they can pick as their optimal year, a time before the catastrophic event—the accident—when they were able to walk. The only thing that regenerative therapy does not do is regenerate body parts, limbs, fingers, toes, eyes. So, if a limb was amputated or they lost an eye in an accident, that will not be restored."

"Amazing. This pill gives you the ability to essentially live forever?"

"Our studies have shown that regenerative therapy does not necessarily prolong your life. Only God can do that. We find, for example that our ninety-three-year-old patients who regenerate to their twenties—say, twenty-two—they don't live ten or more years. On average, they live four or five more years. We find that regenerative therapy allows them to avoid some of the geriatric illnesses, such as Alzheimer's, rheumatoid arthritis, Parkinson's disease, but we haven't found that it prolongs life to a noticeable extent."

"No wonder you are called the 'Billion-Dollar Doctor.' You even allow people to bypass the aging process all together."

Dr. Morninglory's 'RYY' therapy grossed $73 billion, including one billion within the last year alone. Of the handful of regenerative therapy companies, hers is the only one who holds the patent, has FDA approval, and has a license to advertise. No wonder her company consistently outpaces her closest competitor. The RYY Center is located on 350 acres of which was once known as St. Elizabeth's Hospital. The District of Columbia government lured the RYY Center to that location by giving it tax credits. Employment at the RYY Center is strict. Each of the 800 employees must sign a non-disclosure agreement and are annually scrutinized by the security team. But it's worth it. RYY boasts some of the highest-paid employees in the country. In fact, the receptionist makes $137,000 a year.

But just what is this 'regenerative therapy'? Essentially, it is a cell therapy. Incredibly, Dr. Morninglory discovered a way to isolate the cells in the body that control the aging process. Patients are studied like lab specimens using samples of their blood, urine, saliva, tears and mucus. A research team led by Dr. Ava Ellington in the New Patient Cultivation Department analyzes the cells to determine what biochemical or nutrient is missing, and then Dr. Ellington's team devises a customized pill that replenishes that chemical or nutrient. *The patient then visits the Center every week for lab work and an examination—the results of which are calculated based on the molecular structure and targeted toward achieving the 'optimal age' of the patient. Then, the pill formula is recalibrated weekly, replenishing the body until it has the molecular structure of the desired age. The entire process, amazingly, takes only three months, and after the patient has reached his or her 'optimal age,' they have to continue to visit the Center every week for a customized stabilization pill administered by a team led by Dr. Lloyd Overbrook of the Regeneration Stabilization Department.*

Regenerative therapy has put Dr. Morninglory in the center of a cultural storm. One of the few scientists that can say she has been on the cover of Vogue, TIME, and National Geographic, Dr. Morninglory is routinely feted by heads of state and stalked by the paparazzi. She has received numerous awards and grants, including a John D. and Catherine T. MacArthur Foundation Award, commonly referred to as a "genius grant." Lovely, you may say, but there is a downside to all of this attention. When she had two attempts on her life in the last five years, Dr. Morninglory is now never without a bodyguard.

"You have more money and more fame than any scientist in history. Would you say you have paid a high price for it? There have been two attempts on your life. You have a bodyguard by your side. You can't even go to the grocery store without being mobbed. You've been in court with your ex-husband, Curtis Washington, who sued you twice to gain a portion of your company. Why, why are some people so mad at you?"

"Change is hard for some people. Also, when you get what you asked for, is it what you really want? Lesley, RYY is a lifestyle for me. I try not to think about the attempts on my life and the limitations on my personal freedom. I didn't set out for this. I just wanted to help people, do what I love. I truly love seeing people having years restored to them. There is no feeling that matches when a regenerated patient sees their younger self in the mirror. It's very emotional. They cry, and often, they make me cry.

A lot of people live with regret. It just melts away when they see their twenty-three-year-old self again, and they feel like they are getting a new start. Lesley, for every letter I read where a person is unhappy because of a side effect or some unexpected consequence of being younger than their children, there are hundreds of letters from people thanking me for giving them a second chance."

"Your patients may be happy, but the plastic surgeons aren't. This little greenish-blue pill has caused havoc in the plastic surgery industry. Since you invented RYY, plastic surgeries have plummeted to forty-three percent."

"Yes, I get a lot of criticism from plastic surgeons. What I offer is another option. An alternative. To me, plastic surgery is a gamble. Despite all of these promises, after plastic surgery, patients often look like an entirely different person and some people need corrective plastic surgery on top of it. Also, you have to continue getting plastic surgery, because gravity affects the skin. The more plastic surgery a patient receives, the less they look like they did originally. With RYY, patients know what they will look like, because they looked like that before. Their appearance is no surprise. I do caution that patients have to make a choice. It is either regenerative therapy or plastic surgery. But not both. Plastic surgery is prohibited while undergoing regenerative therapy. The bodily tissues regenerate so rapidly that if a patient undergoes plastic surgery, the sutures will rip the skin, causing damage."

"What about people who have to have surgery, pregnant women who have C-sections, others who have lifesaving surgeries?"

"Our patients come into the clinic weekly to receive their dosages so that we can monitor them closely to make sure they are adhering to the prescribed regime. In the cases of accidents or mandatory surgery, we work collaboratively with the treating physicians to continually customize the regeneration therapy to fit the needs of the patient. It requires intense collaboration. Often, those patients may have to regenerate slower. We may lessen their dosage."

"I'd like to talk for a minute about the societal consequences. Some people say you are directly responsible for the increase in crime. Some people say it is a return to the 1980s and 1990s because of the rampant car jackings, purse-snatchings, and robberies. Credit-card theft and identity theft is at an all-time high. They say that this little blue pill is the crack of the 21st century, because people will do anything to stay on the therapy…"

"Of course, I don't condone patients using criminal means to pay for their treatments. Even though we do a full financial background check on all of our patients and provide financial counseling, sometimes patients end up not being able to pay for their treatments and they end up being discontinued.

"Another sad reality is that, although we have a Collaborative Treatment and Severe Reaction Department that works closely with the patient to minimize side effects, a side effect that the patient may encounter is the loss of the attribute that enabled them to earn the income to pay for the treatment in the first place. For example, we've had patients with beautiful voices regenerate and lose their ability to sing. We've had patients like doctors and lawyers whose cognitive abilities were compromised from regenerative therapy, all of which meant that their incomes were drastically reduced, which resulted in their inability to pay their bills. There are just no guarantees. Oh, and, Lesley, we let them know that when they sign the contract."

"I see. I read that treatments range from $100,000 to $300,000 and up per year for the life of the patient, or as long as they receive treatments."

"Yes."

"What's the most anyone—without naming names, because I know about HIPPA—but what's the most anyone has ever paid for the regenerative therapy?"

"I think the most a patient has paid is…$500,000."

"Per year?"

"Yes."

"Wow. That's a lot of cheese."

"Yes, but look at what they're getting. A chance to live the life again they always wanted."

CHAPTER SIX

The early model silver BMW parked at the curb of Naomi Morninglory's house was a familiar sight—one she looked forward to as much as her annual mammogram. And, like a mammogram, Curtis Washington could detect. He spent his time detecting what he could get from her. Not that Naomi didn't know this. But that did not stop the visits, every seven months or so—nor did it stop Naomi from letting him in.

"You want me to stop and get out, doc? I can get rid of him." Marlon drove slowly to the gate of the former residence of the Indonesian ambassador, Naomi's Northwest Washington home.

"It's okay. He can come in."

The BMW followed Naomi's black Mercedes and stopped at the garage. A few minutes later, the doorbell chimed.

"Hello, Curtis."

Curtis's tall, lean frame perfectly displayed his custom-made Italian suits. Over the years, his weathered creamy chocolate skin had developed a delicious patina. His closely cropped curls—once deep dark brown, now cloudy and soft—were familiar to Naomi in a way nothing else was. His familiar features took her back to when they were married, every single time.

"Hello, Mimi."

Defaulting to the name he called her post-coitus was his way of immediately depositing Naomi in the S.W. townhouse she and Curtis had shared during their marriage. It was also his way of reminding her that she once had been under his control. Naomi walked into the expansive white kitchen, kicked off her shoes, and padded in her bare feet on the glistening black marble floors. She opened her Sub-Zero and reached for a can of chai tea. "Would you like something?"

"No, I'm straight."

Naomi dragged a stool closer to the white-pebbled island and sat on it. Curtis sat opposite her. His fervid brown eyes, red with fatigue, studied Naomi's every movement. "It doesn't have to be like this, Mimi."

There was a time when Curtis's touch sent electromagnetic shocks to Naomi's scalp, then inched down slowly over the map of her skin, resting in pulses in the split of her legs. That time had come and gone. What remained was familiarity. Naomi, an only child born to only children, had no family and no real friends to act as her griots. There was no one in her life with whom she could sit and have a cup of hot tea and eat the sweet, moist cake of remembrance. No one knew how loved she was by her parents. No one knew how, as a small child, her mother sang her to sleep every night with a cup of hot cocoa. No one knew how, for years, her father woke her up at dawn every Saturday morning and drove her for an hour to the National Zoo before it opened to the public to attend the biology classes there, sowing her passion to become a doctor.

There was Haron—her Harry—with whom she stole slivers of time when Quinn wasn't looking. To Harry, her past was an afterthought, as he lived his present with Quinn and his sons. What Naomi was left with was Curtis. He knew her past—at least from the age of twenty-two—and that, though paltry, had to be enough. That was sixteen years ago; now she was thirty-eight. Sixteen years was a lifetime ago, given how her life had changed so dramatically since then. His perfect hazel eyes contained only one gift: the gift of remembrance. In his hands, Curtis tentatively held her history, but to Naomi it was tangible.

Handsome and confident, Curtis could sell anything to anyone—except insurance, which, unfortunately, was how he got paid.

"How much this time?" Naomi popped open the can and took a swill.

Curtis's voice lowered, "Mimi, I said I was sorry. Baby, let's put all of this behind us. I love you, and you know that. Can't we find a way?"

"No, I don't think so." Naomi lifted the can to her mouth and took another long sip. It had been a long day, and Naomi wanted to skirt his usual game of pleading.

"Why not?"

Curtis surmised a situation quicker and better than anyone Naomi knew. His ability to exploit the gaps, the lapses, was uncanny. But she was no longer his novice working for him at the insurance company, fragile and reeling from her parents' death and the breakup with Harry. During their marriage, Curtis ladled her emotions from her reservoir she openly shared, in an effort to please him. He manipulated her, selecting the emotion that suited him on that particular day. And she let him.

As her emotional strength galvanized, however, Naomi noticed that Curtis's strategy changed. He became the supportive husband by working two jobs to pay off her medical student loans. Later, as Naomi experimented with the Renew Your Youth formula, Curtis sold the house his mother bequeathed to fund samples for her to get more investors. Once Naomi got more investors, she used those funds for samples for the trials that led to FDA approval. Curtis's excitement toward her grew as her obligation to him deepened, in his mind tethering them forever.

Curtis traded her name—the famous doctor who invented a pill that restored youth—on the D.C. social stock exchange, using it to elevate and ingratiate himself into a town full of prominent people. His custom-made Italian suits and congenial manner got him in the door, but it was her intriguing Renew Your Youth formula that kept him relevant.

When Naomi left Curtis for Harry, Curtis's social stock plummeted. In a moment of weakness, brought on when Harry missed too many deadlines to leave his wife, Curtis insinuated himself back into Naomi's life. He enjoyed the perks of returning home. His social stock was restored. He was also so secure that he had reclaimed his dominance over Naomi that he believed a dalliance with a young, shapely secretary at the insurance company proved to Naomi that Curtis was still her king. That is, until the secretary did what Naomi could not; she became pregnant. With lightning speed, Naomi demonstrated that she indeed had changed. She moved out, finalized their divorce, paid him a settlement that included repaying her student loans and his investment in the Renew Your Youth Center, and circumvented any chance that Curtis would receive any future proceeds from the Center. He thought he could manufacture her love for him forever—one of the few situations he wrongly surmised.

"Curtis, I just got tired of the façade. How you have to impress everyone. Running over here and there, showing people your latest and greatest gizmo or toy. Those people don't matter. They certainly don't care about you or me. Never did, never will. It's just that I need someone who is all in. Who doesn't need the hoopla. Who doesn't need the adulation of strangers."

"All in? Are you for real?" Curtis strained to keep his voice from rising. "How much more 'all in' can I be? I was there for you. All I did for you. Let's look at this. Who was there for you after your parents died? Nobody did for you what I did. Nobody. Nobody would do for you what I did. I helped you when you worked for the insurance company. I kept you on that job. I saved your job for you. If it wasn't for me, they would have fired you. Or, how about this? I paid your medical school loans. Selling my mother's house hurt me so bad. I held on until I got rope burn, but you needed the money to start all this shit. So, I sold it. For you. That was the house that I grew up in. Prime location, too. Northeast on Capitol Hill. Man, if I had that house now, do you know what it would be worth? For you. That was me, Mimi. The least that you can do for me is be grateful."

"Grateful? Oh, don't confuse gratitude with servitude. Just because I'm grateful doesn't mean that I have to do whatever you want me to do. All the time into infinity. That I'm your indentured servant for the rest of my life because you keep throwing in my face what you did for me. Thank you for helping me. Thank you for being there for me when no one else was. How many more times can I say thank you? But I'm not your improvement project anymore. I've grown. I've evolved. I'm not where I was sixteen years ago, or even five years ago. I'm not that person anymore. So, stop looking at me like I'm broken and it's your duty to fix me. I was broken. I admit it. That was the worst part of my life. But things change. Things have gotten better. I've changed.

"And let's be accurate. Let's not forget, I paid you back for paying my medical school loans and I paid you back every cent of the $250,000 you gave me to start my business, with interest. It's all there in black and white in the divorce settlement decree. And I know you cashed the checks with the quickness."

"Yeah, you're right. You've changed, all right. It's easy to be brand new when you got all this, isn't it? When you're on top of the world, isn't it? It's easy to want something different, somebody different? Isn't it? Let go of what was holding you up when it reminds you of what you used to be. Want a man who's brand new, too. How's that working out for you?"

"Curtis, I don't want to go over this anymore." Naomi did not hide her annoyance that Curtis reveled in the fact that things were not going as Harry had promised her they would.

"Face it, Mimi. If Harry loved you...*really* loved you, he would have left his damned wife and married you. But he didn't. When I took you back, you were collapsed on the floor. He broke your heart...*again*. Why would I do that? Why would I take you back? Because I love you. I wanted to spend the rest of my life with you. Have my family with you. One mistake, pouf, and you were out the door."

"You're calling the baby one mistake? Really?"

"You know what I mean. Mimi, I apologized. You hurt me bad. I was angry and trying to work out some things. The wrong way. I know that. I knew that then. But I thought...I wanted you to hurt the way that I hurt. It was wrong, I admit that. But, I thought together we could overcome anything. We'd been through so much."

"Whatever, Curtis. All I know is I keep writing checks. Just tell me how much, because whatever it is, this is the last time."

"I got bills, Mimi. I'm behind in my child-support payments, my house is underwater, I owe the IRS $75,000 in back taxes. That's not all. I got work trouble. In order to make my third-quarter quota, I wrote these life insurance policies on people who didn't really want them. So, to prevent them from canceling the policies, I've been paying on them. It didn't happen all at once, but I had to do something to keep my job. As long as I was out there working, I could make it up by writing some real policies. But the life insurance market didn't rebound like I thought it would. So, I've been paying for the policies with money I borrowed from Aspacio Aranha."

Curtis walked into the living room, ran his hands through his soft gray curls, and sank into the cushions of the ochre velvet sofa. Naomi leaned against the threshold that separated the kitchen and the living room. "Aspacio Aranha? Who's Aspacio Aranha?"

"C'mon, Mimi. Get your head out of the sand. Everybody in D.C. knows about Aranha."

"Okay, everyone knows him but me. Who is he?"

"He's what they call on the street a businessman. He made a lot of money in the drug game in the nineties and plowed it into other ventures, like real estate, little corner convenience stores, beauty parlors, and barbershops. They're just fronts for him to launder money. He loans people money. People who can't get money any other place. He loaned me the money."

"So, tell him that you'll pay him back when you get the money, because I'm not giving you another red cent."

"You don't tell Aranha that you're going to pay him back when you get the money. When he asks for something, you give it to him." Curtis buried his face in his hands.

Naomi sat in the vanilla-colored suede chair opposite Curtis and crossed her legs. "So, how much are we talking about here? A few thousand dollars?"

Curtis chortled. "I wish."

Naomi stared at Curtis. Disgust seared at his flesh. "How much, then?"

"Just $500,000."

"Are you telling me that you need me to give you half a million dollars so that you can pay some lowlife back? Is that what you're saying to me?"

"No, that's not what I'm saying."

"Good, because I'm not doing that. So, what are you saying?"

Curtis walked around the room. He shoved his hands in his pants pockets and immediately jerked them out to prevent ruining the drape of his suit. "Mimi, he doesn't want the money back. He knows I'm your ex-husband. He knows how lucrative your business is. Hell, the news reports love to say that you're this seventy-three-billion-dollar woman. He wants me to convince you to give me fifty percent of your business. He wants you to make me your partner."

"What does making you my partner do for him?"

"Well, uh, um...if I'm your partner, then I just pass my percentage of the profits to him. We're still talking about what percentage I'd get to keep."

"Oh, that's ridiculous. I'm not making you my partner, and you aren't getting any percentage of my business. I thought the judges made that perfectly clear to you the two times you sued me in court. It didn't work then, and it won't work now." Naomi lifted the can of chai tea toward her mouth and swallowed. "So, if you don't get it, then what? He's going to kill you?" She laughed mirthlessly.

"No, um—Mimi, *he's going to kill you.*"

CHAPTER SEVEN

The department heads never failed to apply on Naomi the pressure to increase the patient pool their own relatives and friends applied on them. The Tuesday through Friday morning meetings Naomi held to discuss the patient reports and discovery updates always ended with a pitch from the department heads to expand the Center to service more patients. Every week, the clamor to increase the patient pool intensified. Last month, the doctors insisted it grow by twenty percent. This month, their request surged to forty-five percent.

Jamal Lindicott adjusted his name plaque so that Prior Art Improvement and Discovery was directly in front of him. "I think it is good that we are victims of our success. Everyone should be so lucky."

"Between the *60 Minutes* interview and the *TIME* magazine cover, my phone has not stopped ringing." Scobey Thomas, Director of Communications offered loudly. "You still haven't responded to the *Vanity Fair* request, Dr. Morninglory. Can you give me an answer by the end of the day?" He reached for the water-pitcher and tilted it toward his mug.

Dr. Vanessa Van Stritton, Head of Collaborative Treatment and Severe Reaction chimed, "I'd like to talk more about increasing the patient pool. If we do that, then we will have to do more staff hiring. In Collaborative Treatment and Severe Reaction, we already have as much as we can handle. The side effects change as the patients regenerate, so we often see some of the same patients every week."

Lloyd Overbrook shrugged. "Listen, there's no dispute that we're all busy. But we all stand to gain by increasing the patient pool. Not just because by increasing the Center's revenue it increases our personal coffers, but also, what this will mean for our new patients. We will be reducing their wait times and, quite frankly, impacting their lives so that they can be younger longer."

Fatimah Webster, Director of Finance, adjusted the brightly colored head wrap arrayed on her head. "Let her see the numbers. Who has the copies of the proposal?"

"Oh, I do." Ava unclipped a large black binder clip and handed the documents around the room. "Scobey Thomas wrote a great business proposal and feasibility study. Just take a look at it, Dr. Morninglory. I think it is worth taking a good, hard look on how to improve operations. I mean, really, as of this morning I have fifteen thousand people on the waiting list."

"And the average wait time is three years," interjected Cyril Macintosh, Director of Maturation and Reversion. "This is unacceptable from a customer service standpoint."

"At the rate of adding approximately a hundred patients a year, the people on the wait-list have better odds of winning the Powerball," Dr. Lindicott joked.

"Some of our older potential clients will die without ever receiving the therapy." Overbrook shook his head in disgust.

Dr. Macintosh leaned forward and spread his hands on the table. "Exactly. I just don't see what the problem of increasing the size of the Center is. Honestly, if what concerns you is the cash outlay to ramp up for the new patients, I'm sure Van Stritton, Ellington, or I could get you a NIH grant, like that." He snapped his fingers.

"It is a big picture, a sustainability issue," Ms. Webster concurred. "Although servicing a thousand patients per year pays our overhead, it just doesn't give us much room to plan for expansion."

Naomi pushed the document away from her. "This is the same proposal from last month. I recognize the cover. Thank you to everyone who is worried about the sustainability and the expansion of a seventy-three-billion-dollar business. And that is seventy-three billion in profit. But right now, I think the best thing we can do to sustain this business is to continue to do our jobs to the best of our ability. And I am not interested in a discussion on expansion right now. I know the waiting lists are long. I get Ava's reports every week, just like you do. I'm the one charged with allaying the fears from anxious potential patients on the waiting list that they will get the regenerative therapy. I also know that some of the older potential patients will die without the therapy. Unfortunately, everyone who wants RYY will not be able to get it. No matter how much money you have, you don't get everything you want. Life is just not like that."

"But it can be," Overbrook retorted.

"Uh, Dr. Morninglory, turn to page twenty-seven." Ms. Webster licked her fingers and paged through the document. "It outlines how patient care will not be compromised if we increase patient load even just by thirty percent to meet more of the demand. And if we do that, it can cut the wait list by just under fifty percent." She held up the page with the chart.

"Forty-eight percent, to be exact." Ava Ellington gently scratched her dusty brown skin, flecks of which fell onto the table like discarded tree bark.

Naomi was in no mood to argue with the latest assault of greed. Her mind was still consumed with the bomb Curtis had dropped last night. "This is all as informative as it was last month. But the Center provides the best care by adding a thousand new regenerating patients every year. Any patients added above that number come from the deaths of current regenerating patients or discontinuation events. That's the policy. And that will continue to be the policy."

"Well, that is what I call an open mind." Lindicott took a swig from his water bottle.

Overbrook bent over the proposal and flipped through it. "Any business that does not seek to grow will stagnate. You may be taking home a seven-billion-dollar-a-year paycheck, but we aren't. If we increase our patient load even by just thirty percent to meet more of the demand, our salaries can increase to—what did you say, Fatimah? By eight million a year, not including our yearly bonuses."

Naomi hissed through her gritted teeth. "That's what this is really about. Salary increases. Not patient care. Not carefully calibrating a patient's regeneration experience."

Bertrand Angenois, who had been uncharacteristically quiet throughout the morning's exchange, suddenly leaned forward and thumped the three-inch document. "Listen, let's do this. Since we aren't going to be able to make a decision today, why don't we separate the new information from the old? Scobey, since you wrote this very comprehensive document, can you break out the new information? Or at least highlight it for us?"

"I suppose so."

"And, Fatimah, I'd like to see a budget on what expansion would cost. From increased staff to building a new wing. Not just if we were to tackle it this year, but what would the numbers look like next year and the year after? Accounting for inflation. Can you find the time in your busy schedule to do that?"

"Sure. I'm sure I can, Bertrand."

"Lovely headdress, by the way. Beauty and brains."

Fatimah blushed.

"Dr. Van Stritton," Bertrand continued, "you mentioned that Dr. Ellington and Dr. Macintosh would have no problem getting NIH grants. I must say that you're all our version of the dream team. Since you are very knowledgeable about the process, can you put together a package to submit? Complete with query letters and bios of the key players? That way, we can target who we submit the package to."

"It would take some time, but I think we could do it between our appointments. What do you all think?" Dr. Van Stritton looked at Ava and Cyril, who nodded in agreement.

"I know that you are all very busy people, but I am wondering if we can we get some dates behind these actions?" Bertrand scanned the calendar on his phone.

"We can talk about dates at the meeting tomorrow—after we've had a chance to think through all the work involved," Dr. Overbrook chortled as his phone rang. He picked it up and whispered into it, "Hello? Just a moment..." He aimed his gaze at Naomi. "Are we done here?"

"I don't know about you. But yes, I'm done." Naomi rose from the head of the conference table and walked out the door.

"Thank you all for your cooperation and collaboration." Bertrand's eyes circled the room and met the gaze of each of the participants, one by one. Then he rose and walked out.

"I'm at work. I told you not to call me here. Ever." Lloyd Overbrook quickly darted down the hall to his office and closed the door.

MGM Grand was not as exclusive as Le Cercle at Les Ambassadeurs Club in London. Nor was Lloyd Overbrook Sean Connery as a Saville Row tuxedo-clad James Bond. Nor, for that matter, did blackjack carry the same cache as *chemin de fer,* the game that James Bond always won. But when Overbrook sat at the blackjack tables and threw down a $10,000 bet, and the men gasped and the women swooned, he *was* James Bond, 007.

Even at fifty-nine, Overbrook surpassed Connery's rakish handsomeness so palpable in *Dr. No.* He maintained his physique by weightlifting six days a week. He ran seven days a week, conquering the icy, frigid D.C. streets in the winter and the humid air in the summer. He guarded every morsel he consumed. Madison, his third wife, was as lucky as the first two women he married.

Naomi Morninglory owed him. She had lured him from the Cleveland Clinic, where he had developed renown as a highly skilled internist who accurately and speedily diagnosed obscure diseases. He was a big star in a big place. As Naomi's second hire for her fledgling Renew Your Youth Center fifteen years ago, Overbrook rounded out the triune of Morninglory and Ellington. His presence at the Renew Your Youth Center lent considerable gravitas to Naomi's impossible endeavor.

He responded to her plea to move from Cleveland to D.C., because she needed him, and the chance to control aging with his very hands excited him. In the Center's first year, Overbrook took home $625,000 a year—a pay cut from the Cleveland Clinic, but *TIME* interviewed him in its feature article about Naomi, which included a dot-sized picture of him.

Annually the money crept up, and though this year he reported $10 million on his tax return, his intimacy with the 21 tables at the MGM Grand demanded he make $25 million. He sat among the men at the tables, who befriended him when he was winning. He sat among the women at the tables, awarding the prettiest a prize to make love to him after he won.

Whenever Overbrook won, he neatly stacked the chips in front of him, feeding a rush that he really was James Bond. It's just that Overbrook won with astonishing infrequency.

Most of the time he sat among the men and the women as they focused on their own game, giving little thought to the fact that a star sat in their midst. He consoled himself with his hands—the hands that held the power to cure aging. No matter how much the other players won, they couldn't compete with that.

"You told us you'd square up last Thursday. It's Tuesday, Overbrook. Oh, I'm sorry—make that Doctor Overbrook."

"I remember what I said. I'm good for it." He logged onto his computer to hurriedly check his bank account online. He wiped his moist forehead when he read his balance of $33,999.72. Overbrook ticked off in his mind the places he could siphon to make up for the shortage. Last month, he drained his savings accounts. Last week, he emptied his retirement accounts. Maybe Madison hadn't spent the household money yet. Overbrook exited his computer and dashed from his office, hoping he could make it to the bank before the two child support payments hit his account. He kept his cellphone pinned to his ear.

"Thirty-five thousand. In cash. Tonight."

"Going running, Dr. Overbrook?" Astrid called out just as he turned the corner down the hallway.

"What? Uh, yeah, going running. I'm going to change in the gym downstairs." He frowned at her interruption to his phone conversation.

"Okay, but don't forget you have a five-p.m. appointment," Astrid bellowed to his back.

He continued to whisper into his phone. "Of course, I have it. Where should I meet you?"

"Seven p.m. You don't need to worry about where. We'll find you."

CHAPTER EIGHT

"Ms. Jones?" Naomi slapped the wall, but the computer screen remained dark. Bertrand reached over her and lightly touched the screen, and it blazed to life. He raised his eyebrow at Naomi.

"It's Ms. Gregory, isn't it? I'm sorry."

"That's all right, Dr. Morninglory, just call me Tangela." The woman eased onto the metal chair, her posture erect as a colonel's.

"Sixty-seven?"

"That's right."

"And you are interested in regenerating to twenty-five?"

"Yes." Her expertly coiffed salt-and-pepper hair lightly touched her shoulders as she spoke. Minimal makeup on her smooth cocoa-brown skin belied her age.

"You understand the risks of regenerating four decades? It can be quite painful, and it's possible that during your optimal age you will experience some cognitive impairment."

Tangela Gregory rose from the metal seat, walked to the window, and placed her manicured hand on the counter, as if she was about to address the U.S. Supreme Court. "Dr. Morninglory, I'm sixty-seven years old, and I make $1.3 million a year. Last year, my bonus alone was $72,000. I sacrificed everything to become a partner in one of the largest medical malpractice law firms in the country. I have a six-bedroom home on Embassy Row and another home in St. Bart's overlooking the beach that I've only been to a couple of times because I don't take vacations. Even if I were able to get away from the office, I don't have anyone to go with me. I'm single. Never married. I've never even come close. I've had two relationships in thirty-three years. Each lasted only six months. I don't have a lot of time. I even work on the weekends."

Naomi looked at her sympathetically.

"Oh, these are not complaints, you understand," Tangela continued, "It was my choice, and...you see, I looked up from my desk, and I was thirty, so I kept working, because that's what it took to be successful at the firm. I figured I had some time. Time to meet the right man. Time to have a family. Then, I looked up again, and I was forty-two. And I said, 'Oh, I'd better do something quick, or I would be completely alone.' Even then, I looked young for my age. And I began at least trying to meet men. But, when they found out how old I was, they...they ran for the hills. I never heard from them again. To my face, I had men tell me I was just too old. Some of them were even older than I was. I didn't know it would all go by so fast. Don't get me wrong. I have met many, many men. But they were divorced and wanted a woman who could help them meet their child support payments, help them raise their kids. I didn't want to invite that drama in my life. You see, my job itself is very stressful.

"On the other hand, I saw my male colleagues, my male friends... they made the same choices I did; work long and hard. But when it was time to marry, they chose these younger women and had their families. It was like they were rewarded for spending so much time working into the night and on the weekends. When it was time for them to go home, there was someone there to go home to. I can't tell you how many times I've celebrated with other people. Their weddings, their anniversary parties, their bridal showers, their baby showers. The graduations for their children. Now, I'm sixty-seven years old, and the eligible men I know who are my age, they want me to be their nurse or their purse. I don't want to be either."

Bertrand clasped his hands together and fixed his gaze on the non-existent pattern on the linoleum floor. Dr. Morninglory handed Tangela a tissue. Her posture concaved as tears streamed down her elegant cocoa-brown face.

"They say you can have it all, and foolishly I believed them. Well, I guess some women can. You know, I can buy anything that I want—houses, cars, jewelry. But that doesn't really matter much to me anymore. What I most want now is time. I want to be loved, to get married, to be a mother. Have a family. I want to matter to someone. I want someone to matter to me. I read all about your illustrative list of side effects. I suspect that there are some that aren't even listed. I read the pamphlets, and I perused the website. I even did a background check of your Center and the doctors. I'm well versed on what to expect. I've come to a decision. I don't care whatever these side effects may be; I want what you have to offer. I want what only you can give me. I want time back."

After a long pause, Naomi placed her hand on top of Tangela's and finally said, "I see that you have given this a lot of thought and want an opportunity to make another choice. Live life differently. A chance to get back what you've missed. I do understand that..." Her earpiece buzzed. "Please excuse me for one moment." She pressed the button on her earpiece. "Astrid, I asked not to be disturbed. I'm with a patient. Who? MJ is at the front desk demanding to see me? Who's MJ?"

Bertrand glanced up from his seat. "Michael Jordan?"

"Michael Jordan?" Naomi repeated into the phone. "No, the *other* MJ. Manassas Jurica..."

Bertrand rose excitedly. "Manassas Jurica, the shooting guard for the Boston Celtics? He's only the second-best shooting guard of all time!"

"Please tell Mr. Jurica that we will be right with him, and for him to wait in the reception area. I'll be there in a few moments. Thanks." Naomi returned to Tangela, who was dotting her eyes with a tissue. "Are there any questions I can answer for you?"

"No, Dr. Morninglory. I just want to get started. I've wasted enough time."

Bertrand searched Tangela's face. "Have you considered what will happen if cognitive impairment is the side effect you experience? How this will affect your law practice and your ability to maintain and sustain your treatments?"

She met his gaze. "When I met with the pre-screening counselor and she mentioned that, I considered the impact of the side effects. Of course, it would be most unfortunate if the side effect I experience is cognitive impairment. But, if I understand the heart of your question, and that is, whether I have the ability to pay for the treatment should I lose my job due to cognitive impairment, I have extensive savings and real estate holdings that I can liquidate if need be to cover it. I don't care about any of that. What means more to me than...than anything is to start a family...have a family. Love someone...have them...love me.... Do you understand?"

Naomi rose. "Yes, I understand completely. Let's talk about next steps. There is a thirty-day decisional period, which our finance department will discuss with you when you meet with a representative. After all of the paperwork is completed, you will meet with Dr. Ellington, whose team will coordinate your Renew Your Youth formula. As you know, the formula will be administered here, in the Center, weekly for the rest of your life. If you have any questions, Dr. Ellington will be able to answer them thoroughly and completely for you. We want you to be comfortable in becoming one of our patients. Once you join the Center and become part of our family of patients, Dr. Ellington will be your personal physician available to you at all times. Thank you for choosing us to go on this journey with you."

Naomi firmly shook Tangela's hand. "I'm sorry, but I have to take care of something. Please excuse me. Please let me know if there is anything I can do to make your transition to youth smoothly."

CHAPTER NINE

No one said no to Manassas Jurica. In fact, the last time someone said no to him, he was in the sixth grade—about the time the twelve-year-old, almost overnight, grew to six-foot-three. News spread quickly that a preteen phenom was sprouting in the sleepy town of Harrisburg, Virginia, garnering him national attention. And he just kept growing. By the time Manassas reached Harrisburg High School, his amiable squared-jaw politeness and easy smile endeared him to the community and the nation as he perfected the 'aw, shucks, ma'am' move.

His flaming auburn heavy curls fell into his eyes, shielding his shyness from the camera, while his light brown freckles shone beneath his blushing cheeks. Manassas finally stopped growing at seven-foot-six, breezed through four years at Stanford on a basketball scholarship, and went pro the day after graduation. He played for the Detroit Pistons for two years and then hopped to the Boston Celtics, where he stayed until he retired thirteen years later. The nineties were all his—of course, when he wasn't being dominated by the other MJ.

In retirement, Manassas transferred his photogenic looks to sports commentating, overseas product advertising, and the occasional acting role, tripling the income he earned while playing ball. But something was missing. Every evening, he sat in the darkness of his home theater dissecting the current crop of players, imagining how they could match up against him at his best. While he slept, Manassas dreamed nightly about racing up and down the court.

"Mr. Jurica?" Naomi held out her hand. "I'm Dr. Morninglory. This is Mr. Angenois. He is the Center's Chief Operating Officer."

"Man, it is good to meet you." Bertrand shook Manassas's hand and embraced him like an old friend.

"This way." Naomi ushered Manassas into an examination room closest to the reception area. "I'm sorry we haven't much time, since you don't have an appointment. My assistant Astrid mentioned there was a problem. What can we help you with?"

"Yes, there is. Look here, I've been on this waiting list for two years. I think I've been very patient. But, ma'am, I'm ready to re...you all call it regenerate..."

"Yes."

"I'm ready to regenerate. I'm sixty, and I want to play again. I've tried business, and I like it. Done well in it. I've tried TV and commercials. I'm no actor, but I like it and done well in it. Even done a few movies. They were bit parts, mind you, but I think I did okay in them. But, ma'am, there is nothing like the smell of the locker room. Being on that court, the crowd, the adrenaline. Nothing like it." He turned to Bertrand. "Man, I look at these young guys. They can't hold a candle to me. I got more in me. I know I'm not done yet. Since I was a little kid, all I've ever done every day of my life was play basketball. All of this other stuff, it really isn't living. I know...I know. They told us in college, there's going to come a time when...when you have to do something different. When it's all going to go away. They prepared us for injuries, for getting older. Getting slower. They told us, 'Love the game, but prepare for something else.' They told us, 'Make room for the young guys.' I heard them. But ma'am, it's one thing hearing it, and another thing doing it. Doing it so that...life is meaningful. You know what I mean?"

Manassas looked at Bertrand wistfully. The former basketball giant's famous flaming auburn curls had cooled to silver tufts along his retreating hairline.

"I'm no pro athlete," Bertrand said as he sat in the seat beside Manassas, "But I understand where you're coming from, man."

"Ma'am, my life is on that court. I'm not done yet," Manassas entreated, studying Naomi's inscrutable reaction. A simple phone call was all it usually took for him to move any mountain. In the rare cases where a phone call didn't work, an in-person meeting always did.

Maybe it was the allure of being *People* magazine's sexiest man alive in 1992. Maybe it was his charisma that vacillated between confidence and wholesomeness. Men wanted to befriend him. Women wanted to mother him or lie beneath him. Or maybe it was admiration for his undeterred persistence—the same persistence that got him MVP awards six years straight. Whatever it was, Manassas Jurica always got what he wanted, and this time would be no different. He was not leaving Naomi's Center without an appointment to regenerate.

Naomi smiled patiently. "Sir, we hear that a lot. We have many talented athletes who successfully return to their sport."

"Boxers, mainly," Bertrand gratuitously offered, "loath to give up the sport. We do have a few basketball players such as yourself. Interestingly enough, very few football players. I think they get fed up of being pounced about on the field. No footballers, though—I mean, soccer players. For some reason, none of those."

"Yeah, I know about the basketball players. I got a few friends who did it. They're the ones who told me about this regenerating thing."

"I'm glad. Then you're familiar with the process?"

"Pretty much, ma'am. I just know they're back on the court where... where I gotta be."

Naomi read Manassas's pining deep-sea-blue eyes. "Mr. Jurica, our therapy can indeed restore you to, say, twenty-four or twenty-five, or whatever age you think was your best playing age. But there are side effects that you should be aware of. Of course, everyone is different, but the side effects can be anything from dizziness, impacted depth perception, joint-pain, digestive issues. I have even seen people lose their sense of smell."

"I don't care about that. I don't care about any of that."

"Yes, I've heard that before." Naomi's voice lowered in weariness.

"All I need to know is, will it get me back on that court? If the answer is yes, then let's get this thing going. Where do I sign?"

"Mr. Jurica, it's never going to be the same. You'll get back on the court, but just know that things will be different. *You're* different. Older. You've lived years of life that your teammates haven't. They're experiencing all of this for the first time, and you're not. We can make you twenty-five years old, but you won't *be* twenty-five years old. Times change. Things change. People change."

Bertrand's puzzled expression was almost undetectable as he squirmed in his chair.

"Hey, what is this?" Manassas retorted. "You're not trying to talk me out of it, are you? You did it for Kammau Wheatley, didn't you? So, do it for me."

"Mate, we can't reveal our patients, but, believe me, we can take good care of you." Bertrand gingerly took Naomi's laptop from her and began to tap on it.

Naomi's doctor smile returned. "If a patient has revealed to you that they've undergone our therapy, then you also know that there is a waiting list. Everyone has to wait. We don't allow anyone to jump ahead." She crossed her arms and leaned against the counter.

Manassas stiffened, unable to hide the flash of fire in his deep-sea-blue eyes.

"Let's do this." Bertrand snapped the laptop shut. "I'll check to see where you are on the list, man. You never know if someone has cancelled and just hasn't told us yet." He shook Manassas's hand, gripped Naomi's arm, and led her out of the door. "Stay put. Excuse us for a moment. We'll be right back."

He closed the door and went over to Astrid with Naomi in tow. "Astrid, check to see where Manassas Jurica is on the list."

Astrid gushed, "Bertrand, I told you about ordering me around. You are not the boss of me."

"Please."

"Does this mean you're buying lunch today?" She batted her newly purchased eyelashes at Bertrand.

"Morninglory, what was all that about?" Bertrand handed Naomi's laptop back to her.

"Astrid, we're in a bit of a hurry," Naomi ignored him.

"Yes, Dr. Morninglory. I'm checking." Astrid scrolled through her tablet and found Manassas Jurica's name on the list. "It looks like he will be up in the fall. Maybe in about eleven or twelve more weeks."

"Anything we can do to hasten his time? What does the call/check list look like?" Bertrand hovered over Astrid's shoulder.

"I'm checking...but you're crowding me." Astrid feigned annoyance and moved her shoulder closer to Bertrand.

"And you love it," he whispered in her ear out of Naomi's earshot.

"Based on what I see on this list, it can probably be shortened to a month, maybe five weeks. I'll stay on top of the Call/Check List Department for them to ping me each day with their results. But I'm not promising anything."

"Good enough. I want a steak sub today." Bertrand waved as he walked away, gripping Naomi's forearm tightly.

"You know I'm a vegan!" Astrid called after him.

Naomi tapped on the door, and she and Bertrand entered. She folded her arms and stood beside Manassas Jurica, who, sitting, was almost as tall as she was standing.

"We checked, and based on where you are on the list, you can begin the therapy in eleven or twelve weeks."

Manassas rose from the chair, towering over Naomi. "That's not what I came all the way from Boston to hear. I was supposed to board a plane for the Philippines this morning. I'm supposed to be there as a guest coach for an exhibition game. But, instead, I came here to see what was taking you all so long."

Bertrand stepped forward. "Uh—however, there's a chance, mate, that we may be able to get you in as early as a month. Rest assured, you're on our radar. It's going to happen, whether it's twelve weeks from now or a month from now. Just be patient for a little while longer. You'll see. We can work together to make your dream a reality." He squeezed the basketball star's shoulder.

"Okay, man." Disappointment bubbled in Manassas's voice. "I'll wait."

"Meanwhile, go on about your business. You'll see everything happens in its time. And sooner than you know it, we'll be in touch. I'll see to it personally." Bertrand smiled and handed Manassas a business card. His hand remained on the man's shoulder as he led him to the door.

CHAPTER TEN

Bertrand Angenois intentionally sandwiched his office between Dr. Van Stritton's office and the fourth-floor conference room so that Naomi was in his full view. He declined the numerous suggestions from Astrid and promptings from Naomi to move down the hall to a larger office. He wanted an unobstructed vantage point at which to watch Naomi.

Besides, Bertrand didn't really care about his surroundings in the United States. Nothing matched the natural splendor of his Freeport home—the dirt roads that ended at the warm sparkling green ocean, the sugar cane or aloe vera plants saluting in the wind, the bright green trees fragrant with soursop and wild lemons, or the blue-black nights dotted with diamonds. It wasn't that Bertrand pined or longed for his homeland. It was just that nothing here compared.

*　　*　　*　　*

"When you finish wiping off the tables, take these bottles to the back." Manshed Linville lined up the empty bottles on the bar. He ran a tight ship at Forsythia's pool hall. "You forgot the trash yesterday, Boy. I shouldn't have to keep reminding you." He smiled as he ordered his young protégé around. Forsythia had hired Manshed, who had hired Forsythia's son, Bertrand, to help him each day after school. The boy was good company, except for one thing.

Bertrand wiped his hands on the white apron tied around his waist, assembled as many bottles in his arms as he could carry, and disappeared into the back of the pool hall and bar.

"Did you ever find that eight-ball for Table 2?" Manshed pushed the clean glasses further on the shelf.

"No, I looked for it, but I think it's another one that's gone. Guess you have to add that to the order."

The wooden door creaked and banged against its sill. "Now, *this* is authentic." The tourist swung her long light brown hair from her shoulders and held the door open for her friend. "Do we seat ourselves?"

Her friend stood by the door and tugged at her micro denim shorts so that they covered more of her buttocks.

Manshed picked up two menus and walked over to the women. "I can find you ladies a seat. Come on with me." He laid the menus at a side table near the window. "This all right?"

"Yes." The tourist with the long light brown hair giggled.

Bertrand returned from the back room. He rinsed a cloth at the bar's sink and approached the women's table, wiping it with ungainly fervor.

"Thank you." The tourist's friend lifted her menu as Bertrand wiped her place, scattering crumbs into her lap.

"Oh, I'm sorry." He picked at the wayward crumbs in her lap. The ladies giggled.

"I'm not." The friend giggled. "Now, *he's* authentic," she whispered to her friend.

After the women ordered and ate, they settled with two beers at the pool table that offered the best view of Bertrand.

Manshed cautioned, "Forsythia don't like you staying too long after dark. That's enough for today. Your mama expecting you home soon."

"Not too soon. She gone to take her lettuce, tomatoes, carrots, and such to the Luxbury Hotel. She won't be looking for me to be home no time soon." Bertrand sat on a stool by the bar, enjoying the attention.

The tourist struck a ball that went airborne. Bertrand turned in time to catch it. "You ladies look like you could use a few lessons."

"It depends on who is doing the teaching."

The one thing Manshed was unable to cure Bertrand of had reared again. He warned Forsythia that lonely tourists smelled her son's brilliance and his promise. His warnings fanned Forsythia's worry that her son's appetite and arrogance was too large for the small island.

Manshed, who had lived next door to Forsythia all of her life, reminded his employer how the local magistrates had picked off each of her older brothers like ripe sapodilla when they reached fourteen years old. The magistrates scrutinized the teenagers, finding them guilty of something—anything. He told her that Bertrand displayed the same traits as his uncles. Manshed should know. The teenagers maturing into sweet men with strong flavor and sharp intellect were his friends. Forsythia argued with Manshed and insisted that her love protected Bertrand from the magistrates' reach, but in quiet moments *she* even feared it was not enough. Determination stirred within Forsythia to ensure that her son had more than the two paths offered by the small island—the magistrates, or soul-diluting island work. She saw how jail had sucked the sweet ambition from her brothers and how farming her family's land had dulled their brilliant flavor.

Wrestling with Manshed over an unrepentant Bertrand's future, coupled with piloting an adolescent Bertrand on the cusp of manhood around the island's minefields, exhausted Forsythia. He was growing into a fruit well beyond her reach.

But nothing clamored her alarm as loud as when Manshed had summoned her that day to her pool hall to see her thirteen-year-old son lying on flour sacks with two tourists in the kitchen. The faces of the women were burned into Forsythia's memory—one at each end of her son.

Forsythia, expressionless, walked slowly to the phone that hung on the wall, dialed a long-distance number that—despite her best efforts to forget—had been seared into her memory. Bertrand's father in America. For years, the man had begged her to send him his son. It took three days for her to finalize the arrangements. The fear of Bertrand's future with her was far greater than the pain of sending him away. She relented, released Bertrand, and put him on a plane to Washington, D.C., wrangling one condition from his father: to tell Bertrand he was his uncle.

Consoling herself to be her son's compass, she declared 'that way, I will always be his home.'

Bertrand arrived in the U.S., excited that the ocean no longer hemmed him in on the island and that long drives on the roads actually took him somewhere else.

Everything in the U.S. was big. Washington, D.C. was big. His father's home there was big. Yes, big, fine homes existed in Freeport, but Bertrand had never been in one. He shared his one-bedroom rambler with his mother and slept on the pullout in the living room. The biggest buildings Bertrand entered were the boutique hotels while on errands delivering his mother's sought-after vegetables. The limitless variety of this big, new land engendered gratefulness in a boy famous for ingratitude.

Grateful that his uncle opened his big home to him, gave him his own room with his own bed, and cared for him so willingly. Grateful that his aunt opened her heart to him as if she had birthed him. Grateful especially that this couple poured their largeness into him, expanding his borders so that he became large, too.

So, Bertrand endeavored to make his mother, his uncle, and his aunt proud by voraciously seizing this opportunity with a hunger he never knew and never displayed at any time before. With that, he spread his young wings wide and alighted on the breeze of America's waves, graduating from high school at sixteen.

So now, as Bertrand sat in his closet office, watching for the sway of Naomi Morninglory and listening for the intermittent click of her heels as she darted by his door, his gratitude for Forsythia's sacrifice to send him to the U.S. was personified.

His aunt...even after her death all those years ago, he dipped from her well of love retrieving strength, confidence, integrity, and humor. But gratitude to his uncle, father, whatever, that he left in the folly of his youth.

CHAPTER ELEVEN

The tenseness from Naomi's face drained as she involuntarily released her clenched jaw when Bertrand strode into her office.

He returned her smile. "Interruptible?"

Naomi removed her glasses and rubbed her eyes. "The vultures are circling in the air, and the piranhas are chomping in the water."

"Oh, I don't know about that."

"I do. Everywhere I turn, people are trying to get more money. Senior staff are relentless for more money. Now, even the support staff are angling for raises. Even Liliya stopped me in the hallway and asked me when the cleaning staff were getting a raise. There is no other place in the world where the cleaning staff make $100,000."

"Look at it from their perspective. They know how much this place is making. It's always in the news. They're the miners, working day in and day out. You can't fault the miners for wanting a little bit more gold."

"Yeah, but they're very well-paid miners."

"I read Thomas's proposal and feasibility study. It's pretty sound." Bertrand walked around Naomi's desk to get her full attention. "You're pretty far away today, Dr. Morninglory. It sounded to me like you were trying to dissuade Manassas Jurica from regenerating. I noticed the dosage you prescribed for Mr. Darchow. If he took the dosage you prescribed, he would not regenerate from seventy-six to forty-seven, the age before his dementia set in. He'll age hover. You know, the board of his tech company is pressuring us to regenerate him as quickly as possible so they can thwart this upcoming takeover. I even saw Mrs. Hueng's chart. Overbrook forgot to consult both the Collaborative Treatment Chart and the Regeneration Chart to avoid complications with the twins. I'm not trying to be critical, but it's not like you to miss when Overbrook miscalculates his formulations. I've always known you to catch his mistakes and make the necessary adjustments. Clearly, your head's not in the game today."

Naomi plugged her iPad into her desk computer and watched her notes download. "What did you say?"

"I said, I'm trying to keep us from any lawsuits. This is what I mean, Naomi. Your head's not in the game. What's wrong? Marlon told me Curtis was over last night. Did he say something to upset you? Is there something wrong?"

Tears fell furiously from Naomi's eyes. The faster she wiped them away, the more that appeared.

"Hey, hey, look at me." Bertrand raised her chin to his face and said, above a whisper, "You want to talk about it?" The familiarity in his touch, in his manner, was new.

"Curtis is in trouble." Naomi measured her words, parceling them out as she struggled to understand it all herself.

"So, what else is new? Don't worry, he got himself in it, he can get himself out of it. He always does."

"Not this time."

"Really?"

Naomi turned her head from him.

"Tell me." As Bertrand stood next to her, his closeness enveloped her, and his warmth and strength confused her emotions. "You know what I love most about my work?"

Naomi shook her head, wiping her eyes with a crumpled tissue.

Bertrand bent down to be eye-to-eye with her. "What I love most about my work is being with you. You have to know that by now. It shouldn't surprise you." His large weathered dark-brown hands slid up her neck and rested around her chin, pulling her face to his. His lips kissed her lightly, testing her.

She stiffened and drew away. Bertrand tasted like heaven. Naomi had not imagined the two of them like this.

"You're beautiful. Intelligent. I like being around you. Very much."

She inched away from him, but he only moved closer. "Please, Naomi. Don't shut me out." He had said Naomi's name many times before, but this time when he said it, it landed between her thighs and dripped down her legs. He nestled his face in her neck. "Please."

Since her divorce from Curtis ten years ago, Naomi operated on autopilot, focusing on two things—the Center and Haron—and that was only when he allowed her to. Now, Bertrand set fire to her skin in a way that could be doused only by his touch. She turned toward him, and he parted her mouth with his lips. He pressed against her until she found herself weakening on the soft leather camel-colored couch in her office. His lips never left hers.

Bertrand held her chin. "Look at me. Stop for a minute and look at me."

"What? Why?" She opened her eyes.

Bertrand brushed her hair from her face. "I want you to see my eyes. This is me. You're a renowned doctor. You meet with kings and queens. Presidents, in fact. I'm a nurse. I don't know if I have the pedigree you're after. I'm just a plain ol' bloke who happens to be the COO of your company. Let's not forget that I work for you."

"I know that," Naomi cooed, leaning into him.

"My father always told me not to get involved with anyone at the job. He would say, 'Bertrand, don't stir your pecker in your money pot.' He'd practically pop a vein if he knew about this." The corners of his eyes creased at the memory. Yet, he followed the paisley pattern of Naomi's white, gray, and yellow DVF silk blouse with his nose and then lightly touched her nipples with his index finger. As she writhed beneath him, he deftly unbuttoned her blouse and traced her cleavage in her midnight blue lace bra with his tongue. "I have always loved your breasts." His baritone echoed in her skin.

"We are not going to talk about body parts." Naomi reached to cover her breasts with her arms, but Bertrand pinned them away.

"I love your body. It is a treat for me to watch how you move every day. I see you walk down the hall. I walk next to you. It makes me just want to hold you. You don't know how much that this is my dessert."

He licked Naomi from her neck to her armpit and made small circles around her breast until he reached her nipple. He sucked gently, then feverishly, until she begged him to stop.

"I can't stop. You don't really want me to stop, do you?" His heavy lips pressed into her ear. He reached beneath her skirt, and his fingers passed her lace underwear to feel the wetness. He inserted his meaty digits, simulating himself until she groaned. "I'll stop, if you want me to." He guided her hand to unzip his pants and touch his growing bulge. His hands gripped her wetness, and he held himself inside of her so she could feel him involuntarily pulse. "Tell me, 'Stop.'"

Discovery between the two friends lasted hours. With each kiss and caress, Bertrand healed Naomi's shattered heart. They unwrapped their sticky entwined limbs. They glowed from each other's sweat. Naomi stretched as if his touch had awakened her for the first time. She looked at the smiling Bertrand. "This is not what this couch is for."

"It should be. And, for a few more things, I'd be glad to show you if we had more time." He kissed her deeply and sucked her willing tongue, as he lay wedged between the back of the leather sofa with his leg anchoring her on the cushion. He brushed her curls with his finger. "You know what?"

"Yes, I know. Things will never be the same between us." Naomi reached for her silk blouse.

"That's not a bad thing. Everything changes." Bertrand took the blouse from her, balled it up, and threw it onto the guest chair. He positioned her to face him. "Marry me."

It slipped out. The years of watching her summed up in two words.

"What? What did you say?"

"I love you. Marry me."

Naomi's phone pinged. She got up, padded in bare feet toward the sound in her purse, and squinted at the message. "Overbrook. He doesn't ever sleep."

"If he doesn't sleep, maybe he should do some more of this." Bertrand embraced Naomi and lay his head on her shoulder, biting her neck. "Let me tell him that." He grabbed her phone and peered at the message.

"Harry: I'm sorry about yesterday. I miss the softness of your skin. I can still smell you and can't wait to be inside you again."

Bertrand stiffened, pushing Naomi away.

"Haron Fitzgerald." Bertrand stepped in his underwear and lifted his pants from the chair.

Naomi reached for her phone, but Bertrand held it high above her head. She avoided his accusatory gaze and quickly dressed.

Bertrand pressed. "Oh, I get it. I'm a placeholder for the good Dr. Haron Fitzgerald. A dalliance until he's free. I'm not good enough for you. Not part of your precious talented tenth. Not some bloke from Harvard with the fancy manners."

"Where is all of this coming from, Bertrand? I mean, really, it was just sex. Good...very good sex, but..."

Bertrand's glibness was muted by anger. Naomi's intractable arrow had just hit an unintended target. His eyes dulled with a wound she knew she caused. A picture of the pain in his eyes streamed like a video in her mind each time she blinked.

After the seconds that seemed like hours elapsed, Bertrand finally spoke. "You know what, Naomi? You're what women say men are. With you, it's the thrill of the conquest, isn't it? That's what happened between you and that poor sap, Curtis, isn't it? Once you got what you wanted from him, you were no longer interested. You left him flapping around in the wind."

Naomi's face hardened.

"It's all fantasy with you, isn't it? I mean, with Dr. Haron Fitzgerald. Snagging him gives you a rung up, is that it? I mean, really, Naomi, rung up from what? Then, once you get him, then what? And at what cost?"

"You don't know what you're talking about. Give me my phone back."

"Don't I?"

"I don't even know why we're having this conversation." Naomi sank into the plush camel-colored leather couch and pushed her feet into her black patent leather Ferragamo slingbacks.

"You want to take this man from his wife...his kids. I mean, really, the man has a family, Naomi. But I guess that doesn't matter to you, does it? Doesn't quite fit into your plan. The only thing that matters is that you get what you want."

"Harry's children are grown."

Bertrand paced up and down Naomi's office suite, his anger seeping out like pus in an open wound. He paused at the door. "You know what? This I'm not going to do."

"What do you mean?" Naomi's voice strained.

"You're not God."

"Don't be ridiculous."

"It's just an illusion, isn't it? This RYY. Yeah, you invented a way for people to appear young. A seventy-five-year-old who looks twenty-six, an eighty-three-year-old who looks twenty-two, or some such shit. But it isn't real. All you really did was give them a whole different set of problems."

"Well, I don't hear them complaining. I don't hear Mrs. Hueng complaining, now that she's about to have twins, after experiencing menopause for fifteen years. I...I don't hear Mr. Darchow complaining, now that he...that he has reverted to an age where he doesn't have dementia anymore. I do a lot of good."

Bertrand stood in front of Naomi. "You don't hear their complaints. I do. I read the letters, the emails from patients who have problems for which there are no solutions. Like when they look younger than their grandchildren. You acting like God gave them a choice. And now you're so used to playing God that you think you can do that with me. With Haron. With Curtis. But this is real life. Not an illusion. Not a fantasy. My fucking life." He gripped her arms tightly. "And you know, Naomi, if he loved you, he would have left his wife a long time ago. Try loving someone who isn't an illusion. Someone with real blood flowing through his veins. Someone who is right here."

Naomi writhed away from Bertrand's grip. "Oh, I'm supposed to... to drop everyone out of my life because now you're in it? Everyone else should be gone. You're in love. You want to marry me so I should be able to give you an answer just like that." She snapped her fingers.

Anger flashed in Bertrand's eyes. "Darling, it should be an easy answer. If you know what's good for you. If you're smart."

"I *am* smart. You said it yourself. You work for *me*, remember?"

"Careful. Don't confuse me with your adoring public, your employees. Those people who run around you like little pups, trying to appease and please Naomi Morninglory. Or, at the very least, make you think they're trying to please you. Sweetheart, I don't need you to make me feel important like your boy, Curtis, does. And I don't need to be your bed warmer until Harry has nothing better to do. When a woman is important to me, I show her. And I don't sneak around with her in the dark, hiding from this person or that one. Sexting like a fucking teenager." He threw her phone on the couch beside her.

Naomi watched as a swirling river of complications sprang up between them. "I...I wasn't expecting this. I wasn't expecting any of this."

Bertrand walked to the door and stopped, fingering the doorknob. "You weren't expecting it? Or you didn't want it? Careful, think before you answer."

"Is this some kind of test?"

"No, baby. I don't want you to wrack your brain. Put you in some kind of quandary. But understand that this $11 million you pay me, it ain't for fucking. Let me be very clear: I have six offers from pharmaceutical companies in my inbox right now. All I have to do is press 'Send.'"

"Oh, so now you're going to quit?"

"No, I didn't say I was going to quit. But don't think for one single second that I won't."

Bertrand opened the door and walked out.

CHAPTER TWELVE

Overbrook was convinced that, although someone was following him, no one would be foolish enough to disturb him in the fitness center at the prestigious Army/Navy Club. After all, how could they get in without a membership? He lay back on the weight bench, thinking what exit offered the best cover from anyone watching from the street. To give them the slip, as James Bond would say. He had the money, but it was his, and he wanted to keep it that way as long as possible. Perhaps after rush hour, he could make it to the MGM Grand and all his troubles would be over, since it was a Tuesday, and Overbrook was lucky on Tuesdays. He could win enough to cover his losses and pay his two ex-wives.

He was bench pressing his two-hundred-pound weights, silently mapping out his route to avoid the traffic to the MGM Grand, when somehow, from somewhere, a twenty-five-pound weight rolled onto his foot.

"What the fuck?" Overbrook writhed in pain. "Get off my foot!"

"Dr. Overbrook, you have our money?" A man in a dingy Nats T-shirt that matched his dingy, scraggly beard crouched down to stare eye-to-eye with Overbrook.

"Get off my foot! Of course! Just get off my foot!"

"Well, I'd like it now, please."

"It's...it's in my locker." Overbrook rubbed his beet-red left foot as it swelled before his eyes. "What the fuck, man..." He eased from the bench and limped toward the men's locker room. "You didn't have to do that. I need my foot. I told you I had the money." He located his locker, opened it, and shoved a heavy manila envelope into the man's chest.

"Look, Overbrook. We don't like to take the extra steps. You said last week you had the money, and I had to call you to ask where it was. Timely payments."

Overbrook sat on the bench in front of his locker. "You got your money."

"Oh, so you're dismissing me." The man bucked toward him and stopped. "You know you're not even worth it." He turned to leave, then turned back. "One more thing, Dr. Overbrook...as much as we like doing business with you, you should find another hobby. It don't seem like those tables like you very much."

*   *   *   *

"Doctor, your five o'clock is early." Astrid watched Dr. Overbrook limp to his office. "What's wrong with your leg?"

"It's my foot—I—uh—I hurt it running. It'll be all right."

"Want me to bring you some ice from the cafeteria?"

"Maybe later. Which examination room is his file loaded onto?"

"Four. It's Cinander LeGrande."

Cinander LeGrande sang better than he danced, he danced better than the best hoofer on Broadway, and his acting was better than both his singing and dancing, crowning him with an EGOT—an Emmy, Grammy, Oscar, and Tony. The Iowan, who stood at five-foot-eleven, once had a muscular frame that belied his effortless agility. His sun-streaked, fluffy hair tousled in every appealing direction. When Cinander peeled his eyes on you, even if it was only virtually through a movie screen, his green and hazel eyes mesmerized you, and everyone else simply disappeared.

But at sixty-three, the passion Cinander had channeled into performing was extinguished by food and liquor, ballooning his weight from a compact 178 pounds to 323. His bank account vanished along with his sexiness, but when he unleashed his charisma, aiming his green and hazel eyes at you, he remained unrivaled. Forty-five days ago, Cinander began regenerating to twenty-seven, his age when he won his second Tony and first Oscar.

Cinander sat on Lloyd Overbrook's examination table in the Regeneration Stabilization Department, struggling to cover his girth with a sheet, because their largest hospital gown had failed to fit him.

"Puzzling, Mr. LeGrande." Overbrook studied the file on his laptop. "I have gone over the calculations for your formula with several of my colleagues, and we still find it puzzling."

Cinander swung his doughy legs, hitting them against the table's side. "What's the problem, Dr. Overbrook?"

"According to this formula, you should be regenerating, but you're stagnant. It's like you're in age limbo." Overbrook stared at his laptop and tapped his temple. "Open your eyes wide again." He shone a light into each of Cinander's green-and-hazel eyes. "You know, this only happens when one of two things are occurring." He clicked the light off and placed it in the pocket of his lab coat.

"Really? What's that?" Cinander flung the sheet across his shoulder like a toga.

Cinander was unaccustomed to interrogation. Fame shielded him from skepticism, and most everyone believed everything he uttered, except his bill collectors, who hounded him daily. Cinander had found a way to pay them handsomely for their patience.

"Number one is, the patient is missing some of his or her appointments, or, number two, the patient isn't taking his pills with the prescribed frequency, which can be caused by number one."

"Well, Dr. Overbrook, you can attest that I'm here dutifully every week. You give 'em to me and I just take 'em. Swallow them. Dr. Overbrook, you know that. I think I just need a stronger dose of that stuff."

"Interesting. You know, we did some checking. The staff called around to some of the hospitals." Overbrook lied.

"You did? For what reason?" Cinander's earnest expression did not change.

"We do that when we can't match the symptoms with our treatment. When there's an anomaly and things don't add up."

Overbrook crossed his legs as he sat on the stool. His foot throbbed, and its swollenness strained against his shoe. "We found out that George Washington Hospital had a patient in their emergency room last week—sallow skin, shallow breathing, heart palpitations, excruciating joint pain, headaches."

"Oh, yeah? Sounds terrible. Poor guy. So?" Cinander ambled his girth so that his feet touched the floor.

"They ran some tests, and they all came up negative. That's when we asked them to check for regenerating."

"So?"

"So, these are symptoms of pill-sharing. This is an indication that the patient is not receiving enough of the dosage to regenerate, but enough so that they do not revert."

Cinander cocked his head at Overbrook, smiling with EGOT earnestness.

"You wouldn't be pill-sharing, would you, Mr. LeGrande?"

"Oh, no, Dr. Overbrook! How on earth could I do that? I have to come to this Center every week to get this damned pill. And swallow it in front of you so that I can't share it with anyone else. You've seen me." He crossed his arms.

"Correct. I've seen you. But one thing I've learned from all my years as a doctor at this Center is not to ask how a patient does anything. I just know there's a black market out there. Patients can make thousands of dollars sharing their pills with someone unable to receive the therapy through normal channels. At the Center. We've seen it before. Patients pill-sharing with people on the waiting list, or with people unable to afford the therapy, so they buy pills at a cut rate—on the black market, if you will. We take these things very seriously. It's against your contract, and there are consequences that accompany such an action. RYY could sue you for breach of contract and refuse to provide anymore therapy. Send you to Maturation and Reversion immediately to set your course for reverting."

Cinander's eyes blinked with the slightest recognition of fear.

"Also, remember that your pills are customized for your

regeneration, carefully calibrated to your cell composition based on your age, physical condition, etc. There are health ramifications for all involved. The body isn't designed to be in a state of non-aging. The stagnation can cause irrevocable damage to your organs."

"Doctor, I don't like where you're headed with this. I already told you, I'm not pill-sharing. I think the problem lies with this crackpot clinic. Go back to the drawing board and fix what's wrong, then give me a stronger dose."

Overbrook limped to the door, his throbbing foot a reminder of a problem in need of a solution. He pushed a black button beside the light switch, turning off the video and audio recording that was always used during every patient visit. "Because, if you *are* pill-sharing, I'm sure that you and I can work something out."

CHAPTER THIRTEEN

Attorney Oliver Steinberg massaged and pushed the womb of Naomi's mind until her contractions signaled the birth of her crazy idea—a pill that restored youth. He acted as a midwife, easing the baby Renew Your Youth pill from her. Then, tottering on his newly minted lawyer legs, he crafted her business. Symbiotically, the twins—Oliver's fledging solo practice and Naomi's Renew Your Youth Clinic—grew side by side.

Oliver filed Naomi's patent and trademark applications, compiled her trade secret formulas, played hardball to get the FDA approval fast-tracked with exclusive advertising rights, and negotiated her contracts. His baby grew from an intellectual property law firm, run at a table at Starbucks on Reservoir Road, to one of the world's preeminent IP lawyers, with a sprawling office complex on prime real estate on Connecticut Avenue in downtown D.C. His practice mushroomed into publishing, media law, franchising, corporate, and antitrust, with offices on the West Coast and in Atlanta. The two friends grew in tandem in their fields: Oliver into a titan of law, Naomi into an unrivaled doctor of regeneration therapy. Fusing his future with hers, Oliver kept his palatial headquarters on Connecticut Avenue so he could answer Naomi's call quickly. In these sixteen years, they spent so much time together, ruminating over every angle of RYY, that Oliver knew Naomi better than he knew his wife, Ellarie.

In fact, he considered himself an expert in solving all matters concerning Naomi Morninglory. But this, he was not prepared for.

Oliver perched his champagne glass atop the turquoise-swathed cocktail table. The annual Renew Your Youth Foundation gala was in full swing at the Robert and Arlene Kogod Courtyard of the National

Portrait Gallery. The pillars were bathed in turquoise, fuchsia, and yellow lights, the colors of the RYY Foundation. Confetti in those colors dotted the cocktail tables and were scattered on the floor.

"Naomi, I don't know how Curtis got mixed up with Aspacio Aranha, but I have a feeling this is not going to end well," Oliver whispered through his smile as he shook hands with the visiting doctors who had flown in from China. "Welcome, welcome. Yes, please, have a glass of champagne." He handed them glasses as a waiter held the tray.

"What can he do to me? I have a bodyguard twenty-four hours a day. There must be *something* we can do. Oliver, I've worked too hard to give half of my business to some lowlife like Aspacio Aranha or anybody else. What about the FBI? There are laws to protect against extortion." Her plastered smile hid her worry. "Please review the story boards on the wall. It shows how we are putting your money to good use. We have eradicated homelessness in Washington, D.C. We built apartment homes for them all across the City, and plugged them into social programs that will keep them in their homes. Those are the two state-of-the-art hospitals in Ward 7 we built." She strolled with the guests along the walls, pointing to the enlarged photographs that hung as murals.

Dr. Leonardo Ho encircled Naomi and inserted himself between her and Oliver. "Dr. Morninglory, my colleagues and I are wondering when you will open up a satellite Center in China. It's much better for your patients in Asia. Easier than traveling weekly to the States. Especially when they are in the early stages of regeneration and the pain is most acute."

"Dr. Ho, this evening is not to talk about business. It is to highlight the work of the Foundation. Have another glass of champagne." She handed him a glass.

"Dr. Overbrook promised us that RYY would be opening a Center in China. We want to know when."

Naomi smiled her most authoritative smile. "Dr. Ho, Dr. Overbrook is an excellent doctor, committed to regenerative therapy and an expert in anti-aging methods. But make no mistake about it, I make those decisions. And right now, I have no intention to open another Center anywhere. Please excuse me, I have a few other matters to attend to with my assistant."

Astrid twirled multi-colored ribbons in her fingers. "Mr. Steinberg, you don't have your ribbon. I made them myself." She pinned a turquoise, yellow, and fuchsia-looped ribbon on his lapel.

"Aren't they beautiful? She's very talented." Naomi hugged Astrid and stroked the ribbons pinned to her Armani Privé, liquid-silver silk sequined gown.

"And very creative." Oliver winked.

"Thanks. I have one for Bertrand, but I haven't seen him yet." Astrid stood on the tips of her toes, surveying the crowded courtyard.

"Keep looking. I'm sure he's around here somewhere." Naomi tipped her glass to her mouth, and then handed it to Astrid.

"You're getting pretty good at this." Oliver leaned toward Astrid.

"Yup, fifth year in a row. Thank you. I'll take the compliment." Astrid lifted the folds of her lemon-yellow chiffon gown, letting it fall like petals to her ankles. "Do you like my dress? I picked it especially since it matched the color of the ribbon."

"Very much. And you clean up nicely."

"Thank you, and you, too." She smiled at Oliver, then turned to Naomi. "Now, Doc?"

"What?"

"The students. You want them to start now?"

"Yes. I think we have a critical mass now."

Oliver watched Astrid depart toward the stage. The panels of her lemon-yellow gown billowed behind her. He whispered to Naomi through his smile, "Listen, I didn't have time to go to my office when I got back from L.A. this afternoon, so I locked my bags and briefcase in the Foundation's temporary office upstairs. It's quiet, and we can talk in there without being interrupted. We can steal upstairs during the performance."

The Duke Ellington Show Choir's voices soared to the cathedral ceilings, imprinting the swing sound of Ella Fitzgerald on the rafters.

"Let's go." Oliver nodded toward the stairs.

Bertrand waded through the crowd, finally resting his eyes on Astrid, and pushed until he reached her.

"Hi. Aren't they terrific?" Astrid bounced to the choir's rendition of *It Don't Mean a Thing* as her dress swayed around her like a yellow cloud.

"Yes, they have quite a future in front of them." Bertrand scanned the crowd. "Seen Dr. Morninglory around?"

"You didn't say anything about my dress."

He eyed her up and down. "How'd you get all that hair up there?"

She frowned petulantly. "Is that all you noticed?"

"Lovely. You look very lovely, Astrid."

"Thanks. You look almost perfect." She swooned.

He smiled and sipped from the champagne flute. "You haven't answered my question."

"You know what I've noticed?" She giggled.

"What is that, Astrid?"

"I noticed that you like thick steaks medium-well. That's what you get whenever we have our monthly corporate lunches."

"Guilty. Very observant of you. You are correct. I love a good steak."

"You know what else I noticed?"

"No. What is that, Astrid?"

"I noticed the way you're always watching her. Dr. Morninglory. You don't think I notice, but I do. You do more patient appointments with her than any other doctor. I checked."

"You did, did you?"

"Yes, I did."

"One thing's for sure."

"Oh, yeah? What's that?"

"You need to mind your own damn business. Back to my question:

Do you know where she is?"

"Oh, all right. I saw her and Oliver go up the stairs. They're probably in mission control. That's what I call the temporary office I set up for the gala. Room 3412. Right at the top of the steps."

As Bertrand turned away, Astrid tugged his arm to stop. "Oh, I forgot. I have this for you." She lingered as she pinned the multi-colored ribbon swirl on his lapel. "Now you're perfect."

Oliver unlocked the Foundation's temporary office and clicked on the light, holding the door open for Naomi to follow him. The door shut loudly behind them. "Good turnout, don't ya think?" He unpinned the looping ribbon from his tuxedo jacket, tucked it into the pocket, and laid his jacket on the long table beside the door.

"You asked me what I know about Aranha." He unstacked two chairs and placed them at a round table. "You've heard about the fire in that housing development in Southeast. Twenty-five people were killed. Well, that was Aranha. I heard that it was all because a family pulled their son out of his crew. Some of the people who died were children. That entire neighborhood is gone. Winthrop Estates. So tragic. I have to tell you, Naomi, whoever his talons touch, they end up dead. Everyone knows he's behind it, but in all these years, the police can't link him to that crime. Or to any other. That fire was awful. It was on the news. The people who are left are too scared to testify."

He reached beneath the tablecloth. "I know I left my briefcase and laptop under one of these tables." He bent under two more tables, swatting the tablecloths until he found his items. He returned to the table, where Naomi sat staring at the closed curtained window. "And that's just that crime. I've heard so much about Aranha. Kidnapping, drug distribution, money laundering, money lending, I really could go on. He seems to be made of Teflon. Nothing sticks. Naomi, what has your security team said about all this? You know those bodyguards you pay so handsomely?"

"I just heard this yesterday from Curtis. It threw me for a loop, since Curtis is involved in getting me to negotiate with an extortionist."

Oliver plugged in his laptop and signed on. "Well, you need to beef up your security while you figure this out. But, quite frankly, if he wants to get at you...I just don't have a lot of faith that they can protect you."

"Think, Oliver. This is America, not some third-world developing country where corruption rules..."

"Say you go to the FBI. Right now, all you have is what Curtis told you. No direct threats from Aranha. You don't even have any evidence. No emails from Aranha, no tape recordings of phone conversations. Nothing. Who do you think is going to back up your story? Curtis? Really? At this stage, he can deny it all, and what would you look like? Some lady in fear for her life, because of what? They'll think you're crackers."

"You think I'm making all of this up?"

"No, of course I don't. I know you. They don't. I'm just saying you're going to need more to go on than what Curtis said."

Naomi walked to the large floor-to-ceiling window and drew the heavy curtains. She looked down on the busy Friday night on G Street—the couples, the groups of young people laughing on their way to dinner, the movies, or just a plain night out before Memorial Day weekend. They were completely unaware that her life and the lives of her patients were rapidly shredding. Little did they know in an instant everything in life could just change. Worry washed over Naomi's face.

"Why is my word not good enough for them to do something? At least investigate. Isn't anyone interested in catching criminals?"

"Right now, they'll say no crime has been committed."

"What do they need, my dead body?"

"No, but they do need proof. A little something called evidence." Naomi cried into her hands.

"Hold on. Calm down." Oliver ripped a sheet of paper towel from the roll on the table and handed it to Naomi. "Say they believe everything you say, Naomi. Aranha is so dangerous that they're likely to put you in witness protection to keep you alive so that you can testify. Everything in your life will change. Your identity will change, and you won't be Naomi Morninglory anymore. How will you be able to treat your patients? Operate your Center and conduct your research? Hold meetings with your staff? If you do it remotely, say, from Oregon or Montana, everything, nowadays can be traced. It's just a matter of time before he finds you. Even out there. I don't know. Maybe it won't be so bad, if you gave up half your business. You have all the money you could possibly need."

"What are you saying? Your money or your life?" Naomi leaned against the window sill, glaring at Oliver. "Why do lawyers always give such bad advice?"

He bit down on a half-chewed No. 2 pencil and placed his laptop on the table. "Bad advice? Let me remind you that if you had listened to me, you wouldn't be in this fix."

"What?"

Oliver tapped on his keyboard. "I told you when you were divorcing Curtis that he was bad news, and to give him fifteen percent of the valuation of the business as of five years after the date of the divorce. You didn't even want to give him stock. I said, let's just give him prospective cash. Put it in writing in the divorce decree. Bam! All at once the man gets cash. Plus, he could've gotten monthly dividends for life. Give him dribbles every year so that he will go away and stay away. Poor cheap bastard, I told him to hire a lawyer. If he had hired a lawyer, he probably would have gotten a better deal. He was broke then. Cash at that time would have been worth what...?"

Oliver clicked on the calculator function on his computer and tapped in numbers. "Ten billion dollars, give or take a few. You'd be done with him. But no, you didn't want that." He leaned in his chair, removed his left shoe, and rubbed his foot. "Fancy shoes always hurt. I've seen it before."

"Seen what before?"

"This."

"This what, Oliver?"

"D.C. is full of professional women who got it together on the outside. Head of this department, run this government agency, partner in this law firm. Congresswoman or Senator This or That. But when the sun goes down and the door closes, they get lonely, like everybody else. I'm not judging. I'm just saying when you're lonely, you become a prime target for a pussy run. All it takes is the wrong man to say the right thing...to the right woman at the wrong time." He pulled off his other shoe.

"A pussy run?" Naomi laughed mirthlessly.

"Naomi, D.C. is still a small town. I play tennis with Marlon, a.k.a bodyguard and driver, every Sunday. I know how to protect my investment. He's a fount of information. He told me that Curtis comes by every few months or so to get him some. In the nineties, we used to call it a 'booty call.' In this Internet age, it's a 'pussy run.' Everything's quicker. Microwave sex." He twirled his half-chewed pencil.

"Oh, please. This is not about sex."

"Naomi, *everything* is about sex. Even *money* is about sex. The more money you have, the hotter the chick. The hotter the chick, the better the sex."

"I'm not sleeping with Curtis."

"Sure, you're not."

"Seriously, I'm not."

"Tell me, how does he smell?"

"What? Why?"

"I just want to know. C'mon, humor me. How does the man smell?"

"Good. A deliciously fresh scent...like he just stepped out of the shower. His shirts are always crisp. They smell freshly laundered all the time."

"See, if you noticed how he smelled, then he's poundin' it."

"Oliver!"

"What? Oh, Naomi, look at it from where I'm sittin'. A man goes to his ex-wife's house every few months at night and leaves two hours later."

"That's because he's always hurting for money. He looks at me with those lost puppy dog eyes...I don't know...I just feel..."

"Guilty. Please, I could've solved that years ago. We could have set up an automatic monthly bank wire transfer. No. Naomi, don't tell me he comes over and you give King Asshole money. Good God, Naomi, no wonder you can't get rid of him! Why should he leave you alone? It's like those neighborhood cats. You feed them once, and then they just keep coming back. Meow...meow."

"Oh, Oliver!" Naomi wiped her eyes. A faint smile crossed her face.

"Tell me, how much?"

"What?"

"I'm curious. How much have you been giving him?"

"I just give him a little. You know, something to tide him over."

"How much is 'a little'? The truth." Oliver's voice deepened, emphasizing his seriousness.

"Just a few hundred thousand dollars every time he comes over—"

"Two hundred thousand dollars every *what?* Every six or seven months? I can't believe you've been doing that! What the hell were you thinking?"

Naomi pressed her forehead against the window.

"Deep-fried mess. I told you—brilliant woman plus honey-talking man. Deep-fried mess."

Naomi shot Oliver a withering look. Feeling the heat of her gaze, he sat up in his chair.

"Steinberg, are you going to help me?" Her words sizzled with anger.

"I've been with you since the beginning. The late nights. The filing deadlines. You remember how I'm the one who had to keep visiting those FDA people...God, the bureaucrats...to ram through the approvals. That's where all this gray hair came from." Oliver ran his hands through his chestnut-brown hair with gray strands and leaned back in his chair. "Just think about the paperwork it would take to add this man as a partner. Surely, it would flag the SEC. Then, how does it affect the Foundation?" He rubbed his temples. "I mean, for years they've been blaming you for the uptick in crime. The thefts, car jackings, burglaries...anything people could do to pay to keep up their treatments—buy more time to stay young. Now *you're* the one being hit up! I guess this is what it means to be a victim of your own success. By the way, I caught last night's *60 Minutes* segment. I thought it was unfair. I don't think you're a twenty-first-century crack queen."

"You know, yesterday everything was working. People thought I was doing a good thing. Today, it's just a total disaster."

"I'm sorry this is happening to you, Naomi. I wish I could say something different. Something comforting. I hate to see you so upset."

Naomi smiled wearily at her longtime friend and reached for his hand. "You ever wonder why we didn't get together?"

"Oh, I know why. You had me working so hard on your business. Calling me night and day. And we both know how you are about keeping your money right. Am I right?"

Naomi smiled. "You're right."

He narrowed his eyes on her. "Speaking of your business, while I have you here, I just want to make sure I have your electronic signature on file. Small things come up, and I don't want to keep bothering you for your signature."

"Yeah, like what?" she said through a fog.

"Oh, like *pro forma* stuff. Renewing your trademark registration... other routine government forms. Which reminds me: I should review your patent portfolio while I'm at it."

Naomi leaned over Oliver and signed a form, which he slipped into his briefcase. "Thanks. I'll just scan this in the morning. Hey, stop worrying." He squeezed her shoulder. "I have a law school classmate at the FBI. I'll run this Aspacio thing by him. I have another friend at Justice. Maybe they'll have a different take. I'm supposed to leave in the morning for Japan and then spend two weeks in Germany and Switzerland to wrap up some business ventures. And then, Ellarie and I are taking the kids to Paris and then Provence until the 3rd of July. But I can change all that. You need me here."

"No. Don't rearrange all of that for me. Just call me when you hear from your friends. In the meantime...I'll beef up my security."

"Promise?"

"Yes."

Oliver tapped on his calendar. "Okay, but it really is no trouble. I'd feel better if I was around."

"No, Oliver. Go. My security team can handle this."

"Okay, then let's schedule a meeting for when I get back on the third. Does six p.m. work for you?" He snapped his laptop shut.

"Yeah. Six should be fine."

"Get some sleep. Things always look better in the morning. I'm sure we can figure this out."

A staccato pounding on the door startled Naomi.

"Easy. I'll get it." Oliver opened the door. "Hey, Bertrand."

"Hello." Bertrand looked at Oliver, and then at a still visibly shaken Naomi. "Am I interrupting something?"

"No. Not at all. I was just on my way downstairs." Naomi skirted past Oliver, and then Bertrand, who stood at the door.

"Hey, Naomi, don't forget our appointment. I'll call you from Japan after I hear from my friends." Oliver called out.

"Yeah," she answered from the hallway.

Bertrand trailed closely behind her as she ignored him and walked quickly down the corridor. "Is everything all right?"

Naomi briskly walked toward the staircase, ignoring him.

"Naomi, I can tell something is wrong. Tell me what it is. Maybe I can help." He grabbed her hand before she reached the mouth of the stairs.

"Bertrand, I'm fine. Just leave me alone. Everything is fine."

CHAPTER FOURTEEN

"Dr. Morninglory? Dr. Morninglory?" Astrid waived her hand in front of Naomi's face.

"Oh, Astrid. I didn't hear you knock."

"I did, but you didn't say anything. You've been dragging around all day. But that's to be expected since everything ended so late last night. It was a great turnout. I just checked. Fundraising said we're still getting some online donations."

"Yes, I know." Naomi's voice sunk deep into her chest. She struggled to hide her worry from Astrid's inquisition.

"I would have thought you'd be floating on air. Are you getting enough sleep? I've been drinking kale and apple juice before bed. I mix in a little chamomile tea. I sleep like a baby." Astrid smiled and pushed her black frame glasses on the bridge of her nose. Her dreadlocks carefully wound into two charming buns.

"Yes—no, I mean, yes, it was a great event. No, I didn't sleep very well. Next time, I may have to try your kale and apple juice concoction." Naomi spun to face her computer to end the conversation.

"I thought you should know that New Patient and Finance are beefing again. Dr. Ellington wants an answer about the waiver for El Hadid Mohile, since he may not be able to get a visa from Turkey to enter the country as often as his treatment requires. They want you to weigh in. Dr. Ellington said she sent you an email about it yesterday but you haven't responded. Apparently, they need an answer in the next few hours. Oh, and don't forget that the annual review of the updated employee security clearances is due by COB today. I put the flash drive in your top drawer. Bertrand gave me his recommendations yesterday. I passed with flying colors." Astrid smiled.

"Anything in here I should be concerned about?"

"Well, Doc, they did report that Dr. Overbrook spends a lot of weekends at the MGM Grand. VIP member. Apparently the twenty-one tables are not his friends. Bertrand is concerned that this may be the beginning of some kind of problem. He explained something about Dr. Overbrook being susceptible to undue influence. He said he wanted to meet with you about that. But, you know, Bertrand, he thinks everything is the beginning of some kind of problem."

"Yes, I know. I'll talk to him about it. Anything else?"

"Not that I saw."

"Thanks. I'll work on it before I leave tonight."

"Okay, Doc. Then can I leave early? It was a long night for me, too."

"Sure. Go home."

"Thanks. Have a good evening."

Naomi inserted the flash drive in her computer. Safe and Sound Security always did a good job on the comparison charts of the previous and current years of her employees' lives, highlighting major changes such as marriages, divorces, deaths in the immediate family, and large-scale purchases. Perusing the report, it was clear that her employees enjoyed lives that didn't even faintly resemble her own. Lives filled with people they loved and people who loved them. Their wives, husbands, boyfriends, mothers, fathers, children, grandmothers. The extended trips to exotic locales, the real estate purchases to places they regularly visited. Inside lives that did not revolve around waking up to arrive at work in the dark and staying at work, leaving only when it was darker. She imagined how much laughter their inside lives engendered.

The Safe and Sound Security report read like a TMZ article. Lindicott recently purchased a fifteen-acre ranch in Arizona and stocked it with five thoroughbred horses. He hired a trainer, a jockey, and a liveryman. *Interesting. Lindicott was setting himself up to race horses. Possibly getting ready for retirement,* she surmised. Fatimah

Webster, the preacher of endless fiscal responsibility at the Center, recently purchased a twenty-six-unit apartment building in Oahu.

Naomi flipped through the gorgeous pictures. *Nice.* Van Stritton purchased a New York penthouse apartment on the Upper East Side. *Didn't her mother live in New York? Or was it her daughter? Interesting. McIntosh divorced his wife and replaced her with a twenty-four-foot speedboat and a twenty-three-year-old girlfriend.* Scobey Thomas founded a school for children with disabilities in Lusaka, Zambia. *Gruff old Thomas, really. Who knew he was such a softie? As usual, Ava made no changes from last year's report and just stockpiled money.*

Naomi glanced through Bertrand's recommendations, which he had annotated in the report. She agreed that they should speak to Overbrook about his gambling, and in six months, review his income/debt ratio for improvement.

Usually, when Naomi thumbed through the security report, she skipped Bertrand's entries, as he hadn't changed anything in the six years since joining the Center. He still had his penthouse condo in NE. He still sponsored a soccer club for elementary school girls in SE. He still paid the college tuition for five of his former players. He still sponsored a soccer club for middle-school boys in Freeport. There was nothing new. As Naomi speed-read Bertrand's entries, she paused. Winthrop Estates. Oliver had mentioned that Aranha had destroyed an entire neighborhood. *Wasn't it named Winthrop Estates?* Maybe it was because this new death threat singed Naomi's nerves, or maybe it was because Aranha now possessed her every thought, that Naomi kept reading.

Bertrand's first address in the United States was at Winthrop Estates. He closely guarded the details of his life. When pressed, he charmingly and deftly diverted the subject. He spoke adoringly of his mother in Freeport, the delectable vegetables she grew, the brilliant blue skies that stretched across the island, the lush vegetation that sprang along the dirt roads, the warm, transparent water. He mentioned that when he had arrived in the U.S. from the Bahamas, he had lived with an uncle and an aunt. In unguarded moments, he released dribbles of information about his aunt but rarely mentioned his uncle, and, to Naomi's recollection, never mentioned his uncle's name. She tapped on her keyboard, searching to see if their home was among those the fire had destroyed.

She Googled *Winthrop Estates, 131 Sterling Street, Washington, D.C.,* the first address listed for Bertrand in Safe and Sound's security report. She squinted at the results, hoping her eyes were deceiving her. Property owners: *Aspacio Aranha and Mandolin Aranha.*

CHAPTER FIFTEEN

Caprice knew every step that it took from Gate 17B to reach the Enterprise Rental Car kiosk of Reagan National Airport. Each Wednesday, she boarded the red eye from LAX and when she arrived in D.C. Thursday morning, drove straight to the Renew Your Youth Center for her evaluation and to receive her next pill. Because Findlay complained about the mounting costs, Caprice stayed overnight at a hotel only if the pain was too excruciating for her to sit through the plane ride home. The sympathetic first-class flight attendants had hot tea and blankets waiting for her when she boarded. Their compliments on how Caprice looked younger with each treatment buoyed her spirits and soothed her intense headaches, nausea, dizziness, and aching joints.

Caprice adamantly resisted Dr. Ellington's suggestion to visit the Center's Collaborative Medicine and Pain Management Department fearing it would slow the progress of her regeneration. The process had to go as fast as possible, because regeneration was pulling apart her marriage the younger she became. Worrying that Findlay would pull the payment plug any minute, she wished she had listened to Aurora and saved more of her money. But even if she had, her savings wouldn't be able to cover the regeneration therapy payments on her own for the rest of her life. So, she felt that the sooner she became twenty-four, the sooner she would return to A-list actress status and pay for the treatment herself.

Caprice was forty-five days into the treatment and halfway to youth. It was easy to remember as Caprice spent Memorial Day weekend in bed. The doctors had warned her about the side effects, but no one told her that her once luminous skin would be a tinted green color or that her eyes would be constantly bloodshot. She had to hold onto walls as she walked to keep her dizziness in check. First, Findlay showered her with adoration and care as his "little patient." This did not last very long. He hated that she was sick from her treatments all the time, and her sickness tapped the last dredges of his sympathy. His thinly veiled resentment toward her spending most of her time in bed was pushing both of them to the brink.

Findlay did not hide his belief that Caprice stopped caring for him or their business. Every day when he came home, he made snide comments about paying $300,000 annually for the therapy. Every time he looked at her, she could practically see him calculating the cost of the treatment floating above his head.

Yet sometimes—with increasing rarity, however—Findlay was really sweet. When he sensed she felt better, he gave her a stack of client applications to review and project sites to visit. He hired a temp to help him at the office and a caretaker for Caprice at home. He hired a maid and a cook. Caprice knew it unnerved Findlay for strangers to invade their home, as he barked that there was no difference between his home and a train station. In fact, he argued about everything, including the way the maid folded his underwear, which made him feel as if he was in the military.

In their first years of marriage, Caprice landed the occasional role as the mother or older wisecracking best friend of the ingénue, jetted to location, staying away for weeks or months at a time. Findlay seemed proud of this, and displayed patience with the infrequent demands of her wilting career. She noticed that her fading star power in Hollywood brought out tenderness and heightened ardor in Findlay, as if he relished that she was home more and that he no longer had to share her with the public.

But in the last ten years, Caprice's work had dried up, to the point where she could not even book voiceover work. This worried her, for she knew Findlay still banked on her star wattage to be good business. He beamed at his clients' reactions whenever he trotted Caprice Deveaux out at his business meetings.

Now that she was regenerating, he didn't seem to know her at all anymore. He didn't share her excitement as she paraded the subtle changes to her body in front of him. She could not contain her delight at seeing her face gradually transform from wrinkled to tight and smooth. On it shone a peachy dewiness she had forgotten she once possessed. Her posture straightened, her bust perked, her waist whittled away three inches, the flabbiness under her arms disappeared, and the buoyancy returned to her hair. She slept better, because her hot flashes disappeared. She had more energy. She didn't need glasses anymore. She wanted sex all the time.

The closer Caprice reached her optimal age of twenty-four, the less frequently she vomited. She managed her side effects by fighting through the excruciating joint pain in her arms and legs. The episodes rarely lasted longer than a few hours, so she waited for them to pass. However, she preferred that pain to the odd pain that cut through her stomach so sharply she fainted. She hid her side effects from her doctors for fear they would dilute her dosage to slow the regenerating pace. Squeezed between trying to return to her Hollywood A-list spot before the next "it" girl was discovered, eclipsing her second chance forever, and Findlay's obsession with the cost of the therapy, Caprice felt pressed.

Ava handed her a small white paper cup containing her final regeneration pill.

"Six more weeks, doc. This little thing is a life saver." Caprice placed the pill far back on her tongue and swallowed a large sip of water.

Ava tossed the small white cup in the trash receptacle. "Yes, you are half way there."

"But to me, I look like I'm all the way there. I mean...just look."

"Yes, patients always feel that way. They look in the mirror and see the dramatic changes but you still have a ways to go. Believe me, there are more changes to come."

Caprice turned the two-carat diamond stud in her left ear. "What about if I need to go on location, Dr. Ellington? In my line of work, I could be away for months at a time. In order to take the pill, I can only go someplace for what...four or five days at the most, since I've got to be back here every four days? And take this weekend. It's the Fourth of July. Findlay and I usually go to Jackson Hole, but this pill has me pretty tethered to D.C."

"It's a sacrifice, Ms. Deveaux. This is something you'll have to do for the rest of your life. You'll have to budget your time accordingly."

"Yeah, Findlay is pretty disappointed about spending the Fourth at home. And I'll just have to make sure that there is a rider in my contracts that location shoots can't last more than a few days," she thought out loud.

Ava's chestnut-brown eyes narrowed at Caprice. "At your initial consultation with Dr. Morninglory, she explained the side effects of reversion, correct? We can't overemphasize how important it is for you to have your pill every seven days. You have to understand that the reversion process is...is different for everyone, and the stress, the toll it takes on the body can cause problems that are not reversible. For example, if you don't get your stabilization pill in the forty-eight-hour window, your organs can go into shock. Your liver, kidney, heart. We can do everything we can for you, but once your organs are affected, the problems may become irreversible. For some of our patients, especially the older ones who have other health challenges before they regenerated, it has meant death."

"I got it, Dr. Ellington. Okay?"

"Good. Take all the time you need to get dressed. Don't forget to make your next appointment with the receptionist before you leave." Ava smiled efficiently.

Caprice stepped into her yellow suede mules and reached for her floral printed linen shirt. "Thank you, Dr. Ellington. I mean it. This regenerating stuff, it really is saving my life."

CHAPTER SIXTEEN

It was the weather. It was the weather that first drew Lloyd Overbrook to Case Western Reserve University in Cleveland, having been admitted to every medical school at which he applied. It was the weather that kept him in Cleveland, as he stayed to become chairman of the Cleveland Clinic. He reveled in the fall's sunless days and the winter's snowy, ice-filled ones. The summers suited him. Cloudy. On the rare occasions the sun escaped, it scurried back behind the clouds where it belonged, knowing Overbrook detested the heat.

It would have to be something revolutionary to lure him to D.C.'s humidity. To be on the cutting edge of age-reversing medicine was irresistible. He chanted to himself over and over that working at the Center was worth it, especially while wading through D.C.'s hot July humidity.

He rounded his second lap of pacing the Police Memorial across from the Judiciary Square metro station. It was that small-minded Naomi's fault. She had stopped listening to him. He stood sentry beside her from the day she opened the door to the Center. He and Ava, her first hires, did everything at that Center, except mop the floors. And what did his loyalty get him? She had closed up her ears and stopped listening to him.

That Center made $73 billion last year. How much did he see of it? Morninglory sure got her share. What was it? Overbrook sharpened his mental pencil and quickly calculated at least $8 billion. What did he get? Ten million. Yes, it was more than the newer doctors and the other senior staff, but one million less than Bertrand, and he wasn't even a doctor.

If Naomi were to listen to Overbrook's plea to expand the Center and add more patients, then he would make more. Didn't she know he...the other staff had needs? Just because Naomi sat in that office day in and day out didn't mean he was going to spend his life that way. She had no children, and she rattled around in that behemoth estate. He had two ex-wives to pay alimony to—child support payments. His current wife, Madison, binge-watched luxury channels surfing for ideas to solicit proof from him that he loved her.

To top it all off, his daughter at Middlebury wanted a Tesla for her birthday next week.

The other doctors and senior staff counted on him to persuade Naomi to expand the Center. After all, they had needs, too. Lindicott was trying to raise a triple-crown-winning horse. Fatimah endeavored to become a real estate mogul in Hawaii. Van Stritton hoped to retire to her New York penthouse apartment. McIntosh was enamored of his speedboat and impressing his new supermodel girlfriend. And Thomas wanted a Nobel Prize, so he was planting schools in Africa for children with disabilities. Even Bertrand did something with his money: running those two soccer clubs. That couldn't be cheap. But all Naomi did was prance around in her designer clothes. No one could even see them under her smock. Sure, Ava didn't do anything with her money, but maybe she would if she had more of it. Ten million didn't go as far as everyone thought it did.

Overbrook helmed the effort to get Naomi to expand, but she had stopped listening to him.

Overbrook's stare would have melted Cinander LeGrande had he bothered to gaze up from the bag of pistachio nuts he picked at as he sat on the cool stone bench.

"When is he going to get here?" Overbrook broke through Cinander's daydreams.

"He'll be here." Cinander blithely sat on the stone bench, shucking nuts. "You want some?"

Overbrook shook his head. "Why are criminals always late? I have somewhere I have to be. I have appointments to keep. Patients, you know."

"Dr. Overbrook, I guess you forgot. Once you started this enterprise with me, you are now a criminal too...and you're not late. Ergo, not all criminals are late." He smiled impishly.

"I'm not a..." Overbrook blustered.

"Look, see, I told you he'd be here."

Lolly approached the two men and dapped Cinander. "Hey, man. I'm sorry if I kept you all waiting, but I had to stroll around a bit. Check out the perimeters. Make sure you weren't doing nothing stupid."

"What does that even mean?" Overbrook quizzed Cinander.

"It means that my introducing you into the equation made my friend Lolly nervous. Man, I've been doing business with you now for...how long? You know you can trust me. Sit." Cinander returned to the stone bench. "With Dr. Overbrook here, it'll be easier for us. I won't have to resort to hiding the pills in my molar. He'll just give them to me. There are other advantages. Volume that I couldn't accomplish with sneaking one pill out every other week. Dr. Overbrook can make this happen for us. He's an important ally."

"So, how can you help us, Dr. Overbrook?" Lolly reached into Cinander's bag of pistachios and drew out a handful. "Can you get us bottles filled with these pills?"

"No, it doesn't quite work that way. But I'm pretty sure I can get at least five patients to cooperate. I can give them double dosages one week, and the next week they can sell us their pill, which will also contain a double dosage. Hopefully their bodies will tolerate double dosages. But I can't guarantee it. There is a downside to all of this. The patients' regeneration will be slowed, but I can calibrate the dosages so that they won't revert. Mind you, the people...the patients outside of the Center will not get a customized pill, so you'll have to find people who have mirrored conditions."

"Five people—that don't seem like very much." Lolly turned to Cinander, who looked at Lolly and then back at Overbrook.

"What's this about mirrored conditions?" Lolly flicked a few empty shells into the bushes that rimmed the memorial.

"Term of art in age reversal medicine. It means patients with similar characteristics. For example, same age at time of regeneration, patients who desire the same optimal age, patients who are in the same general health condition. Same gender. It won't work otherwise."

Lolly and Cinander read each other's expressions. The latter finally spoke. "I think we can handle it, man. It will just mean, Dr. Overbrook, you'll have to give us the stats so we can make the matches."

"I can do that."

"We'll just have to be careful who we offer the pill to." Cinander held his bag of nuts open in front of Lolly, who nodded in agreement.

Overbrook viewed the men intensely. "You'll have to warn these out-of-the-Center patients—or, let's call them 'off-line patients'—that they won't receive the same support for their side effects, the monitoring of their regeneration, and if they choose to discontinue, they'll be on their own. I don't want to be on the hook for another set of pills."

"Explain that part to Lolly, Dr. Overbrook. I've heard this spiel."

"Patients who decide to discontinue the therapy are sent to another department so that they can ease back to their actual age. It can be hell on the body to just revert cold turkey. But I won't have access to that formula, because it is in an entirely different department, and, quite frankly, it is a lot of trial and error. I don't have time to do that *and* work with you *and* keep up with my patients."

Lolly and Cinander shrugged their shoulders at each other.

Lolly spat a pistachio shell into his hand. "I can live with that. After all, nobody's forcing them to take this shit."

"All right, let's talk numbers." Cinander sat between the two men to facilitate the conversation.

"The best I can do," Overbrook explained, "would be to provide five pills every other week, ten pills a month. We, of course, will have to offer my patients a cut for the use of their pills."

Lolly shucked the pistachios and flicked the shells onto the ground.

"This don't seem very sustainable. Just five patients. I don't know a whole lot about medicinal and what not, but I do know there's Bayer and there's aspirin. There's Aleve and there's naproxen. What I'm saying is there's the brand of a pill and there's the generic one. Because my grandma is always taking the generic because of the cost. Seems to me, it would be more sustainable to wait her patent out. That way, the barrier to market entry would be lower and we would have more customers. That would be sustainable. How long does a patent last?"

"Twenty years," Cinander chimed. "We've done our research. He has a point, Doctor."

Overbrook stood as a professor about to lecture his class. "The beauty of Dr. Morninglory's invention is because each pill is customized to the patient, the drug's patent isn't subject to expiration. It just continues. There will always be a high barrier to market entry. You see, she's the only one. Her competitors are frauds. Cheap imitators."

Lolly and Cinander frowned at each other.

"How tasty for her. Let's look at our options again." Lolly pursed his lips.

"Dr. Overbrook, then you can only add five people to our enterprise?" Cinander clarified.

"And if we sell the pills at $5,000 a pop, that means $50,000 for ten pills a month." Lolly sorted through the nuts in his hand.

"Dr. Overbrook, we can offer your patients $1,000 for each pill they contribute, and then split the remaining $45,000 three ways—you, me, and Lolly," Cinander surmised.

"Meaning, I jeopardize the career that I worked my entire life to get for a measly $15,000 a month?"

"Think big picture, Dr. Overbrook. It's tax free. All yours." Cinander crumpled the empty plastic bag and deposited it in the trash receptacle.

"Yep, Dr. Overbrook, $15,000. That's icing, man. Tax-free icing. And just think—if you get us more patients...more patients, more pills.

More pills, more money." Lolly wiped the salt from his hands.

Overbrook paced around the circular memorial, stopping in front of the concrete bench where the other two men sat. "$15,000 a month, huh? More patients, more pills. More pills, more money. Okay, that's a start."

CHAPTER SEVENTEEN

Bertrand rapped his knuckles on Naomi's open door. "Truce? I don't have a white flag to wave, but it's a truce nonetheless. Can we talk?"

"About?" Naomi shrank toward her computer blocking the screen. How could she have thought Bertrand was her moor, anchoring her and her business, when he was secretly conspiring with his uncle to take her business? And if she refused, he would kill her. She thought she knew him, but now everything about him signaled 'stranger.'

"We both said things we shouldn't have. Did things we shouldn't have. Let's leave it at that," Naomi spat out too quickly.

"Naomi, I'm sorry for getting angry, but I'm not sorry for expressing how I felt. It's still how I feel. I want us to work out." Bertrand swallowed and leaned on her desk. She angled in front of her computer and moved nervously away from him. "Oh, I see. It's like that now?" He retreated, gliding into her office chair. "Wow. It's like we never happened. Morninglory, you can turn people on and off faster than anybody I've ever met. But me, I don't operate like that. I don't switch my emotions on and off quite so quickly."

"Neither do I." She feigned brightening her mood. "You're right. Let's talk about it over dinner. I ordered a cheeseburger from the cafeteria. They can't deliver it, because they're short-staffed today. Would you mind picking it up for me? While you're there, why don't you get something and bring it here? We can eat together and talk."

"I didn't hear there was a problem with the café. Funny, I usually have my ear to those kinds of things."

"Uh, it was sent by email. Probably got lost in your inbox. You can check when you get my cheeseburger."

"I have an even better idea. Let's get out of here and go get Italian. I know you love lasagna. I have a luscious little spot in mind. Soft music...dim lights."

"I already ordered the cheeseburger. Plus, I really do have to finish these security reports. We can talk, and I can flip through the reports."

"Morninglory, ever the romantic. As you wish." He lightly touched her cheek and walked out the door.

Naomi grabbed her silk coral jacket from the back of her chair, reached for her purse in her desk drawer, and peeked around the door. Bertrand was hovering at Marlon's cubicle at the end of the hallway. The two conversed and laughed as they strode down the corridor and turned the corner. She quietly shut her office door behind her, tiptoed toward the elevator, and pounded the down button. She heard a set of footsteps grow louder on the linoleum floor and listened intently. They sounded like the familiar steps of Bertrand.

Sure enough, he spotted her darting to the ladies' room. As the door swung closed, he walked over to it and tapped on it. "Naomi?"

"Oh, yes."

"Is everything all right? Why aren't you using your suite's bathroom? The toilet's heated, for heaven's sake."

"Uh, something's wrong with my commode. The flushing button malfunctions. I've called it in to maintenance—something about ordering a part. Well, oh, is my food ready that fast? I'll be out in a minute."

"No, I haven't gotten it yet. I forgot to ask you what you wanted to drink. Do you want fries?"

"Yes, a Coke and regular-size fries. It's all on my order. Thanks."

Naomi waited by the door for a few minutes, pressing her ear against it. Bertrand's footsteps grew faint. She looked down the empty hallway then ran into the stairwell, where she galloped the steps two at a time to the floor directly beneath her. There she swung the door open, looked up and down the corridor, boarded the elevator, and pressed "G."

Once she reached the ground floor, Naomi ran through the

underground garage, stopping at her vacant parking space. "Fuck," she muttered as she realized that Marlon had left her Mercedes at the dealer earlier that afternoon for routine servicing and had the keys to the loaner on him.

In the distance, Naomi heard the squeal of a car's brakes. Caprice's rented late model Audi screeched as she navigated the turns of the underground garage. When she drove by the building's garage entrance, Naomi hurled herself in front of the car, drummed on the hood and motioned for Caprice to stop.

"Dr. Morninglory?" Startled, Caprice rolled the window down.

"Yes, yes, please let me in." Naomi ran to the passenger side door and furiously lifted the handle. "Please, quickly."

Caprice pressed the button and unlocked the door. Naomi climbed in and ducked down into the passenger seat.

"Go, please. Just drive off as fast as you can. Hurry!"

CHAPTER EIGHTEEN

Bertrand put the tray of food on the glass conference table in Naomi's office. He lifted his own plate of blackened salmon, rice pilaf, and steamed broccoli from the tray and placed it beside Naomi's. He sucked deeply from the straw, swallowing iced tea while glancing around her expansive, empty office.

"Naomi? They didn't have your order, so I had to wait for them to make it." He sat at the conference table and fiddled with his knife and fork, arranging it on a napkin. Hearing no answer, he bellowed, "Did you hear me? They couldn't find your order, so I had to wait for it."

He took inventory of her spacious office. The jacket that normally hung on the back of her chair was missing. He checked her drawers. Her purse was missing, too. He knocked on her office bathroom door. No answer. He opened the door, switched on the light, and held the toilet handle down. Water gushed and swirled around the bowl.

He peered out into the hallway as Liliya stopped at the cubicles and made her rounds emptying the waste cans.

"Hi, Liliya."

"Hi, Mr. Bertrand."

"Can you do me a favor?"

"What's that, Mr. Bertrand?" She eyed him suspiciously.

"Don't worry, it's a quick one. Check the ladies' room for me? I'm looking for Dr. Morninglory. She was supposed to meet me in her office, but she's not there. I think perhaps she's in the ladies' room. Can you just pop in for me to see if she's there?"

"Sure, Mr. Bertrand." Liliya pushed through the door to the ladies' room, returning moments later. "No, sir. No one's in there."

"You sure?"

"All gone home. Or at least gone somewhere else."

Bertrand smoothed his hair and walked back to Naomi's office where he sunk in her black leather chair and swiveled back and forth, tapping each finger on her gleaming cherry desk. He ran his fingers across his beard and scratched it absently. Her computer screen was in power save mode. He flipped the power off and on and then logged in with his password.

Where *was* Naomi Morninglory, and why had she sent him on a wild goose chase?

*   *   *   *

"Where are we going? What's going on?" Caprice tightly gripped the steering wheel.

"It's a little hard to explain. Oliver should be back by now. Please take me to 1737 Connecticut Avenue. Turn right here." Naomi pressed Oliver's cell and office numbers on her phone at least ten times as Caprice navigated through the afternoon traffic. It went straight to voicemail.

"Oliver? Who's Oliver?"

"My lawyer."

When they reached Connecticut Avenue, Naomi fidgeted. "Here. Stop right here. I'm going to get out. Pull up behind that blue car and wait for me. I won't be long."

Naomi sprinted from the car to the building where Oliver Steinberg had his office. As she stepped toward the revolving door, glass shattered, raining shards down around her. An ominous thud landed a few feet away. She jolted toward the direction of the sound and saw a motionless man clad in a suit with limbs twisted like a discarded marionette. Instantly recognizing the suit, she braced herself as she headed toward the familiar body in it and bent down beside the motionless figure. His limbs splayed in impossible directions. His head was smashed flat against the concrete. His blood escaped toward the curb.

Naomi ignored the screams of the onlookers and felt Oliver's warm, blood-soaked neck: no pulse. She beat back tears to see something sticking out of his jacket lapel pocket. She reached into it to retrieve the turquoise, fuchsia, and yellow-looped ribbon pin from last night.

"Don't touch nothing." A burly police officer sweating in the hot July sun admonished Naomi kneeling beside Oliver's broken body. "You know what happened?"

"No, I don't know. I was going into this building, and then the next thing I know is, there was a crash and a loud thud. There he was."

The police officer removed his cap and ran his wrist along his forehead in a futile attempt to remove beading sweat. He radioed for an ambulance.

"You know him?"

"Yes, yes, I do," Naomi stammered.

"What's his name?" The officer pulled a miniature tablet from his pocket and began to scribble on it.

"Steinberg. Oliver Steinberg."

Dorinda, Oliver's long-time secretary, rushed out of the building, flailing her arms toward the body. Naomi caught her, preventing her from reaching the contorted body. "Dorinda, what happened? Are you all right?"

"Yes, I'm all right. Dr. Morninglory, I don't know what happened. I went to the eighth floor to the valet to pick up Oliver's dry cleaning. You know, he just got back from Asia and Europe. He just came back to the office to take care of a few things. He said he had to meet with you. He was going to Chicago tonight. Meetings all day tomorrow. He didn't have time to get his dry cleaning, so I went for him. When I came back to give it to him, the window in his office was broken..." Dorinda heaved, crying between sentences. "Why would someone hurt Oliver? I just don't understand. I just don't get it."

Another woman ran toward the scene and placed her hand on Dorinda's shoulder. "Charmaine...it's so...awful!" Dorinda cried heavily into the woman's shoulder.

"Ladies, I need a statement from you. Peters, take a statement from these ladies." The police officer motioned to a smaller officer wearing mirrored aviator sunglasses.

Peters directed Dorinda and Naomi through a growing crowd of onlookers to a parked squad car. "Folks, behind the yellow tape. C'mon, get behind the yellow tape. Ladies, can you wait for me right here? I gotta get these people away behind the tape."

"Doc, what is going on?" Caprice approached Naomi. Her gold bracelets jingled as she put her hands on her hips.

Peters pushed against the crowd as many onlookers held up their cellphones. "C'mon, folks, show some respect. You wouldn't want to see that on YouTube if you were his loved one, now would ya?"

Sirens blared. A news cameraman and reporter ran up to Peters. Another cameraman set up a tripod beside the police cruiser.

Naomi grabbed Caprice and ducked down, weaving through the growing crowd. "I'll explain, but not here. Where are you parked?"

They drove in silence, stopping on 16th Street in front of Meridian Hill Park, where Caprice parked the car and turned to Naomi. "Okay, so tell me. I can't go any further until I know what this is all this about. Who was that unfortunate creature on the pavement? Good God, death in real life is a lot different than in the movies. For one, they don't get up and walk away when the director yells, 'Cut.'" She leaned her head against the steering wheel. "Geez."

Naomi shook her head as her eyes filled with tears. She exited the car and treaded heavily on the russet-colored pebbled steps, pushing the overgrown vegetation that obscured the path to the park. Her feet steadied on the uneven pathway she was feeling through her yellow suede sandals. This was real. Oliver was dead. And, unless Naomi gave Aspacio Aranha what he wanted, she would be dead, too.

Naomi ambled to the cracked large concrete fountain and listened to the water trickle through the intricately carved spout. She splashed her fingers in the refreshing water, startling the ducks that swam in the fountain to honk and fly above Caprice's head.

"That man—he was Oliver Steinberg."

"Tell me again, who's Oliver Steinberg?"

"He is my lawyer, the man we were going to see. He was the closest thing I've had to a brother. Poor Ellarie. And his kids."

"Wow. Ellarie?"

"His wife."

"How many children did he have?"

"Two. A boy, three. A girl, nine." Naomi threw a handful of pennies in the fountain.

"Oh, Doc, I'm so sorry. A shame. A real shame."

Naomi wiped her eyes and leaned against the gurgling fountain. "You have to help me. There are some people...a person who wants ownership of the Renew Your Youth Center. If I don't make him my partner, fifty percent ownership, then he's going to kill me. I can't go back to the Center. Oliver Steinberg was trying to help me, but...but he killed him. As a warning to me."

"Wait a minute, Doc. That's quite a leap. Oh, I'm sorry. I mean, that's quite a stretch. How do you know this? It...it could have been an accident. Or something...something that didn't have anything to do with you."

"It could, but it didn't. See, I found this in Oliver's pocket." Naomi rubbed the entwined ribbon pin between her fingers.

"What is it?"

"We gave these out yesterday at the gala for my foundation. Everyone was asked to wear them. It's a sign from this man to me."

"Who is this person? Doc, what are you talking about?"

"I'd rather not say who. But obviously, he is making good on his threat."

"Doc, wait a minute. This can't be. You just can't snatch a person's business from him—I mean, her. You have resources. Hire another lawyer. Can't you fight this thing? What about the police?"

Naomi sat on the lip of the fountain. "Well, that was what I was doing with Oliver. And you see what happened to him. This person is very powerful. Very dangerous. I wouldn't say above the law, but definitely beyond it. Oliver said the cops can't keep me safe. They couldn't keep *him* safe."

"Doc, I heard you have bodyguards. Where are they?"

"Yes, I do, but at this point, I can't trust anybody. I suspect he's co-opted them, too. He has someone working on the inside. One of the persons I trusted the most." Naomi's voice broke.

"What do you mean?"

"It's like a cancer that's infected my whole business, and I don't know how to eradicate it. I'm worried about myself, but I'm more worried about my patients. There are a lot of lives at stake. People... patients who are regenerating need their weekly pills, or they will revert to their actual ages in twenty-four to forty-eight hours."

"Yes, I know, you said that in our consultation, and Dr. Ellington explained that to me again this morning at my appointment."

"The problem is that, even with medical assistance, the reversion process is very dangerous. Some people die."

"That's what Dr. Ellington told me. I get it. But, Dr. Morninglory, other doctors administer dosages. Dr. Ellington has been giving me my pill since I started the therapy. Just call them up and tell them to keep giving out the pills until you get this thing sorted out. No offense, but no one is that irreplaceable. Not even the president." Caprice hugged her black python Lanvin handbag to her chest and adjusted her buttocks so that she sat beside Naomi on the lip of the fountain. "Besides, if you ask me, you could use a vacay."

"They only think they're administering the dosages—"

"Okay, what are you talking about, Doc? What do you mean, 'They only think they're administering the dosages'? Doc, I'm telling you, they *are*. In fact, Dr. Ellington gave me mine."

"Listen. A few weeks ago, I implemented some quality control measures. A few checks and balances, if you will. So, I had a chip installed in my hand that unlocks the Dosage Delivery Machine. We call it the Dosage Dispenser. The other doctors don't know about the chip." Naomi rubbed the slight bumps that resembled bar codes in her right hand. "The teams devise the formulas, which I review. Based on those formulas, the lab technicians upload this information into a dosage machine that manufactures each customized pill. Every morning, my chip automatically updates the patient's identification number with the corresponding dosage. Not only that, but my chip also unlocks the dosage dispenser for the patients scheduled to receive medication that day so the doctors can administer the pills."

"So, let me get this straight. Without you, this dosage machine won't update with the people's new formulas? And even if it did update, you wouldn't know which pill goes to which person? And even if you could get the machine to update, and you could find out which pill goes to which person, no one can open this machine to get the pill out, but *you?*"

"Correct."

"Whew, sounds pretty complicated. And I thought my husband Findlay was a control freak. But what is your Plan B? Say, what happens when you go on vacation or out of the office for a few days? I mean, you do leave D.C., don't you? Even I saw your TED Talk. I had to reschedule my initial appointment with you several times because they told me you were out of town." Caprice peered at Naomi skeptically.

"I just implemented this new system a few weeks ago. I haven't been away from the Center since."

"So, tell me, what would happen, say, if you, God forbid, died? All of your patients, including me, would suddenly just revert because we couldn't get ahold of our meds?"

"No, there is someone else with a chip."

"Who? Let's get 'em on the phone."

"It's Bertrand Angenois, my Chief Operating Officer."

"I know that name. He's the guy I met that day when you were explaining the process to me."

"Yes, him. But he's working on the inside—against me."

"Mmmm, that's a shame. I rather liked him."

Naomi shot Caprice an exasperated look.

"Just being honest." Caprice leaned over and watched the fountain water churn and bubble. "Geez, and I thought my life was mess...and he is the only one with a chip."

"And his chip is only activated when...when my pulse is silent."

"Silent? You mean, like, dead?"

"Exactly."

"Okay, then let's *not* call him." Caprice leaned on the edge of the fountain and held her bag protectively against her. "Doc, this thing is getting scarier and scarier. I really don't see how I can help you. I think we need someone else. Like the police...the FBI...the fire department. Someone other than me."

"I wish I could ask them. Even if we did go to them, they wouldn't understand. At this point, they'd think I'm crazy. We don't have a lot of time. I'm afraid when you turned that corner in the garage, you drove right into my life and into this problem. You...you're all I have." Naomi put her hand on Caprice's shoulder.

Caprice stared pensively at the fountain. "If I understand what you're saying, if I don't help you, I'll revert to fifty-eight tomorrow, or the next day max. And in the process, I might die."

"Yes."

"If I don't help you, all your other patients will revert, too, and some of them may also die?"

"That sums it up."

"Wow, how'd I get myself into this mess? Findlay told me to keep my ass on the West Coast, but no, I didn't listen to him."

"You have to help me."

"Okay, okay. What do you want me to do?"

"This all started with my ex-husband, Curtis. Maybe he can end it. He lives in SW on the waterfront."

CHAPTER NINETEEN

Curtis's SW townhouse was just like him—exquisitely well-groomed on the outside. The light red brick façade was freshly power washed. The small, expertly manicured lawn, with its perfect bright green blades of grass, had floral sprays of irises and amaryllis, drenched in purple and pink, lined along the perimeter fence. Clusters of jasmine bushes hugged the bottom of the front steps, floating fragrance in the air.

It was the house he and Naomi had bought in 1990 and shared as newlyweds clinging to a tentative promise. A house—but neither of them made it a home. Then, the house sat across the street from the dingy middle school with a playground overtaken as an open-air drug market. The druggies hungrily eyed Curtis and Naomi like fresh prey, memorizing their schedules to seize any deliveries to their house that they could resell for drugs. The druggies, the men and the women, prowled day and night, shopping Curtis and Naomi's house like a department store.

Their neighbors were no better. They smiled and nodded while perched like hawks on their front porches, lulling Curtis and Naomi into believing they cared for their safety. The neighbors watched Curtis and Naomi, mentally logging when they bought clothes, when packages and mail were delivered, even when they went grocery shopping. Curtis and Naomi's packages were swiftly stolen from their front porch and their mail ripped open. Every time Curtis or Naomi returned home, toting a bag of groceries or a shopping bag from a store, someone ransacked and robbed their home the next day. It got so bad that Curtis and Naomi arranged for the Post Office to deliver packages and mail to them at the insurance agency at work. They only bought as many groceries as they could conceal in their briefcases.

How times changed. The home they had purchased for $79,000 was now worth more than $800,000 because of its proximity to the revitalized waterfront. Curtis knew, to the penny, how much the home was worth as he secured two mortgages on it.

Change found its way to the decrepit middle school. School officials sandblasted the imposing columns of its entrance and regularly power washed its newly replaced windows. They modernized its 1968 façade. The aluminum siding received annual coats of inviting mint-green paint. The druggies had dispersed long ago to some unknown destination. The neighbors, who once watched like hawks, had sold their homes to pioneering yuppies now reaping the benefits of a city in the throes of revitalization and used the proceeds to flee the area for suburban life.

Now Curtis's mail remained untouched in his box and the packages delivered to his front door lay undisturbed.

The metal squeaked when Naomi lifted the gate latch. She peered into Curtis's front door window. A gray cat with a white face and pink-dotted nose slinked from behind the cluster of jasmine bushes and rubbed her face against Naomi's leg in a greeting. She purred, burying her face in Naomi's bare leg. She lifted the cat and cradled her in her arms. "Hi, Misty. Hi, sweet girl. Where's your Daddy?"

"Hello, there." A squat man in khaki shorts holding a rake in the adjacent yard approached the common fence. His face was flush with perspiration under his oilskin hat. "You looking for Curtis? Hot, isn't it?" He removed his hat and wiped the sweat from his forehead with his large forearm. "I'm his neighbor, Jack. I've been feeding Misty. I've been trying to get her to stay over here, but she wails loud as a baby when I keep her in the house. I think she just likes waiting for her master to return. I haven't seen Curtis for a while. It's been at least a few days. His car is parked in the back alley, though. When I see him, can I tell him who's calling after him?"

"I'm his ex-wife—"

Jack interrupted Naomi. "Oh, yeah, I know who you are. I've seen your pictures, seen you on the news. Naomi Morninglory. Glad to meet ya. I'd shake, but I'm planting pansies and begonias. The ones I planted earlier in the season died. You know, with this hot July sun beating down on them, I have to keep replacing them." He ogled Caprice. "But her, I don't know."

"Mrs. Deveaux."

"Oh, my God! Say it isn't so! Imagine both of these stars on my street! Caprice Deveaux. I've seen so many of your movies. It is incredible to meet you. I have to say, you look so much better in person. Much prettier." He scrambled out of his yard and entered Curtis's.

Curtis never bothered to change the locks, so Naomi used her key and pushed on the door. Caprice accompanied her into the home. Jack followed closely behind Caprice, who suddenly turned around. "Easy, Heavy-Duty. We'll call you if we need you."

"Okay, I'll be out here, waiting."

Curtis's townhouse was different on the inside than on the outside. The smell of mildew and stale air engulfed Naomi's nostrils as she walked the length of the dank front room. She cupped her hand to her mouth and shouted between coughing spells, "Curtis?" She circled the large, dark front room, made darker by the heavy burgundy curtains, drawn shut to prevent any light from escaping the bay windows. With each of her steps, the floorboards creaked.

When they were married, Curtis hated cleaning up and did minimal upkeep. But this was out of the ordinary, even for him. His bookcase lay across, spilling books, an ashtray, and Curtis's salesman-of-the-year trophies onto the brown-stained area rug. The cushions of the once brightly patterned chintz sofa were split open, revealing tufts of batting. Soiled, crumpled newspapers dotted the floor. A trail of stuffing and batting from the sofa cushions led to the kitchen.

Clearly, Curtis had gone elsewhere to spend the money she had given him. In a contest for the greatest eyesore in the house, the metal light-pink kitchen cabinets would have won, had it not been for the hideous blue-and-white, duck-printed wallpaper. Unwashed dishes were stacked high in the chipped pink sink. The kitchen table, a relic from their marriage, was covered in piles of unopened mail. A framed picture of Naomi and Curtis on their wedding day sat on the kitchen window ledge, its glass smashed within the frame. Beside it was an ornately framed picture of Curtis's nine-year-old son smiling while blowing out the candles on his birthday cake.

Naomi opened the refrigerator. It was empty, save for three decaying oranges and half a jar of mayonnaise. Misty jumped from her arms and bolted to her food and water bowls, purring insistently.

"I'll feed her—that is, if I can find some cat food." Caprice held the water bowl under the faucet. She opened each of the warped pink kitchen cabinet doors. "You're in luck, kitty. Your dad did leave you a few cans."

"Curtis?" Naomi called again as she climbed the narrow, squeaking stairs. She flicked the light switch to relieve the darkness, but no light bulbs were in the ceiling light fixtures. She turned the doorknob to the first of the three bedrooms. Curtis desperately needed to hire a housekeeper. The king-size bed had no sheets, and a rumpled pill-worn blanket lay at its foot. In the closet were more hangers than clothes. Naomi nudged her foot against the few pairs of very worn shoes at the bottom of the closet.

In the bedroom converted to an office, junk and books were piled neatly around an L-shaped desk. Naomi opened the desk drawer to find an assortment of knickknacks, paperclips, pens, and pencils.

She peeked into the last bedroom, which seemed to be Curtis's catchall room. Clothes were piled on top of a treadmill, a set of weights was lined against one of the peeling gray walls, and boxes of more junk filled much of the space.

Naomi trekked to one of the full bathrooms. The black-and-white tile on the floor was cracked. No towels were on the broken rack. Toothpaste and soap were missing. She clicked on the light in the other bathroom. Curtis was fastidious about his appearance but had no razors, aftershave lotion, or toiletries of any kind anywhere. The showers and tubs were bone-dry.

Naomi returned to each of the bedrooms, this time opening each closet and carefully inventorying its contents. All that remained were a few outdated suits, a navy-blue sports coat, and two pairs of shoes well past their prime—stuff she knew Curtis wouldn't be caught dead in. His suitcases were gone.

Naomi placed one hand on the wall of the stairwell and gripped the handrail with the other, descending the small winding staircase one step at a time. Landing back on the first floor, she surveyed the front room to the kitchen, where she located Caprice leafing through the endless piles of mail on the table.

"Well, one thing's clear."

"What's that, Doc?"

"The son-of-a-bitch left town."

CHAPTER TWENTY

Bertrand swiveled in Naomi's chair and picked up her desk phone. "Hey, man, Bertrand. Do you know where Dr. Morninglory is?" He hid the alarm in his voice from Marlon.

If she didn't want to talk, if the time wasn't right, why didn't she just say so? Bertrand fumed. The next time he saw Naomi Morninglory, he intended to break her of the bad habit of lying to him—slipping out and sending him for food, as if he were her errand boy. His time was just as valuable as hers. There were plenty of other things he had to do, including review tomorrow's dosage summary charts. With the mistakes Naomi was making lately, he prioritized scrutinizing her dosage recommendations. It was unusual for her to be so...dotty. Something was definitely wrong.

Marlon sounded surprised to hear from him. *"Hey, Bertrand, after I left you, I went to the loaner to get my wallet. It dropped between the seats. The dealership texted and said Doc's car was ready, so I was about to head out. But no, I don't know where she is if she isn't in her office. I haven't heard from her."*

"She asked me to pick up some food for her from the café because she wanted to work late, but when I came back, she was gone."

"That's weird. No, she didn't buzz me that she wanted to go anywhere. That's what she usually does. Have you called her on her cell?"

"Of course. She won't pick up."

"That's really weird. She always picks up."

"Yes, I know."

"Well, she can't be very far. I still have her car keys. Maybe she's in a meeting with one of the other docs."

"No, that can't be because her jacket and purse are missing. She wouldn't take those to just go down the hall for a meeting."

"Okay, well, if I see her, I'll tell her you're looking for her."

"Thanks."

Bertrand sat pensively for a few minutes, then redialed Marlon. "Pull up the surveillance video of her hallway for the last hour."

"I think that's a little drastic. If something was wrong, she'd tell me. She's probably around...somewhere."

"Just do as I ask. I'll be by in a bit."

Bertrand took two large bites of the blackened salmon, scooped two forkfuls of rice pilaf, finished the dregs of his iced tea, and shook the cup so that a few ice cubes fell in his mouth. On his way out, he picked up Naomi's carton of fries.

"This is not like her. Real weird." Marlon lifted four fries from the carton as Bertrand offered it to him.

"Yeah, I know. You got the surveillance video?"

"Right here. You said one hour, right?"

They watched the tape. Naomi was leaving the ladies' room and entering the stairway. Marlon pulled more fries from the carton in Bertrand's hand. "Look how she's looking around. Like she's avoiding someone. Weird."

"Pull up the stairway video so we can see where she went."

The pair watched Naomi exit the stairway and get on the elevator.

"Where's the front door video?"

Marlon fast-forwarded that video. They observed a stream of patients and employees exiting. "Just normal stuff. People leaving at the end of the day. I don't see Dr. Morninglory."

"I don't either."

"Maybe she's somewhere still in the building. I've never known the Doc to leave without me. I mean, after all, I'm her bodyguard and the one who gets her from place to place. Except that lately she drives herself to work in the morning. She asked me to stop and come to the Center later to drive her in the afternoon on errands and such, and then back home."

Bertrand stared at the younger man. "So, you haven't been with her all the time?"

"No." Marlon winced as if he instantly knew that was the wrong answer.

"Why didn't you tell me about this?"

"She asked me not to tell anyone. I thought maybe she felt I was crowding her. I just follow directions."

Bertrand scratched his head, pacing around Marlon's cubicle. He decided it wasn't worth upbraiding Marlon about his lapse in judgment and their time was better spent finding Naomi. "I've called her five times, and she won't pick up. The garage. What about the garage?"

"I told you that I have her loaner because her car's being serviced. She doesn't have that key. I do." Marlon held out his palm.

"Run the video anyway. I'd like to see it."

Bertrand bent over Marlon's computer screen. The two observed Naomi walking out of the building's garage exit and standing in front of a moving car. She banged on the hood of the car, extended her hands, knocked on the window, bent down to talk to the driver, scurried to the passenger door, opened it and got in. Then, the car sped off. Bertrand had never seen such a look of panic on Naomi's face before.

"Who is that?" Bertrand insisted.

"I don't know. I can't see who the driver is."

"Is this the only vantage point? What about the south end?" Bertrand no longer hid his alarm.

"South end wouldn't pick up this view. Just the door and the side."

"That's an Audi, isn't it? Make it clearer so I can make out the license tag." Bertrand hastily jotted the number. "Find out who the fuck that driver was. I need to know, now."

"Bertrand, how am I supposed to do that?"

"Cross-reference the patient appointments with the time-clock on the surveillance video. See who had an appointment about an hour before. I need it quickly. The surveillance video is too fuzzy to see who's driving that car. Clear up the definition so you can see the driver clearer. I'll call you in half an hour. Make sure you have an answer for me. If you need help, get Astrid back here. Call her on her cell."

Bertrand dashed into the hallway to the elevator and mashed the 'G' button. Alighting on the ground floor, he quickly ran to his parking space, got into his Porsche Spyder, careened onto the street, and dialed Naomi's cellphone, which went straight to voicemail. He dialed another number.

"3d. Officer Brian Logan speaking."

"Francis James, please. Bertrand Angenois is calling."

Moments later, *"Officer James."*

"Hi Francis, Bertrand. How's your mother getting on with her therapy?"

"Hey, Bertrand. How you doin', man? Yes, Mom loves it."

"She likes it, does she? Good to hear. A bit wanky having a mother younger than you, isn't it?"

"I'll say. I can't keep her home, now that she's twenty-five. Said before when she was twenty-five, she was busy raising me. This time, it's all about her. Thank you again, man. Her winning the lottery for that community slot was a blessing. Amazing. What you all do for the community is excellent. Thank you."

"No problem, man. Hey, look, I do have a favor to ask."

"What can I do for you?"

"I have a tag number. Can you run it for me? It's a bit of an emergency. I wouldn't ask otherwise."

"You know I'm not supposed to. But you did say it was an emergency. What's the emergency?"

"It's Dr. Morninglory. She's missing. She got into some car, and we need to locate her. Quickly."

"If she got into a car, then it's voluntary. It doesn't sound like an emergency."

"There's a lot going on, man. Really, I haven't much time to explain everything. You'll just have to trust me that when I saw her face, it didn't look very voluntary." Bertrand recited the license number and make of the car from the notes he had taken.

"Okay, Bertrand, I'm looking. Just a minute. Here, an Enterprise rental in the name of Findlay Fourchette. A Caprice Deveaux signed for it. That help you?"

"Yeah. Can you locate the car?"

"Bertrand, you need to come in and file a missing persons report," Francis whispered, *"I can get in big trouble."*

"Francis, don't worry. I got your back, man. I'm having lunch with the Mayor next week. You're okay."

"Okay, let me see. Heading west on Rock Creek Parkway. Wait a minute...it stopped. 5500 block of Broad Branch Road."

"Got it. Thanks." Bertrand ended the call just as Marlon's name blazed across his dashboard console.

"Yeah, Marlon?"

"I found out who the driver is."

"Caprice Deveaux."

"Yeah, how'd you know?

"Sources, my friend. I have a multitude of sources. Thanks. Oh, if you hear from Dr. Morninglory, call me." The call ended just as an unfamiliar number appeared on Bertrand's dashboard.

"Bertrand Angenois—"

"Oh, hi, Mr. Bertrand. This is Sheila, Shequi's mother—I mean, Shequillah."

"Hi, Sheila, I'm a little busy right now. I'll have to call you back."

"Oh, wait. I'm calling to see if you need any help with the Fourth of July party for the girls tonight? I don't mind bringing the beverages."

"Oh, shit! I'm sorry—shoot! I forgot about that. I'm afraid I'm going to have to cancel that. Something's come up. A work emergency."

"Oh, no, the girls will be too disappointed. They were looking so forward to it. I can take care of everything. You don't even have to show up. Just...just don't cancel the party. Please."

Bertrand thought for a moment as he sped toward the Kennedy Center and veered onto the Rock Creek Parkway. "All right. I reserved the spot at Fort Dupont Park ages ago. Call my office and tell the switchboard to put you in touch with Astrid. Ask Astrid to help you. I have an account with Pizza USA. Ask for Juan Carlos, have them deliver the pizzas, do the set-up, the drinks, everything. Have you got all that?"

"*Yes, I've got it.*"

"If you run into any hiccups, Astrid can take care of them for you. Tell the girls I'm sorry that I won't be there."

"*No problem at all, Mr. Bertrand. I'll handle everything, so don't you worry. I hope you get your work emergency worked out.*"

"Thanks."

"*Bertrand?*"

"Yeah?"

"*Let me know if I can help you do anything else.*"

CHAPTER TWENTY-ONE

"Now what, Dr. Morninglory?" Caprice handled the speeding Audi like a professional, weaving around cars on the Rock Creek Parkway and maneuvering the sharp hairpin turns.

"Where'd you learn to drive?"

"Oh, this. I did an action picture with Tom Cruise in the nineties and trained with a stunt driver for four months. I knew it would come in handy sometime."

"Can you slow down, please? I've seen enough blood spilled today."

"Yeah, that was pretty gruesome. Poor—what was his name again?"

"Steinberg. Oliver Steinberg."

"Since he is obviously out of the picture, do you have any family we could go to for help?"

"No. That's why Oliver and I bonded so tightly. We both lost our parents when we were younger. We both have no siblings." Naomi's mind drifted to Ellarie, Oliver's wife. *What can I possibly say to comfort Ellarie when I visit her? If it weren't for me, Oliver probably would still be alive.*

"You know, Dr. Morninglory, when I first saw you at my consultation appointment, I thought to myself, 'She is so beautiful and accomplished.' That you had it all together, and your beauty, your accomplishments were your armor. That it somehow protected you against life's random bullshit. But it doesn't, does it?"

"No, it doesn't protect you from anything. Except maybe it makes you more of a target." Naomi sank into the seat and stared at the curving road.

Caprice broke the silence. "I think we should go to the police."

"No. Absolutely not."

"Why not?"

"I explained why. They can't do anything about this."

"Are you sure they can't help? I mean, I think they are better equipped to handle this sort of thing than I am."

Naomi shot an exasperated look at Caprice. "I know you're trying to help, but—"

"Okay, Doc. But isn't there anyone we can ask to help us? I just feel this is out of my league. I don't know anything about D.C. I just come here every week for my pill. Now, if we were in L.A., that would be a different story. I could call around to some of my friends out there. Maybe they know someone who could help."

"Oh, no, I don't want anyone else to know. But maybe—"

"Maybe who? Who, Doc? Whoever it is, I think we should try them. Please, Doc, who?"

"I guess I don't have a choice. Pull over at that landing on Beach Drive. I'll drive."

"Okay, but where are we going?"

*   *   *   *

"Oh, hell, fucking no!"

"Quinn, I have to talk to him. Is he here?"

Quinn loudly slammed the intricately carved wooden door, shaking its stained-glass window. Through the closed door, Naomi heard a man and woman's muffled screaming voices. Naomi and Caprice looked at each other and began fidgeting standing on the travertine alcove.

Twenty minutes later, the door flew open. Quinn pushed past Naomi, almost knocking her down with a large Louis Vuitton duffel bag slung over her shoulder. Quinn threw the bag into the backseat of a black Lexus and sped off.

"I feel welcome. How about you?" Caprice stood beside Naomi as they stared at the open door of Haron Wilson Fitzgerald, and then held her hand out. "After you."

Naomi entered the black-and-white-marbled foyer. A large bouquet of freshly cut fuchsia hydrangeas sat on an antique table beneath an ornately carved spiral staircase with gleaming ebony railings. The scent of the flowers wafted into the living room, where sumptuous navy velvet sectional sofas spanned the arc of the large mahogany bay windows. *Minefield,* Fitzgerald's latest book on the intersection of politics, race, and justice, sat on top of a finely polished cherry coffee table. Underneath it was an elegant Oriental rug saturated in reds, oranges, and blues.

Naomi charged into the living room, finding Harry, clad in blue-and-white seersucker shorts and a butter-yellow Polo shirt, fuming on one of the navy velvet sofas. "Naomi, you can't be here. Quinn goes bat-shit crazy at the mere *hint* of your name. And you show up here. I can't imagine what she's going to do."

"The only reason why I'm here is I need your help. Harry, it's an emergency. I wouldn't be here otherwise."

"All right. But still..." Harry's dimples creased the cheeks of his creamy milk-chocolate skin. His hair curled perfectly, and his temples were lightly flecked with gray.

"Who's this?"

Caprice reached out her hand. Harry shook it.

"She's a patient of mine. Caprice Deveaux."

"The actress?"

"The same." Caprice held Harry's hand.

"Haron Fitzgerald. It is a pleasure to meet you." He placed his other hand on top of Caprice's and lingered it there.

Caprice blushed. "I've seen you on TV."

"I've seen you in the movies."

"I read your thriller, *Diseased*. Pretty clever. Congratulations on making the *New York Times* bestseller list with *Minefield*. I haven't read it yet, but I want to."

"You're too kind. Please, call me Harry. I'll make sure you get a signed copy."

"Harry, I have to talk to you. Privately." Naomi yanked Harry's hand out of Caprice's.

"All right, come into the kitchen. Ms. Deveaux, make yourself at home. Can I get you something to drink? Lemonade, perhaps?"

"If I call you Harry, will you call me Caprice?"

"Absolutely."

"Nothing for me. I'm fine. Thanks. I'll just meander around your beautiful home. Is that all right?"

"Mi casa es su casa." Harry smiled and squeezed Naomi's arm, led her into the kitchen and closed the pocket doors behind them. The turquoise glass-tile backsplash glistened in the reflection of the silver cabinets. He pulled a transparent ghost chair out from the round glass table in the breakfast nook and firmly pushed Naomi into it. "Want something to eat? Drink?"

"No. Thanks."

"Well, *I* sure need something. It's been a hell of a day, and I still have fallout from Quinn to deal with." He reached into the cabinet for a bottle of scotch, unscrewed the top, and poured some into a glass. "I got some chips over here. They're sweet potato chips. I'd love some good-old-fashion Utz, but I promised Quinn I'd lose weight." He patted his non-existent stomach, slid the bag on the table toward Naomi, and placed a yellow-and-white-striped paper napkin in front of her. "Before you get started, I heard. I still got friends in this city, you know."

Although Harry occasionally practiced medicine as an anesthesiologist, the bulk of his time was spent as a consultant traveling around the country, testifying in court as an expert witness in medical malpractice cases, and being handsomely paid for it. A prolific writer, his two suspense novels made the *New York Times* bestseller list, and his social commentary, *Minefield,* propelled him to the top of the speaker's bureau circuit. He regularly appeared as a guest on television and radio programs. Ever camera ready, it did not hurt that Haron Wilson Fitzgerald was simply gorgeous.

"I heard about Steinberg. That's a shame. Good guy. I'm sorry, I know how much he meant to you." Harry leaned over and placed his

warm creamy milk-chocolate hand on Naomi's. "I even heard that
Curtis is MIA. By the way, the police are looking for him. I believe it's
just for questioning, right now."

"Then you also know that Aspacio Aranha is trying to kill me
because I won't give Curtis half of my business."

"I did hear your name mentioned in connection with Aspacio's.
I didn't hear what the particulars were. You know how things get
muddled on the street." Harry leaned back and folded his napkin into
origami.

"That's why I'm here. It's imperative that you help me."

"Help you do what? What can I do? Once your name gets mixed up
with Aspacio, it's very difficult to get it unraveled. That's why no one
tangles with Aspacio."

"Well, like you said, you still have friends. Can't you get to Aspacio?
Get him to stop this craziness."

"My friends don't do that anymore. They're old, retired, and slow.
They sit back and watch the young ones fuck things up. Besides, what
you need is someone who can extinguish this quickly. Knock on some
doors. Make some calls. Meet face-to-face with him and his crew.
Explain to him how it is in his best interest to leave you alone. But
meeting with him at this point, honey, quite frankly, it could go either
way." Harry stared at the yellow swan he had folded from his napkin,
avoiding eye contact with Naomi.

"What do you mean by that?"

"What I mean is, when you get in this kind of trouble, you know
who your real friends are. Once you start messing with Aspacio,
meeting with him, you get dragged into his cause. And the people
I know want to avoid that kind of commitment. They have their
reputations, their jobs, their retirements to protect." He repositioned
himself in his chair. "I mean, promises to Aspacio go on forever. Say,
for instance, they get him to back off. Then they have to give him
something in return. First, he asks for something pretty innocuous...a
job for a friend...expedite a building permit for a business associate.
Then, he just keeps upping the ante. It never ends with him. The next

thing you know, it's money laundering, kidnapping, God only knows what else. And you can't say no, because there are consequences attached to that, too. You end up owing him. Forever."

Naomi shook the bag and stared at the potato chips that fell onto her napkin. "You seem to know a lot about all of this."

"Let's just say...I do my research."

An invisible rope of silence lassoed Harry and Naomi together—a rope he could extricate himself from at any time and walk away without giving Naomi's situation another thought. Yet, always adept at reading her thoughts, his dark brown eyes shone with the good times they had shared. "I'm not abandoning you. I do love you. That'll never change."

He reached for her hand, but she jerked it away and stood. She walked around the kitchen, stopped at the stone double farmer's sink, and rested her gaze on the pictures taped to the Sub-Zero. The frozen, joyous smiling faces beckoned her. She instinctively ran her fingers over the photos depicting the evolution of his life with Quinn and their sons. "Funny, I always thought that would be me. I always thought that if I just hung in there long enough that you and I"—she pointed at each one—"the Grand Canyon, that gondola ride in Venice, that prom send-off. I just knew that woman you're holding so closely would be me. Fool, stupid, stupid fool." She crossed her arms, rubbing them protectively.

"Cold? I can turn down the air conditioning."

"Your sons."

Harry stood so closely behind Naomi that she felt his warmth through her clothes.

"They're men now." Tears streamed down her face as her finger lingered on a magnet-framed picture of Harry and Quinn hugging a tall handsome teenager in a black cap and gown.

"That's Hughes. That's Dubois." Harry's voice deepened in obvious pride. "Yeah, they think they're men, but I say men pay their own bills." He pressed his lips in her ear. "I am still their father, and they still expect me to hold it down. I can't just up and leave. Quinn...she still needs me."

"Damn it, Harry! There has never been a time when I did not need you."

"Not like she needs me."

"You said you'd leave her when they went to college. Well, they're both in college now. We had a deal."

"Baby, we've been over that." Harry returned to the large glass table and dropped wearily into his seat. "You know, at work at the hospital, or when I'm testifying in a case. Or even when I'm on the speaking circuit or a book tour. All I get is sharp elbows. With you, it's more—sharp elbows. But Quinn, there's no sharp elbows. She's soft. All she wants from me is to come home and be her man. You see, if I leave, there isn't anything else for her. But you, you're stronger than anyone I know. You can take care of yourself. With those sharp elbows. You don't need me. You have your Renew Your Youth Center. According to *TIME* magazine, you're one of the most influential people in the world. And what did *Forbes* say about you— 'You single handedly changed the entire medical industry.' Naomi Morninglory is one of the most famous wealthiest women in the world. No matter what, you are making it happen for yourself. But Quinn, I'm all she wants..."

"Is that it? *That's* why you picked her. And...not...me. Ego? The male ego. She pretends to need you. Don't you see that? She's no competition for your spotlight. You like that she just orbits like the moon around your sun. Without you, she'd just die. That's bullshit, Harry, and you know it. She's just better at playing the game. That's all. Stroking the male ego."

"Don't knock the male ego, baby. That's how all these roads and bridges got built. That's how planes and trains were invented. That's how man got to the moon. Ego, baby, will drive a man to do anything." Harry smiled. His deep dimples creased his cheeks.

Not amused, Naomi refolded her arms and paced the length of the kitchen. Her Kate Spade mule sandals clicked against the washed white oak floors.

"It's not quite that simple, and you know it." Harry pushed his chair from the table.

"It is for me."

He rose in anger. "Well, shit, if I meant all that much to you, then why...why didn't you stop me from marrying Quinn?"

"Nobody and nothing could have stopped you from marrying her. She was your prize. Her money. Her prestige. Her father's famous seafood restaurants in San Francisco. Her mother, the debutante from Fisk with all those doctors in her family."

"Revisionist history."

"Also known as the truth. She had everything you needed to wipe the stain...the stench of the West Philadelphia projects from your life. They dangled that anesthesiology fellowship from Harvard in front of you, and you couldn't get away from me fast enough."

He removed his horn-rimmed glasses, rubbed his eyes, and cleaned his glasses with the hem of his shirt. "I was young. I wish I knew then what I know now."

"And what is that, Harry?"

"I can't, Naomi. I can't go over this anymore. I do love you, but I can't...leave Quinn."

Caprice knocked on the door and slid the pocket doors open. "Doc, excuse me, I don't mean to interrupt you, especially when you're talking to such an important, accomplished man. I know his time is valuable, but, Doc, your cellphone rang. I answered it thinking that, under the circumstances, you may want to take this."

She handed the phone to Naomi, who wiped the tears from her cheeks. "Who is it?"

"Bertrand."

CHAPTER TWENTY-TWO

"*Naomi, what's going on?*"

"Like you don't know."

"*No, I don't know. You just disappeared. What the hell is going on with you?*"

"Knock it off, Bertrand. I know that Aspacio Aranha is your uncle."

"*I never said I wasn't related to Aspacio Aranha. So what? What's this all about?*"

"You put him up to it."

"*Up to what? No, wait a minute, Naomi. Not on the phone. Meet me—*"

"You must be out of your mind. I'm not going anywhere near you."

Bertrand spoke slowly, in a measured tone. "*Naomi, I know where you're at. Haron Fitzgerald's house.*"

"You followed me?"

"*You're very predictable to someone who knows you well. Meet me, please. Let's talk about what's bothering you.*"

She held the phone away from her ear and looked at Harry. His deeply dimpled smile appeared as he pointed to his watch. "I have to run. I have an appointment on the Hill before the staffers break for the Fourth of July weekend." He lightly pecked her cheek.

"Okay, I'll meet you. But not here." She mentally checked off crowded places where Bertrand wouldn't dare harm her. "Tomorrow at the MLK Memorial. Right in front of the statue. At four o'clock." She laid her cellphone on the glass table as Harry wiped the table and threw the potato chip bag and napkins in the trash cylinder. Their drinking glasses clinked against each other when he set them in the sink.

"I'm sorry, Naomi. I wish...I wish I were...two people. One for you, one for Quinn. No, that's not it. What I really wish is to start all over again. Not like your regenerating process where you get to pick your age but keep all your baggage...your mistakes. I want to never have made my mistakes."

"So, you admit that Quinn was a mistake?"

"Don't get me wrong. I love Quinn. I love the boys, and without her, I wouldn't have had them. But with you, I know things would have been different. Better for me. Better for you. I wish I could just go back in time and start over and make different choices. You know, maybe if I had made a different choice then, this wouldn't be happening to you now." He drew Naomi close and dug his nose into the crook of her neck, inhaling her perfume.

"Yeah, and there's no pill that can do that." She wiped her tears, pushed herself away from him, picked up the white crocodile Birkin bag, and slid her cellphone in its inside pocket.

"Now, that would be really something. If you invented a pill that rewound time. Where you could just start all over again."

"Harry, when I left Curtis, you said you were leaving Quinn, too. Do you remember that?"

Harry returned to the sink.

"And then you hemmed and hawed, and when I asked you why, you were dragging your feet. Do you remember what you said?"

"No, not really. Maybe...probably."

"You said, 'I'm going to keep them both. One to have, one to hold.' And all along that's exactly what you've been doing, isn't it?"

Harry ignored the question, opting instead to concentrate on scrubbing the drinking glasses. He wiped his wet hands on the dishtowel and folded it on the lip of the sink.

Naomi sank into a chair at the table, studying Harry's movements. "Were you really ever going to leave Quinn?"

"Every single time I'm with you, nothing else matters. Just you. I get this feeling, you know, like time suspends. Your arms around me, it's a feeling like no other. But then I get back home. Reality hits me.

Quinn...the boys. I need to go to the store. We need more milk. Quinn needs me to get this or that. Hughes called from school. He needs something. Pick him up from practice, or band, or something. Dubois texted, he needs information for a paper—or can I arrange for him to meet this person, set up this job interview? Then, it's not that I forget how much I love you. It's just that my life crowds in and they don't stop needing me just because I love you."

The light of the setting sun broke through the kitchen window, bathing Harry as he scrubbed the glasses. Naomi realized his dimples were deep creases along his jowls. His smooth milk-chocolate complexion was patinated with large, dark age-spots. His dazzling smile was as hollow as his heart.

Harry escorted Naomi to the patio door off of the breakfast nook, unlocked it, and slid the heavy door open. Caprice slipped around them to the patio and stood under the bright red canopy of the outdoor kitchen.

"Goodbye, Harry."

"Goodbye, baby."

CHAPTER TWENTY-THREE

"Do you know where Dr. Morninglory is? I know tomorrow is the Fourth, but I checked her calendar, and she's not scheduled to be out. I've been looking for her all morning. I haven't been able to find her." Ava steadied her laptop on her hip and plucked at the keyboard, examining the charts, not looking at Astrid.

"No, I don't know where she is, Dr. Ellington. She was expected in the Center today. I actually have been calling her all day myself. It's unusual for her not to answer. Earlier, even Marlon went to her home. He said it didn't look like her bed was slept in."

"Marlon doesn't know where she is? Should we be worried?" Ava placed her laptop on the corner of Astrid's cubicle. "Maybe we should call the police or something."

"Dr. Overbrook said not to. Said he didn't want the publicity. I think Bertrand—"

"Oh, for heaven's sake, doesn't anybody know anything around here? Where's Bertrand? Maybe I can get some answers from him. I have ten patients scheduled today for dosages, and we can't get the stupid dosage delivery machine to work. The techs are going crazy. I already told two of my patients to come back later. We're going to have a lot of sick people around here, if we can't..." She snapped her laptop shut, aiming her frustration in the direction of Bertrand's office.

"Bertrand, where's your girlfriend?"

"I'm sorry, I didn't hear you knock." Bertrand held his cellphone to his ear and swiveled his chair around at the sound of Ava's voice. "Just a moment, Murano, can I call you back in, say, twenty minutes? Yes, yes, I promise. Thanks."

"You must know where she is. After all, you and I both know you're sleeping with her."

"Sleeping with whom, exactly?"

"Oh, stop it, Bertrand. I don't have time to play with you. Where is Dr. Morninglory?" Ava filled the doorway.

"If I didn't know any better, I'd think all this huffiness was jealousy. Could it be? You do know there are other ways to get me to notice you."

"Oh, please."

Bertrand sighed and rubbed his face with both hands, buying time to collect his composure.

"I just want to know where Naomi Morninglory is."

"To be honest, Dr. Ellington, at the moment, I don't really know where Dr. Morninglory is. Is there something I can help you with?"

"You do know that the dosage delivery machines won't open. We've tried all three. They won't open. I sent two patients away and told them to come back on Monday. By Monday, those patients will be perilously close to the forty-eight-hour reversion window. I have eight more patients scheduled today. What the hell am I supposed to do?"

Lloyd Overbrook brusquely brushed past her. "Excuse me, Ava. Angenois, do you know where Morninglory is? Astrid is tight-lipped. She sent me to you. I must see Morninglory. I have twenty-five patients scheduled for treatment, and I can't seem to get the dosage delivery dispenser to open. My doctors are keeping them busy with examinations, side-effect reviews, and customer surveys, but that won't last too much longer."

"I can't get the damned machines to open, either." Ava pushed around Overbrook, settled into Bertrand's office guest chair, and glanced up at Overbrook. "Oh, did you want to sit?"

Overbrook smirked. "What the fuck is going on around here? Where is Morninglory? Can't you call some maintenance person or something? Someone has to open these God-awful machines."

"I sent Maintenance over earlier. They report that it isn't a malfunction they can fix. We're in touch with the manufacturer. They're flying someone in, and they should be here by three p.m. Meanwhile, I am doing all I can to have Morninglory respond."

"Three p.m.? Geez, leave it to the business people to think

everything can wait," Overbrook hissed. "I don't think you understand the urgency here."

"Yes, I do. Very well, Dr. Overbrook."

"If we can't get these people their therapies, there will be a flood of patients..." He planted his palms firmly on Bertrand's desk. "Let me speak in a language you will be able to understand. If these patients don't get their treatment, the liability to the Center will be enormous, because if these patients don't get their therapies, they will..."

Bertrand met Overbrook's glare and finished his sentence for him: "Die."

CHAPTER TWENTY-FOUR

"Hey, Space. You're going to love this." Lolly reclined into the sofa, reached for the remote control that wedged between the cushions, and hunched his shoulders so his cellphone fit in the crook of his neck. "I got us a little side enterprise. That residual income you're always talking about."

"What you got going on?"

"Well, one of those patients from that Center you've been trying to bore a hole into...Cinander's been coming to me to sell his pills. We've been splitting the profits."

"I didn't know about that. Go on."

"Well, we found us a way to expand this enterprise. He got us an in with one of the doctors." Lolly smiled proudly.

"Lolly, Son, what are you talking about?"

"Well, Cinander got a Dr. Lloyd W. Overbrook to agree to work with us." He read Overbrook's business card aloud. "He's going to work with us and funnel even more pills from his patients to us. At first just five a week, but it'll pick up as he gets more comfortable with us and we get more comfortable with him."

"How is he going to do that?"

"We're still working out the details, but the important thing is, he's willing to work with us." Lolly's voice rose with excitement. "The best part is our cut of $15,000 a month."

"Man, that's chickenshit. I have in mind something bigger. Much, much bigger."

"Wait a minute, Space, it's not chickenshit at all. We don't have to do nothing but drive over and collect the cash every month like clockwork. And that's just the beginning."

"That's hardly worth making a trip for."

"I worked hard on...on getting these relationships together, moving these people in place."

"More people, more problems."

"Space, all you do is criticize. Everything I do, you got something to say about it. I thought this would make you happy. Get us a way into that Center you talk about all the time. They...Cinander and Dr. Overbrook are on the inside. A patient and a doctor. Space, it don't get no better than that."

"I'm sorry, Lolly. I didn't mean to insult you, Son. I know you worked hard on it. It shows. It shows. You done good except—"

"Except what?"

"I don't want you to get too caught up in the little. We're going for the big. Where are you now?"

"Home. Why?"

"Listen to me, Lolly. Go pick up Pierre. I have something I want you all to do."

CHAPTER TWENTY-FIVE

"Look, you lowlife shit, you don't have to keep calling me. There isn't anything I can do about it right now. We can't get the fucking dosage machines open," Overbrook whispered into his cellphone.

"I don't appreciate being called names," Cinander admonished.

"Well, I wouldn't have to call you names if you would just stop calling me." Overbrook scampered down the hall and ducked into an empty examination room.

"I'll stop calling you when the people waiting on their next pills stop calling me. At this rate, I'm getting a call every twenty minutes from angry people in a lot of pain. Not good, Dr. Overbrook. Not good at all. You can't start a new business and then fail to deliver the product. We need those pills."

Overbrook sighed. "Morninglory is not here, and we have real problems 'til she shows up."

"You have real problems, and so have I. Solve your problems so I can solve mine."

"I'm trying."

"Maybe you don't understand, Dr. Overbrook. I have a lot riding on this. I can't very well tell these people that the machine doesn't open. They don't want to hear that. They want to hear that it's on its way. They're paying a lot of money for this, and they only want to hear, 'It's on its way.' "

"I know...I know..." Overbrook paced around Examination Room Two.

"Dr. Overbrook, until now, I haven't told Lolly about our distribution holdup. He has entrusted me with getting the pills and delivering them to our customers. I don't intend to disappoint him.

You see, when he gets disappointed, he's unpredictable. You're a smart man. Fix this problem."

"All of this for $15,000 a month? What was I thinking?" Overbrook muttered as he rested his head against the wall.

"What was that?"

"Nothing. Will you just stop calling me so I can concentrate on solving this? I'll call you when...when something has changed."

"Just make sure it changes, Overbrook. And soon. Because after all, you won't be able to practice medicine...in the morgue."

CHAPTER TWENTY-SIX

Ava Ellington was meticulous. Some called it obsessive-compulsive, but to her, it was meticulous. She washed everything five times—her dishes, her clothing—five times. Her clothes became threadbare from washing, such that she always purchased new clothing in pairs: two pairs of jeans, two shirts, two pairs of socks. She bought panties in bulk, because they often could not survive the five-washing ritual. She rated the manufacturers and kept alphabetized files of the ones that made clothes able to endure the impact of her meticulousness.

She took five showers a day and floated in a fragrant cloud of the jasmine body oil she sprayed on afterwards. Her blotchy brown skin was as dry and smooth as an emery board, but she smelled great. Washing her wiry stale brown hair three times daily left it prone to breakage and desperate with static. She alphabetized her makeup, toiletries, and medicine in her bathroom cabinet.

She also organized her pens in holder-cups on her desk according to how much ink remained in them and segregated her pencils in a different holder. She color-coordinated the tablets, Post-it notes, and other paper items, and sorted them in each of her desk drawers according to size and shape.

Though people bemoaned her meticulousness, especially her family, Ava celebrated it because it was what had brought her to the Renew Your Youth Center in the first place. While researching the best dermatologists in the United States to treat a recurring skin condition that erupted in scales on her nose, she had happened upon Naomi Morninglory's name. Ava had traveled to D.C. from Bolivar, Tennessee for treatment, and during a consultation, Morninglory had mentioned her plans to found the Renew Your Youth Center. An internist at a

168 · Caryn Hines

small Tennessee hospital at the time, she was so excited by the idea that she faxed her resignation from the hospital and had joined Naomi in birthing the Renew Your Youth Center, starting on staff as a doctor the same day as Overbrook.

So, in the selfsame spirit of meticulousness, Ava reviewed the chart of every one of her patients five times. She also kept the recording on in Examination Room Two for her listening pleasure.

"Hi, Lloyd, do you have moment?" Ava rapped on Overbrook's office door and entered.

"No, not really." Overbrook looked up from his computer screen. "I'm studying this chart before my one o'clock. This is a sticky one. Joshua Shin, seventy-nine. Can't get him out of fifty-seven. I'm trying to get him to thirty-two."

"Isn't it interesting that men typically don't like to go as young as women? Women seemed to always be shooting for twenty-two."

"Not very. Are the machines open yet? "

"No, not yet."

"Then what is it, Ellington?" Overbrook snapped his laptop shut and reached for his lab coat.

"Been spending much time in Examination Room Two?"

"Is there something on your mind? If so, then spit it out."

"Examination Room Two. I usually have my appointments in there. So, I keep the recording on. I was going through the tapes. You know, about to delete them, but then I heard your voice."

"So what."

"So, I know you're selling pills. I came to you first, because I want to hear your side...before I go to Naomi."

Overbrook finger-combed his closely cropped salt-and-pepper hair. The framed picture on his desk of him emulating a tuxedo-clad Sean Connery smiled back at him. "She earns $7 billion a year. You make $8 million. Doesn't that bother you?"

"I knew it. Pill-sharing." Ava slapped Overbrook's desk. "Don't tell me anymore. I don't want to know."

"So, you won't tell Morninglory?"

Ava shook her head. "Why would I?"

"Okay, then what kind of cut do you want?" Overbrook smirked.

"Uh-uh. No, not me. Too risky. Too many things can go wrong. The patients receiving the pills out of the Center don't have the support they need. No access to Reversion, no access to Collaboration and Side Effects. No access to Pain Monitoring. That's a disaster waiting to happen. I hope it's worth it to you. But not to me."

"So, what *do* you want?"

"Nothing right now. You of all people know that sometimes it's good just to reserve an ace card in your pocket and pull it out when you need it. You just never know when you might need it."

Overbrook sucked his teeth.

"All righty then, what you do with your patients, on your time, has nothing at all to do with me."

CHAPTER TWENTY-SEVEN

Caprice peered beneath the Nationals baseball cap Harry had lent her. She pulled it further down her forehead to make sure she was unrecognizable. She sat a few benches away from Naomi at the MLK Memorial, conceding that this vantage point gave Caprice the best view to see Bertrand approach.

Naomi sat cross-legged on a bench, watching the tourist groups of teens and families weave around the Cherry Blossom trees as they traipsed up to the memorial.

"I thought you were going to be in front of the memorial, over there?" Bertrand sidled next to her.

"That's what I said, but this view is so lovely. You can see clear across to the Jefferson Memorial."

"Here, I stopped by Häagen-Dazs. French vanilla."

"No, thanks. I'm not hungry."

"Okay. I'll eat them both." Bertrand licked a chocolate ice cream cone. "So why don't you tell me what all this is about?"

"I trusted you."

"Trusted? Past tense? You still can."

"And what about Aspacio Aranha?"

"What about him?"

"Like you don't know. Safe and Sound Security reported that you lived with him when you came to this country. You can't tell me that you don't know what your uncle's doing."

"I haven't spoken to Aspacio in five years. We stopped communicating shortly after I took this job." Bertrand bit into the side of his ice cream.

"You don't know about him and Curtis?"

"Can't say that I do. Why don't you enlighten me? Or would you rather I just guess? Lately, you've been the queen of mystery, and, quite frankly, I'm tired of it."

"I can't believe you don't know."

"I said I don't know. All right, Naomi, I'll play. Since it seems that you want me to guess, I'll guess. Curtis and Aspacio are conspiring to take over RYY and kill you if you try to foil their plot."

"Yes."

"I was joking."

"I am not. He...Curtis borrowed a lot of money from Aspacio. Something to the tune of $500,000. I told Curtis I'd give Aspacio the money. But Aspacio doesn't want the money back. He wants Curtis to become a partner in Renew Your Youth and funnel the profits to him. If I don't make Curtis a partner, then Aspacio is going to kill me."

Bertrand crunched on the last of his chocolate ice cream cone, picked up the melting cup of vanilla ice cream, and tilted it toward Naomi. "Last chance?"

"Uh-uh."

"Aspacio is not my uncle."

"Don't start lying now, Bertrand. It's in the report."

"Aspacio Aranha is my father."

"But the security report says—"

"I know what the report says. The report is wrong and they include that every year. I never bothered to correct them. When I came here from Freeport, I was thirteen. Mum and I kept butting heads, and she thought I needed a strong man in my life to reign me in. So, she sent me here to live with 'Uncle' Aspacio." Bertrand gestured his fingers like quotes.

"She believed I'd have better opportunities in the States. I thought Uncle Aspacio was cool. Until that time, I had only met him once...at a wedding. He and his wife, Mandolin, treated me real fine. They had no children. Mum said to be on my best behavior because these people were caring for me. So I was. Gave them no trouble at all. I guess I was grateful to them for taking me in.

"But after a while, it became clear that Aspacio and I were very different people. Aspacio, he craved popularity...you know, the life-of-the-party type. Me, I was more solitary...bookish. So, *we* started to butt heads, too. Mandolin was an angel. I was much closer to her than to him. I think he resented that, too. Three years later, Mum died, and that's when Aspacio told me he was my father. He said he didn't tell me straight away because he didn't want the pressure of being my father in case it didn't work out between us.

"Something broke inside of me. I was sixteen and felt like I couldn't trust anything anyone said to me. I couldn't trust me Mum. Whenever I would ask her about my father, she would clam up and get really mean. I always thought it was some local dude who broke her heart. I don't know why she didn't tell me that Aspacio was my father. It was too late to ask her. I couldn't trust Aspacio. Living under the same roof all that time, and he never told me he was my dad. Made me believe he was my uncle, just to see if it worked out between us. Like he was auditioning me for a bloody part. I was a kid. I didn't know who anybody was. Hell, I didn't know who I was. I did a tailspin.

"I graduated from high school early and went into the military. Really, it was to get away from him. I felt like I could only depend on myself, so I looked to see what kind of job I could get right after military service. Something the military would pay for. That way, I wouldn't have to ask him for shit. I didn't want munitions. Not a lot of future in blowing up shit. I heard that there was a nursing shortage, so I studied nursing.

"Aspacio wrote me letters in the Army. Brimming with contrition. But I couldn't write him back. What was there to say? Now you want to be my father? After lying to my face all these years? Really?"

Bertrand aimed the empty cup at the trashcan and jettisoned it. It loudly ringed the rim of the green metal can and fell in.

"You never answered his letters?"

Bertrand stared at Naomi as if he struggled with comprehending the meaning of her words. "After I started working as a nurse for a while, what really interested me was the business side of hospitals. So,

I went to B school during the day and worked at night. I could study during my shift at night because it was quiet. The patients sleeping and all."

"Not to be indelicate, but what does this have to do with me?"

Bertrand rebuffed Naomi's attempt to turn off his emotional spigot.

"Well, Aspacio retired early from the federal government. Too early. He was an accountant. Something happened there. I dunno what. I just know it was bad. Really bad. He liked business. I liked business. I guess, in that respect, the apple really doesn't fall far from the tree." He finally smiled. "As long as I knew him, he always had a Jekyll-and-Hyde nature."

"What do you mean?"

"At home, he was one way. Moody and dark. Easily provoked to explode. Mandolin and I tiptoed around him to avoid his wrath. In public, he was another. Laughing, telling jokes. Mr. Personality. But that dark side...it was always there. Lurking barely beneath the surface. After whatever happened on the job and he retired...he just didn't give a shit anymore. He didn't have to go to the nine-to-five and had no real structure....he was a young fifty-five-year-old with a lot of energy, nothing to do, and no one to do it with...the Jekyll side took over completely."

"Sounds like an undiagnosed mental illness."

"Yeah, I always thought so. Maybe bipolar disorder. But to get Aspacio in front of a psychiatrist...it would never happen. He remembers the Tuskegee experiments. Made him deeply distrustful of doctors."

"That must have been very hard."

"It was gradual. He liked being around people he felt superior to. People who barely could read. Really poor people, so he could show off his possessions. Brag about being from the Bahamas. A world traveler. What he had seen all over this town...all over this world...impress them with his upstanding family...a wife...a son. Hell, these people hadn't been any further than down their own block. High school dropouts...he drank their admiration. Many of those young blokes remembered when he dressed every day in a suit. It was something they knew nothing about. Going to a job every day. He fancied them because he could be 'street' around them. Maybe it was a self-esteem thing. But he didn't rub off on them. *They* rubbed off on *him*. Drew him deeper and deeper into the street. Sought out the drug runners, felons, lowlifes—the types that had nothing to do all day but cause trouble. Teenagers and young men. In the beginning, maybe he saw himself, I suppose, as a father figure. Most of them never had men with gray hair in their lives. Their fathers weren't around—died from shootings, or stabbed, or some other street ailment. Blokes who never knew their fathers. So, they took mine." Bertrand wiped his hands on his napkin.

"What about Mandolin?"

"Mandolin couldn't take his dark side. No self-respecting person could. She was scared of the people he brought home. I mean, really, they were criminals. She left Aspacio, moved to an apartment, and a few months later, she was diagnosed with cancer of the esophagus. She died eight weeks from the date of her diagnosis. Very painful disease. I'll always believe it was stress." Bertrand's voice strained. He opened and closed his hands, clasping them together.

"So..." Naomi struggled to find the words.

"So, when Mandolin died, Aspacio lost his anchor to the legitimate world. His only other tether was me. He kept trying to lure me in, but his life was dangerous. By that time, he was deep in the drug world. We just drifted further apart. He was hurt. Felt I'd rejected him, but in reality, it was his *actions* I rejected. Oddly, he was proud that I wasn't part of that life. He held me out as his legitimate accomplishment. Jekyll and Hyde. Always a duality to him.

"Well, after the eighties and nineties and that drug thing subsided, he ramped up to extortion, loan-sharking, and the like. Amazing he's still alive. It's amazing he evaded the authorities. I think they just give him a pass because he's so old. But me, I didn't leave Freeport, come to this country to get mixed up in all that bullshit. You only end up in jail or dead."

"Bertrand, you've got to fix this."

He shook his head. "Fix it? You can't fix crazy."

"Bertrand, that isn't fair."

Anger flashed in his eyes. "Don't talk to me about fair. It's not like you and your father. Someone who loved you...claimed you right from the beginning."

"But Daddy gave up and...obviously yours hasn't."

Bertrand sighed. Naomi stroked his arm softly like a wounded wild animal. "I only meant that if you know...think that he has a mental illness then it's not fair to call him crazy."

"Just leave it alone. It's my life."

"Actually, it's my life."

The anger in his eyes cooled, and they flooded with sorrow. "I'm sorry. I'm so sorry."

"Bertrand, tell me one thing."

"And that is?"

"Are you working with Aspacio to take over my business?"

"I wouldn't do anything to hurt you." His soulful eyes engulfed Naomi.

"Why didn't you tell me about Aspacio before?"

"It never really came up in polite conversation, now, did it?

"I think I deserved to know who my COO is."

"And that's exactly why I didn't tell you. I didn't want you judging me based on his actions. And—"

"And what?"

"I didn't want my past to interfere with my future." Bertrand watched the ripples on the Potomac River expand along the Tidal Basin.

"I need to hear you say it. Are you working with Aspacio to take over my business?"

"Have you been listening to anything I've said?" Bertrand kicked the edge of the walkway of the Tidal Basin, staring at the Jefferson Memorial.

Naomi stood next him. He locked eyes with her. "No, I'm not

working with Aspacio to take over Renew Your Youth."

"Excuse me, but yes, yes you are." A young black man in a Washington Football Team jersey and khaki shorts smiled up at them. Dreads encircled his cherubic face. "Dr. Morninglory, how ya doing? I just want you to look over to your right. Over there. A little higher. Over the mound. Beside that 'No Parking' sign. That guy in the pink shirt. Bright, isn't it? Anyway, that's not a camera he's holding. It's a gun. Aimed at your beautiful head. He real good at killing. I seen him do it too many times, yo. His talent is long distances. If you think you can outrun him because he too far, don't worry, I have one, too. Mine, though, is aimed at ol' dude's knee. His daddy'll be mad at me if I did too much damage. But a busted knee, he probably be okay wit'.' But you, I'm told it's pretty painful."

Naomi froze.

"Who are you?" Bertrand demanded.

"Lolly. I feel like I know you, Bertrand. Man, all your Pops ever talk about is you. Look here. I need for you two to come with me, nice and quiet-like. Too many people around here, and they don't need to be involved. We, all three of us, meet with Aspacio. We, all three of us, take care of this. I bet we can make it quick. Then maybe we, all three of us, go out to get some dinner. Y'all like Red Lobster? They're having a Fourth of July special. All the shrimp you can eat." The young man smiled genially.

"Hey, baby boy, you looking for me?" Caprice ambled toward the young man and leaned between him and Naomi, sticking her chest out.

"No, sweet lady, I wasn't looking for you. Excuse me, but I'm in the middle of something. I'll have to get wit' you later."

"Later just won't do. Baby, as fine as you are, I was hoping you were looking for me. I sure am looking for you." Caprice smiled the smile that earned her $20 million a picture in her heyday. "Washington Football Team, huh? You sure fill that jersey out nicely with those big, hard muscles. I can tell you work out. I wonder what the rest of you looks like, baby boy." She lightly touched the man's burgundy and gold jersey. "Washington Football Team…but I'm partial to the Dallas Cowboys, myself."

Caprice shoved hard, sending Lolly airborne. He landed in the Tidal Basin. Bertrand grabbed Naomi's hand, and Caprice ran with them into the crowd that formed to watch the fireworks from the Tidal Basin.

"Help! Somebody help me!" Lolly bobbed up and down, splashing his hands in the dark, murky water. A German tourist knelt beside the Tidal Basin and strained his hand toward Lolly. A group of teens from Minnesota excitedly took pictures with their cell phones. The man in the bright pink shirt ran, pushing through the crowd of onlookers, to the tourist. He yelled out to Lolly, still thrashing about in the water. "Man, stop playing. Did you see which way they went?"

"I can't swim! Help me!"

A lifeguard from Colorado dove into the Tidal Basin and reached Lolly flailing in the water. She gripped his neck and held his head above the water.

The park police officer joined the melee, shoving the crowd back. He heaved a yellow buoy into the water. "Here, grab onto this. Hold on…"

CHAPTER TWENTY-EIGHT

The trio zigzagged between the cherry blossom trees running up to the 14th Street Bridge. "Where are you all parked?" Bertrand herded the women to the side of the bridge.

"We metro'd," Naomi said breathlessly.

"You okay? You need to catch your breath?"

"I'm okay."

"How are you doing?" Bertrand glanced at Caprice, who was bending over, holding onto the steel rails of the bridge.

"Me, too. I mean, I'm okay, too." She gulped as she leaned against the railing.

"I took the subway, too. Listen, we can hide in one of the restaurants on Pennsylvania Avenue. Get you some water or something."

"Good idea, handsome. Besides, I have to go to the bathroom."

The three scampered against the tide of crowds heading toward the Mall for the fireworks.

"Still clear?" Naomi asked, turning all the way around, checking to see if they were being followed.

"Looks clear to me." Bertrand pressed her back so that she remained in front of him.

"This spot looks good. I like Brazilian food." Caprice pointed to *Fogo de Chao* and ran ahead of them, crossing Constitution Avenue.

"One?" the maître d' asked.

"No, three. My friends are right behind me. Is there a long wait?" Caprice removed her Ray-Bans and dropped them in her Hermès yellow snakeskin purse.

"We are quite busy today, since it is the Fourth of July...one of our busiest days, with all the tourists on the Mall. Hey, you look familiar. Say, aren't you...Caprice Deveaux?"

"Yes, I am, and have been for some time." She winked.

"Oh, a pleasure. Such a pleasure." The maître d' pumped her hand.

"You're good, most people don't recognize me without my makeup."

"I'd notice you anywhere. I'm one of your biggest fans. Can I get a picture?"

"Of course you can, honey." Caprice smiled her twenty-million-dollar smile.

Bertrand opened the door to the restaurant. Naomi walked in first.

"Is that...is that...?" The maître d stammered.

"Naomi Morninglory. You really are good. She's my friend." Caprice placed her hand on the maître d's shoulder. "You got a table for us, honey."

"Right this way."

The maître d' escorted them to a secluded booth in the back of the restaurant.

"Honey, if you bring our server over here right now, I'll make sure you get the only picture with both of us." Caprice slid into the booth. "And if you keep us blocked off, I'll give you an astounding tip."

The maître d' smiled. "Of course. Don't worry about anything, Ms. Deveaux."

Caprice turned to Bertrand. "Can you order me a white wine? Any kind is fine. I'm thirsty and need a little something to settle my nerves. It's not every day that a girl stops a kidnapping. I'll be right back. I need to use the ladies' room. Coming, Doc?"

"I'm just going to sit here for a minute and collect myself."

"You okay?"

"Yes, I'm fine." Naomi rubbed her temples. "It's just that I'm used to a quieter life."

"I know what you mean." Caprice patted Naomi's shoulder.

"I've got to make a stop myself. When the waiter comes, I'll just have water with a lot of ice." Bertrand rose and walked in the same direction as Caprice.

Bertrand took deep swallows, emptying his glass of water. He scanned the restaurant for any signs of Lolly or the man in the pink shirt.

Caprice threw her bag down and eased herself around the table. She sipped her wine and grabbed a piece of bread from the basket. She tore it in sections and dipped each piece in the plate of spiced olive oil. "Whew, I feel better. Washed up a bit. Have you eaten here before?" She bit into soaked bread.

"Yes, on several occasions. It's pretty good." Bertrand eyed the venue.

"Yeah, I think so, too. We have one in Cali. I used to eat there sparingly, on account of everything landed on my hips. But now, thanks to the doc, my metabolism has sped up to what it was in my twenties. Man, I could eat anything and everything I wanted to then. Now, I can eat whatever I want again."

She playfully nudged against Naomi, who sipped her water. Caprice held the breadbasket in front of Naomi, who shook her head. Bertrand studied Naomi as she gazed out of the window.

"Well, you two are a barrel of laughs."

Naomi pretended that her water glass fascinated her. Bertrand shifted nervously in the seat opposite the women.

"Okay, fine. I'm going to make a call. Check on the ol' husband before it gets too late and he goes to bed. Excuse me, Doc." Naomi scooted out of the booth to let Caprice out.

Naomi sat back down, lifted a piece of bread from the basket, and tore it into crumbs on her plate.

"So, how is the good Dr. Haron Fitzgerald?" Bertrand reached into the basket for the last piece of bread.

She poured more olive oil into the saucer and mashed at the breadcrumbs with her fork. "Fine."

"I looked around. But I don't see him riding on his white horse, is he?"

"What makes you say that?"

"For one thing...you're here with me."

Her eyes flamed in anger, then turned to sadness. The four years of waiting and planning her life with Haron Fitzgerald had just burned quicker than a lit single sheet of paper.

Bertrand reached for her hand. "Look on the bright side—you won't have to end it with him. That romance was already over when you two started it."

Naomi jerked her hand away from his. Bertrand leaned back into the booth. "But just so you know, I'm no consolation prize. I only want a woman who only wants me."

"I didn't think you were a consolation prize."

"It feels a bit like it."

"It's just that I need to figure some things out."

"Oh, I see. When you had Harry, I was your backup. Something to occupy yourself with while you waited patiently for him to free himself from his dutiful wife. But now that he's gone, firmly ensconced in blissful domesticity...it can't just be the two of us. You and me."

"I didn't say that. Bertrand, I can't talk about this with you right now. I'll be back in a minute." Naomi took her purse and left the booth, pushing through the crowded restaurant in the direction of the ladies' room.

Caprice returned, sliding into the booth. "I'm hungry. You know what you want? Where's the waiter? I'm ready to order."

"Hasn't been by yet." Bertrand fingered the pages of the menu.

"Well, he's sure not getting his picture. Everything all right?"

"Fine."

"Well, I'm ready to order. Did the doc tell you what she wanted? Hey, where is she?"

"I don't know. I think she went to the bathroom."

"No, no, she didn't. I was just there. They only have two stalls, and when I left they were both empty."

"Check again." Bertrand bolted from the booth. Caprice followed him to the bathroom, anxiously pushing the guests that were crowded around the bar. She flung open the wooden door to the ladies' room, startling a young woman in a faded American-flag cropped T-shirt and worn denim shorts with pockets turned inside out. The surprised woman dropped her lipstick in the sink.

Caprice pushed each of the stall doors. They were empty. "Was there a woman in here? About this tall, brown-skinned, in a rocking red sundress?" She motioned Naomi's approximate height in the air.

"Hey, what's the matter with you? You scared me barging in here like that. No, lady. Nobody was in here when I came in. And nobody came in while I've been here." The woman returned to applying her lipstick, then blotted her lips with toilet tissue.

Stunned, Caprice walked back to Bertrand, who hammered the wall with his fist. "Oh, shit, she's gone."

CHAPTER TWENTY-NINE

"Traffic is moving pretty good." Lolly turned onto E Street.

"Yeah, everybody else is headed toward the Mall." Pierre brushed pieces of dry leaves from the shoulder of his pink shirt.

Furious, Naomi sat in the back of Lolly's early model beige Buick, tightly gripping the door handle. She watched the cityscape whiz by as Lolly eased into the left lane to veer onto 395.

"Doc, we're going too fast for you to try anything like jumping out. You could get hurt. You see how fast these other cars is going. Plus, I got the doors and windows on childlock." Lolly pointed to a button on the dashboard, then looked at Pierre. "She's still not talking."

"Guess not." Pierre turned around to the backseat to look at Naomi, who rolled her eyes at him.

Lolly ran his hand down his damp, wrinkled Washington Football Team jersey. "I can't wait to get to Space's so I can change. These wet clothes are uncomfortable. I ain't never had no celebrity in my car before. Dr. Morninglory, I seen you on television and in magazines. It's an honor, ma'am. It really is. Hey, Doctor, where you from?"

"This is kidnapping," Naomi hissed.

"Just relax and be comfortable."

Pierre waved his hand in front of the vent. "Is the air getting to you back there?"

"Not too high. I don't want to catch no cold, since my clothes are still wet."

"I get it, man. You still sore that that lady pushed you in the river. You don't have to keep bringing it up. You survived, so stop complaining." Pierre leaned against the car door.

"No thanks to you. You didn't even dive in to try and save me."

"Look, man, I can't swim either. What did you want? For us both to drown?"

Naomi gripped the back seat. "Listen, I don't know what your plans are. But if it's money you're after, I will give each of you ten million dollars—in cash—to let me go, right now. No questions asked. No charges filed. We can forget this ever happened."

Lolly turned his head toward the backseat. "Oh, we promised a lot more than that."

"Okay, then name a number. How much will it take for you to just drop me off at that exit, right there?" She pointed to the Pennsylvania Avenue exit.

"Ma'am, at this point, it really isn't up to us. We just doing what Space told us to do. All this negotiating you're doing. You can do it with him." Lolly changed the radio station.

"Space?"

"Aspacio Aranha."

Chills slid up Naomi's spine. "Where are you taking me?"

Pierre shifted in his seat. "Don't worry. It's a nice place. We won't hurt you. Man, can't you turn up the air in this thing? It's hot as hell outside."

"You gotta have some patience, man. It'll work in a minute. I bet you wondering why people call me 'Lolly.' It's a question I'm often asked." He smiled broadly at Pierre.

Seizing on the silence, he continued, "Well, my real name is W'Andre Patterson. But growing up, I got the nickname of 'Lollypop' on account of when I was a little kid, I loved me some suckers. Mainly the ones with the bubble gum on the inside. But, really, all kinds of lollypops. Man, I'd run errands to the corner store for anybody who asked me, as long as they'd pay me enough to buy a lollypop. You'd think that after eating all those lollypops, I would have gotten a mouth full of cavities, but, you know, not a one." He turned around and grinned widely at Naomi.

"Man, keep your motherfucking eyes on the road." Pierre nudged him gruffly.

"I know. I know. But, as I was saying, about my nickname, over the years it got shortened to 'Lolly.' As I got older, I tell people, 'Call me Lolly,' 'cause the ladies think I'm so sweet.'"

"I'm going to turn the radio up if I have to listen to any more of this bullshit." Pierre reached over for the volume.

The car stopped at a large mid-century modern red brick house in Southeast Washington, nestled among grand, mature trees and fragrant, brightly blooming honeysuckle bushes. Lolly pressed the garage-door opener and drove inside. The door squeaked shut behind them.

"Come on in here, ma'am. Watch your step." Lolly held Naomi's arm.

"Man, I got to go pick up my lady from work. I catch you and Space later." Pierre pounded Lolly's fist and climbed into a gunmetal-gray RAV 4 truck. "Let me know if y'all need any more help."

Lolly took Naomi into the kitchen. "Hey, Aspacio! We back! I got the doctor with me!" he yelled as he threw his car keys on a round, white kitchen table. The kitchen shined with stainless-steel appliances, lacquered white cabinets, white-tiled ceramic floors, and contrasting dark-gray granite counters.

"I'm in the living room," a man's voice responded. "You all come on back."

Lolly gently pushed Naomi in front of him and guided her from the kitchen into the expansive living room.

"Well, hello there, Dr. Morninglory."

Naomi laid eyes on Aspacio Aranha, an older version of Bertrand. The two men shared every physical attribute. They were the same muscular build and size. The shapes of their broad hands with long, tapered fingers were the same. And when Naomi closed her eyes, Bertrand's cadence rang in Aspacio's voice. His complexion was a richer brown, as if God had stirred one more tablespoon of chocolate syrup into his skin. Street life had a way of aging a person, but Aspacio flourished in it. The eighty-one-year-old man looked young enough to be Bertrand's brother.

The older man stood. "I can see why my Bertrand likes it at that Center so much, if all the doctors there look like you, young lady. Have a seat. Please. Right over there is fine. Just move those clothes over. I haven't put them up yet. Don't have a pretty young woman like you taking care of me."

Lolly pointed for Naomi to sit on the worn, nubby burnished-brown sofa beside a freshly laundered pile of folded, white clothes.

"Lolly, y'all going out to get some food?"

"Probably, Space. Why, you want something?"

"Yeah, I don't cook on wash day. I do my colored clothes in the morning. In the afternoon, I do the whites. Lolly, I have to offer the doctor something to eat. A good host always does. Can you bring me back a fish platter from Horace's? Fries and coleslaw. Doctor, what can I get for you?"

Naomi shook her head and sat stiffly on the edge of the sofa.

"I can't believe you're here. My house. Let me at least get you something to drink. I did manage to make some sweet iced tea. You'll like it. Made it just like my grandmother. She mixed in cranberry juice. Very refreshing on a hot July day like today. I'll pour you a great big glass. Stay right there." Aspacio rose slowly, steadying himself on the arms of the wingback chair, and ambled toward the kitchen.

Moments later, he returned with a pitcher of crimson liquid with ice cubes bobbing on its surface. "The famous Dr. Morninglory. I've seen you on television countless times. You are as beautiful in person as you are on that TV set. Wow. An honor, that's for sure." He picked up a white polo shirt from the laundry basket and shook it. "You happened to catch me during laundry day. I do all my washing on one day and ironing on another. Relax, sit back, Doctor. Nobody here really wants to hurt you."

Naomi sat rod-straight, her hands clutching the edge of the sofa. "Mr. Aranha, I was with friends at a restaurant when your...your men abducted me. You have to know there are a lot of people out there looking for me. If you don't let me out of here...then you are going to be in more trouble than you are currently. I can make this easy for you."

Aranha raised his hand to silence Naomi. "Dr. Morninglory, young lady, before you say anything else, I want you to hear me out."

"I can give you...say, ten-million in cash on Tuesday. Since it is a holiday weekend, the banks are closed. Then we can make arrangements for you to receive, say, ten-million annually for an agreed-upon period of time."

Aranha chuckled. "Whoa, young lady, I can see you're all boss. Used to being in charge. But so am I. And let me tell you, for a lot longer period of time. You know how old I am? I'm eighty-one years old...I earned the right for you to listen to me."

"Isn't that why you brought me here? So, it could be all about you?"

"Oh, no, Doctor, you have me all wrong. It ain't really about me. Well, maybe a little bit about me, but really it's about me and my son."

"Bertrand?"

"Ah, you know about that. Yes. Bertrand. His last name should be Aranha, but his mother didn't want to put that on the birth certificate. We weren't together when he was born."

"Yes. He told me a little about his upbringing."

"Forsythia, his mom, I loved her, but she was one hard-headed woman. She didn't like living here in the States. She missed Freeport. She didn't want to leave that farm. Didn't want to leave all her businesses. That woman had two, three, four businesses going all at once. She tried to run everything, including me."

"I couldn't live in that sleepy little town anymore. No future. Eking a living from hustling every which way. Everything centered around either fishing or tourism. I like my fish on a plate. I don't want to have to haul it in on a net. Tourism. All that is, is watching other people enjoy their lives. That's not for me." He puckered, as if he had just eaten something rancid.

"She came to D.C. for a time but couldn't adjust to life here," he continued. "That was in the seventies. Can you imagine what she would think about it now? All the lights, people, buildings, construction, and hustle and bustle. I have trouble adjusting to how much things have changed now, myself. People walking the streets at all hours of the day and night, walking dogs and pushing baby strollers. Anyway, she went back home. Shortly after she left, she wrote me that, lo and behold, she was pregnant with Bertrand. I was going to be a daddy. I begged her to come back so our family could be together. She'd have none of it. That's what I mean—she was hardheaded. I think that's where Bertrand gets it. Over the years, I tried changing her mind. Finally, I gave up on her. But not on my son. Always wanted a family. Soon after, I met Mandolin and married her. She couldn't have any children. Beautiful woman. She put up with a lot.

"Meanwhile, I kept asking Forsythia to send Bertrand up here to live with us. Better life. More choices. Forsythia didn't want him to be so far away from her. But when he started getting into trouble in Freeport, sassing her and flirting with the tourists, she realized that boy was better with his father. Sent him here. He was about twelve or thirteen. Forsythia made me promise never to tell him I was his father. But that was the deal I made with her. So, I kept my word to her while she was alive. She loved her son Bertrand. I don't know why she didn't want the boy to know the truth. I think she was hoping the arrangement wouldn't work out and he'd go back home to her. But he liked it here. You know, that boy is so smart, he finished high school in three years."

"I knew he was smart. But no, I didn't know that."

"Forsythia died just when he was about to enter college. I didn't want him to think he was alone, so I broke my promise to his mother and told him I was actually his daddy. I ain't never seen that look on anybody's face in my life—before or since. I thought it would be of some solace. Comfort to him, knowing he had at least one parent that was alive. But no. It was like I cut his heart out with a knife. It was never the same between us."

Aspacio ran his palm across the folded pile of white laundry in the chair. He picked up the pile and placed it in the basket. "I like the smell of fresh laundry. I like looking at all the folded clothes. Feels like I accomplished something for the day, you know what I mean?"

Naomi glanced at the clothes and shifted away from the pile of clothes on the sofa.

"I'll take that." He gestured for Naomi to hand him the pile beside her. She did, and he placed it beside the pile in the basket.

"Aspacio, all of this was a very long time ago. I don't see what this has to do with me and the Renew Your Youth Center."

Aspacio chortled and continued speaking as if he had not heard her. "Bertrand is hardheaded. I tried to get him to put aside our differences. I wrote him every week when he was in the army. You know, I never got a return letter. Not one. Things got worse when Mandolin died. She was our buffer. Imagine, I needed a buffer for my own son. He faults me for this rift. My business operations. But, you see, Doctor, I worked for the federal government for thirty-five years. Thirty-five long, hard years. I was the first black accountant in my division. I was the only one in my department with an MBA. I got my MBA in '78. In '82, I discovered that my department was approving and paying invoices from private contractors that were overbilling the government. I took it to my supervisor, Lauralee Laker, thinking she should know and would do something about it. I was naïve. Soon after that, Lauralee eliminated my position and promoted me to be in charge of the whole corrupt department—a setup. So, whenever they did an investigation, I'd be the scapegoat. Nobody ever did one thing about it. I suspect many of them were getting kickbacks. I took an early retirement rather than be blamed for that whole mess."

"Couldn't you report it to the IG or some higher authority?" Naomi wondered aloud.

"Young lady, back then, they didn't have a name for it. All you got was shown to the door. And that's what happened if you were lucky. Hell, back then, they either put you in jail or the loony bin if you went to your so-called 'higher authorities' about all the shenanigans that were going on. Now, they call you a whistleblower. Justice? There's more than one law. One law for black folks, and one law for others. All those years of doing the right thing, and pouf! My hard-fought career was gone. I was fifty-five. How do you start all over at fifty-five? Tell me that."

A brittle cast fell over Aspacio's dark brown eyes as he began to breathe heavily. He reached for the iced tea on the side table and sipped it, calming himself. He replaced the glass tumbler next to the brass lamp that shone an amber cast on the old man's face. He absently wiped the wet ring on the table with his palm.

"I retired and had absolutely nothing to do. Small pension. I still had a house to pay for. I had been working since I was fifteen— sometimes two or three jobs, and going to school at night. Suddenly, nobody wanted to have anything to do with me. The phone never rang. Every day, dead silence."

"Where was Mandolin?"

Aspacio blinked at the sound of Naomi's voice. "Oh, we grew apart. We just didn't have anything in common anymore. She liked gardening and quiet. Her books. She was a homebody. Bertrand may be her stepson, but I swear that boy is more like her than he is like me. Shoot... me, I craved people. Everybody I knew had jobs to go to. Families and such to keep them busy...too busy to have any time for me.

"The only people around during the day were the boys on the corner. It seemed like these boys were the only people who cared that I was even alive. These boys—these men, I should say. They made me feel like I still had something to offer. Not some used-up has-been. Sure, I knew they were drug-runners. Sellers. Small stuff, mostly. I helped them organize their business. Helped with their accounting, plugged some holes in their operation. Made it more efficient. Some of these boys were illiterate. A failed educational system. A shame. Smart, though. They memorized everything. I taught them basic skills...reading...bookkeeping. They trusted me.

"The more involved I became with them, the deeper the divide widened between Mandolin and me. She ended up leaving me. She said she was scared of me. Scared of the boys. Didn't want them in the house. An exaggeration. They were all right. I tried to get her to come back, but soon after she left me, she was diagnosed with cancer. Died fourteen months after I retired. Almost to the day. I wasn't with her when she died. She didn't want to see me. Should have been, though.

Bertrand was incensed. Couldn't reason with him. He blamed *me* for her death. He said it was me and my lifestyle that killed her. He said...I broke her heart. It seemed like when I gained a purpose, I lost my own son. He and Mandolin wanted me to choose. Hell of a choice. Them... or...what was I supposed to do? Go into some corner and just die?"

"So, you turned to selling drugs, loan-sharking, kidnapping, and murder?"

"I don't call it that!" Aspacio snapped.

"Whatever you call it...it is certainly not respectable."

"Respectable? Young lady, I *tried* respectable. I tried respectability. What did it get me? Thirty-five years of nothing."

"I wouldn't call it nothing. Mr. Aranha, you...yourself said what you learned, you taught to...those boys. So, it couldn't have been for nothing."

Aspacio stood, shook the white, flat sheet, and folded it with firm, sure hands, ignoring Naomi. She spoke louder. "Mr. Aranha, whatever you're up to, I just don't want it to have anything to do with me. But now, you've sucked me into this abhorrent, despicable mess."

He placed the folded brilliant-white sheet on the side table and picked up its matching fitted sheet. He shook it and held it between his two outstretched arms.

"Mr. Aranha, what matters to me is my business. I worked really hard and sacrificed everything in my life to make this work. And now, you are trying to snatch it from me. And you'll kill me to do it. And you see nothing...nothing wrong with it!" She yanked the sheet down from his arms.

"That's a bit dramatic, young lady. I fault your ex-husband, Curtis, for that interpretation." Aspacio bent slowly, picking up the fallen sheet pooled at his feet. He shook it, folded it, and placed it in the basket on top of its mate. He sat wearily in the chair, removed his glasses, and cleaned them with a cloth. Then, he smoothed out the folded cloth.

Naomi tried to make eye contact with the older man. "I told Curtis I'd pay you the money he owes. And I've made quite a generous offer.

Very generous. Why don't you just take it...and let me go so we can be done with all of this?"

"Truth be told, I don't want to kill you. I'd rather have you around." Aspacio lit a cigarette. "I keep trying to quit. But every now and then, I light up. My cessation doctor told me to watch what my trigger points are and then avoid them." He fanned the smoke away from Naomi. "From where I sit, you are the glue holding this billion-dollar golden egg together. Why would I want to hurt you? It may affect the value of the company. I figure we could work together on this. Your business can only grow, given that everybody at some point ages." He studied the embers in his cigarette.

"You must be out of your fucking mind if you think I would work with you for one single second, so that you can just take my money from me!" Naomi's voice bordered on hysteria.

Aspacio crossed his legs and inhaled his cigarette. He blew smoke slowly and waved it from her again. "You think that this is about money? Doctor, look around. I have money. I'm eighty-one years old. What do I need with more money? My boy is grown. And he surely doesn't need my money. This house...has been paid off for twenty years. I have everything I need, and then some. My men, those boys— yeah, they do have children to support. But let's be real clear: they have more money now than they ever had. Anything extra would be gravy. But they're counting on me to keep this thing going. Even after I'm gone. I'm trying to make sure I leave a legacy. A legacy for them. A legacy for Bertrand." He tapped his cigarette, and the ashes floated into his palm.

Naomi sat back in the worn, nubby sofa, disguising her repulsion. "Mr. Aranha, just like you have your men—uh, boys counting on you, I have a whole team of people counting on *me*. The doctors and staff at the Center, my patients and I can't just turn it all over to you."

"Don't get me wrong, Doctor. I'm not asking you to. First, I thought I would undergo the process—you know, this regenerative therapy. Isn't that what you call it? I'd fit in more with my crew. You know, not be the old man with the head full of gray hair anymore. But then I got to thinking, why be a consumer when you can be an owner?

"And, to be honest, I don't know about all these people who want to be young again. I wouldn't want to trade places with my boys. Be their ages—they're not even twenty-eight years old yet—again for anything. You know the world is a dangerous place. Cyber threats and drones and what-nots.

"Plus, I like who I am. I think all this gray hair protects me somehow. I mean, who wants to put an eighty-one-year-old in prison? You know, I was reading the other day that the cost of incarcerating an elderly inmate is four times the cost of incarcerating a young one. Did you know that? I figure the city is making a cost-benefit analysis, which is why they don't ever seem to get around to arresting me and charging me with anything."

"I don't know about that. I imagine it depends more on whether they have enough evidence on you."

"You're probably right." Aspacio smiled Bertrand's mischievous smile. "You know, there is one thing I'd do anything to change. I'd like to spend more time with my son."

"Bertrand?"

"Yes. I figured that I'd make him the head of the Renew Your Youth Center. I'd give it to him...as a gift. He'd be so happy. So proud that his old man did this for him. That his old man gave him a business. A legitimate business. We'd finally have something that was ours... Bertrand's and mine. I'd be in his life, and he'd be in...mine." Aspacio's eyes pooled with tears, and his dark-brown face grew ashened.

"Mr. Aranha—"

"Aspacio, please call me Aspacio..."

"Aspacio, don't you think Bertrand will see through all this? One thing we both know about Bertrand is...he doesn't follow anyone else's plan."

"You noticed that, too, huh?"

"I think that if you really want Bertrand in your life, if you really want to change your relationship with him, then *you* have to change. Your actions—what you think is right and wrong—that's what pulled you all apart in the first place."

"Mmmm...I see what you mean, Doctor." Aspacio leaned back in his chair, closed his eyes and began breathing slowly.

"Mr. Aranha? Aspacio?" Naomi raised her voice.

Aspacio opened his eyes, blinking to refocus on Naomi. "What's that you say?"

"Your relationship with your son will only change for the better when *you* change."

"I'm sure that is good advice for some people. But I've given this a lot of thought. I know what to do to make this work for us. Bertrand and me. When a man reaches eighty-one years on earth, he can't hope to live but so many more years. I don't have a lot of time on this earth to be experimenting with what I think might work. I need a straight shot." He sliced his hand through the air.

"And you think stealing my business from me will bring your son back to you?"

"The way you put things, Doctor. You just don't understand me at all."

Outside, firecrackers popped and fireworks whizzed, interrupting their conversation.

"You know, young lady, I think once Bertrand sees I would do anything for him—*anything*—he'll come back to me. My son...will come back to me." A milky film coated Aspacio's eyes.

Naomi picked up the pitcher full of cranberry iced tea and turned the contents of the crimson liquid onto the basket of white clothes. "Listen here, you delusional, horrible man! You'll never fix what is wrong between you and your son *this* way. I will never, ever give you any percentage of my business. I'm getting out of here, and you can kiss my ass."

Naomi ran through the living room to the front door, hurriedly turning each of the locks. She pulled the doorknob harder, when she heard keys hit the kitchen table and the rustle of plastic bags.

"Aspacio, Horace and Dickie's was out of perch, so I got you some croakers." Lolly entered the living room and handed Aspacio a white plastic bag. "And the wait for fries was too long, so I got you some potato salad. You know, Horace's potato salad is the bomb. Your knife and fork and napkins are in the bag. I'm taking mine and eating in the kitchen. What's a matter, man? Space, what's a matter?" He looked around. "Where's the Doc?"

Aspacio stood, staring vacantly and pointing at the front door. "Lolly, she ran out the door. Find her."

CHAPTER THIRTY

"This is us." Bertrand rose from his seat on the Metro and waited for the doors to open at Brookland. Caprice matched his stride as they walked the two blocks to a small luxury condominium building neatly set back from the street. The sun inched lower behind them.

"Hey, Percy." Bertrand waved to the concierge and strode toward the wall of mailboxes.

Percy returned his wave. "Hey, my man. Holiday, you know. No mail today."

"Yeah, I know. Habit. Thanks."

"Nice." Caprice glanced around the lobby with carvings etched into the crown molding and high cathedral ceilings. Inviting seating areas were filled with antiques and plush velvet mustard-colored sofas. Bertrand ushered her up one flight of stairs to the elevator banks, where he inserted a key into the elevator panel and pressed 'PH.' They rode in silence to the penthouse level, where Bertrand guided Caprice down the brightly lit corridor. He lead her around the yellow sign in the middle of the floor.

"Careful. Watch your step. They mop every evening and marble can be slippery when wet."

Caprice leaned against him and rubbed his arm. "Slippery when wet? You have no idea."

Bertrand smiled and pressed his lock combination into the door keypad.

Caprice looked down the corridor. "You the only one on the penthouse floor?"

"No, there's another gent that lives at the end of the other wing. Older dude. Never see him, though, which is good, because I like my privacy."

He pushed the heavy wood door open, and Caprice entered the cavern-like condominium. Floor-to-ceiling windows lined the walls, giving the impression that the condo floated atop the dusky sky. There was no furniture, except for two barstools at the granite kitchen island and an extra-large worn espresso-colored leather chair planted in front of a television the length of the entire wall. The walls were painted a standard white. There wasn't even a rug on the gleaming black walnut hardwood floors.

"Just move in, did we?" She deliberately spun around the vast room, stopping to place her purse beside the door.

"No. Been here almost three years." Bertrand grinned sheepishly.

"Oh, so we're waiting for decorating inspiration, are we?"

"No, not exactly. I just never got around to furnishing the place. I will, though. But I'm in no rush, since I don't have that many people over. One or two every now and then. Have a seat." He pointed to the large leather chair and emptied his pockets on the kitchen counter. He opened the refrigerator and selected a bottle of orange juice. "Can I offer you something?"

"Since you're playing host and my meal got interrupted, I'm afraid to ask, given your attention to home life...but how about some food? I know it's late, and I usually try to eat before seven, but I'm hungry."

"I pay a great deal of attention to my home life, I'll have you know. Just because I don't care about furniture, doesn't mean I don't care about food. I made spaghetti Bolognese last night. Will leftovers suit you?"

Caprice nodded. "Have anything to make a salad?"

"Let's take a look." Bertrand rummaged through his Sub-Zero and placed a tomato, arugula, baby spinach, and a block of mozzarella cheese on his black-and-white-speckled granite-countered island. "You allergic to nuts? I have some slivered almonds."

"No. I haven't got any allergies. And Aurora won't let me go gluten-free. She said it's too California."

"Who's Aurora?"

"I'm kidding. My mother. Aurora's my mother. I'll have some nuts.

I like the crunch."

"Here. You mix the salad dressing." Bertrand put a set of spices and a bottle of red wine vinegar on the counter.

"Smells good."

He arranged the food on a plate and placed it in front of Caprice, who sat on one of the two stools at the kitchen island. He placed another plate opposite her. "To your liking?" He wiped his mouth with a napkin.

"Yes, very good. Let me see. Handsome, a good cook, good job, a few coins in his pocket, and has a beautiful but empty place. No ring. No woman?"

"That's to the point." He twirled the spaghetti on his fork and eased it in his mouth.

"Yes, and that's not answering my question."

"Oh, I didn't know there was a question on the floor."

"There is. I can't imagine why you haven't been snagged, Bertrand Angenois. You must run awfully fast with those powerful, strong legs."

"On the contrary. I'm not running at all. I'm waiting for the right one is all..."

"*Waiting?* You strike me as the kind of guy who goes after what he wants."

Bertrand sipped his wine.

"Perhaps our standards are too high? I bet you're waiting for perfection."

"You sound like you're fishing. You finished?" He reached for her plate, placed it on top of his and placed both in the dishwasher.

"Touched a nerve?"

"No, not really. I'm going to go change." He proceeded toward his bedroom.

"Change?"

"Swim trunks. I like to watch the fireworks in the pool. If you'd like to join me, I probably have something you can wear. A few of the older girls are about your size. Bring your glass with you."

"That's an elegant way of changing the subject. Older girls?"

Caprice muttered to herself.

"Here. Sorry, no bathing suits." He handed her a purple soccer jersey and black uniform shorts. She frowned as she held them high.

"I'm afraid that's all I have. You can just sit by the pool, if you'd rather not."

"No, no, they're fine."

"Good, you can change in the guest bedroom. Straight down that hall to the left."

The automatic glass doors silently slid open, and Bertrand strode barefoot onto the Virginia bluestone patio that framed a verdant green grass lawn. Tall evergreen bushes wrapped around the patio, encircling the entire building and stretching toward the orange setting sun.

Caprice emerged ten minutes later. "This is beautiful. But I don't see a pool."

Bertrand pressed a button on the wall beside the glass doors. The lawn eased into the ground, and a covered pool slid into its place. The cover retracted into the sides of the pool.

"I knew there was a reason I liked you, Bertrand. So Cali, reminds me of home. In fact, it's just like what Jack and Goldie have."

"Jack and Goldie?"

"Oh, excuse me. Name dropping. Jack Nicholson and Goldie Hawn. They each have one just like it in their L.A. homes."

"I like things that do a double-duty. I need a lawn and I need water. This way, I have both." Bertrand sat on the edge of the rectangular pool, absently kicking his feet in the water.

Caprice sank into the khaki-green cushions of the outdoor modular sofa and sipped the dregs of her red wine, trying to hide her labored breathing. "What are we going to do about the Doc?" Her face grimaced as she stretched out on the sofa.

"You all right? Are you hurting?"

"Sometimes at night I get shooting pain in my abdomen that goes down to my leg. I'm all right. I probably shouldn't have eaten so late. I've noticed that eating late can make the pain worse. But it's okay, I'm used to it. The Doc—what are we going to do about the Doc?"

"I know where she is." Bertrand clenched his jaw, focused on the explosion of the multicolored lights arrayed in the sky.

"You do? Where is she? God only knows what is happening to her." She sat up and rubbed her stomach.

"No, we'll wait for him to make a move. I know where he is. He knows where I am." Bertrand sliced into the pool without a splash and lumbered onto a floating chaise lounge. The sky crackled and boomed, dusting the clouds with pastel colors.

"Well, where is she? Doc mentioned that there is this man. What do you know about what's happening?"

"He's just a man." His voice lowered in a way that ended the conversation. He turned his back to her, and the pair wordlessly watched the fireworks. When the show was over, he swam two laps and exited the pool, dripping water. "Hand me a towel, would you? They're in that cabinet."

Caprice did as he asked. He lightly patted the fluffy navy towel across his chest, tied it around his waist, and then joined Caprice on the sofa. She smiled and picked up one of the girls' neon-green sneakers from a row of shoes he had left beside the door to dry outdoors. "You have a lot of daughters..."

The corners of Bertrand's eyes crinkled. "None at all. I run a football club for fourth-grade girls in Ward 8. But it *is* like having thirty daughters. They always need something. Or at least that's what they tell me. While they may advance to the next grade, somehow they never graduate from me or my wallet."

Caprice tossed a shoe in the air. Bertrand caught it, put it next to its mate, and walked in as the glass door slid open. "I love fireworks. Beautiful finale. We don't shoot them back home like you do in the States."

"This them?" Caprice pointed to a framed picture of a group of smiling little girls clad in purple shirts and black shorts identical to what she was wearing that was displayed on the fireplace mantle.

"Yeah. I also sponsor a football club back home. Boys this time.

They're cheaper."

"I thought I detected an accent. Where's 'back home'? Jamaica?"

"Nah. Freeport, Bahamas. Been there?"

"No, I've been to Bimini and Findlay and I swam with the dolphins at the Atlantis in Nassau, but I've never been to Freeport. Is it just as beautiful?"

"Yes. It's a cross between Bimini and Nassau. More developed than Bimini and a little less developed than Nassau. But it's home, you know. More wine?"

Caprice sat in his only chair. Her face contorted in pain.

"Hey, tell me where it hurts." Alarmed, Bertrand knelt beside her and pressed two fingers on her pulse. "Your pulse is weak. Have you ever discussed this side effect with Dr. Ellington? She can refer you to the Collaborative Treatment and Severe Reaction Department. Together, they can find a dose for you that will be easier for your system to digest. This reaction could mean that regenerating to twenty-four was too much for your system. It may be easier on your system to choose a later age. I'll call them."

"No, please don't say anything to her. I don't want my dosage to change. I'm okay. It'll pass." She squirmed in the chair, barely conscious, her legs outstretched and stiff. Bertrand retreated and returned with two tablets of Extra-Strength Tylenol and two tablets of Advanced-Strength Advil. He held out his hand for Caprice to choose.

"Pick a set. I'm afraid this is the strongest stuff I've got."

Caprice lifted the Tylenol from Bertrand's hand and took the glass of water he offered.

He helped her out of the chair. "Come on, you can rest awhile in the guest bedroom."

CHAPTER THIRTY-ONE

Naomi crept into Aspacio's neighbor's front yard, unscrewed the light bulb in the sconce, tucked herself into a ball and hid behind the bushes that framed the house. Aspacio stood in his doorway, straining to see up and down the street, shouting at Lolly to keep searching.

Lolly stood in the street, hands on hips, dodging cars that honked at him as they sped in the lanes. Satisfied that Naomi had left the vicinity, he ran down the street. When he was gone, Naomi stood up and sprinted in the opposite direction to Alabama Avenue. Children lined the sidewalk, setting off firework kits, and teens weaved around them, laughingly lighting firecrackers.

Naomi ran toward an elderly woman sitting in a green-and-white striped lawn chair on the sidewalk. "I need a phone. Do you have a cell phone? I've been kidnapped, and I...I need to call the police."

"Child, I don't have no phone. Reynelle, honey, come here. You got Sonlove's phone?"

"What, Grandmommy?" A little girl with liquid dark-chocolate skin and a single puffy ponytail that shot straight out of her head ran around her grandmother's chair.

"A phone. You got Sonlove's phone?"

"No, Sonlove got his own phone." Reynelle's feet pranced on the sidewalk while she leaned on her grandmother's knees.

"Reynelle, go and get your daddy."

The girl hesitated at the interruption of her fun.

"It's important—please hurry," Naomi pleaded as she ducked behind the elderly woman's plastic folding chair.

"Okay, I'll get him." Reynelle skipped toward the crowd of laughing teens lighting firecrackers.

The elderly woman patted Naomi's hand. "Baby, you're shaking like a leaf. Everything's going to be just fine. You'll see, Sonlove'll be here in a minute and help you out."

Reynelle returned to her grandmother with her father in tow. "Here he is, Grandmommy."

"Sonlove, this lady needs to use your phone. Give it to her."

Naomi instantly recognized the face and the pink shirt. It was Pierre. She stood, fear coursing through her veins like blood, and screamed at the old woman, "He's your son! This is one of the men that kidnapped me!"

"Oh, no, child. You got that wrong. My son would never do anything like that. He's my good boy. No angel, mind you, but he's a good boy."

"Mama, I don't know what she's talking about. See, I'm giving her my phone." Pierre offered his phone to Naomi, who backed away from him, looking around for a place to run. "Never mind, I'll find someone else." She ran onto Alabama Avenue and stopped the first car that passed.

"Hey, Doctor Lady, I'm glad we found you before you got lost." Lolly jumped out of the car. Pierre gripped Naomi's shoulders.

"Get off me! Help me! No! Call the police!" She kicked and screamed as Pierre pushed her into the car.

The elderly woman ambled her girth toward the scene. "Why's she screaming like that? What's going on here, Sonlove?"

"You better tell her that everything's okay, or I swear I'll kill you right here and you won't even make it to Aspacio's," Pierre murmured to Naomi through gritted teeth while pressing his gun deep into her side. "Smile at my mother."

"It's okay. We're okay." Naomi stiffened.

"I'm just taking her home. See Mama, I told you it was okay." He rubbed the hand his mother was resting on the car door. "Mama, Reynelle can stay out a little while longer. But I want her in bed in an hour. I'll be home to tuck her in shortly."

"See, child, I told you my Sonlove was a good boy. I raised him to be a good boy. If you need anything, anything at all, you come on back. Nice to meet you, child. Take care now." The elderly woman walked back to her chair on the sidewalk.

CHAPTER THIRTY-TWO

Caprice awakened when she felt Bertrand's weight on the side of the bed. "Feeling any better?" His face was awash with concern.

"Of course. Who *wouldn't* feel better waking up to you?" She stretched her arms straight.

"You're definitely feeling better." He held her wrist and timed her pulse.

"What time is it?"

"It's almost four a.m. I didn't want you to sleep through the night without checking on you. You had me worried about your reaction. I wanted to make sure I didn't have to take you to the Center."

"You're a nurse, all right." She rolled over and yawned. "It happens all the time. I'm used to it."

She cooed and rubbed his chest with her left hand. He gripped her hand flat against his chest, stopping her, and brought it to his lips. "That's a pretty big canary diamond. Someone must love you an awful lot."

She pressed her breast against his leg as he sat on the bed. "Things change. People change. If it bothers you..." She squeezed the ring off her finger, and it clinked loudly when she dropped it onto the bedside table. "You made me feel better. Now *I* want to make *you* feel better." She raised the soccer jersey above her head. "Your hands are strong." She placed his large burnished hands on each of her breasts. "Make me believe in your hands."

"You're a client at the Center—we have rules against this sort of thing," Bertrand stuttered as he traced the outline of her breasts with his hands.

"Yes, I'm a patient. But you're not one of my treating physicians. Plus, you strike me as someone who knows how to break a few rules."

Caprice put her lips on his and whispered as her tongue moistened his lips, "Prove to me your hands are strong. Let me feel your strength."

He released her breasts, removed her bra, squeezed them tightly, and rubbed them against his cotton polo shirt until he felt her nipples harden. He pushed her into the soft pillows and widened his mouth around her flesh, tickling one nipple with his tongue and the other with the flick of his thumb.

"I can see what you like," she laughed into his ear.

"You have no idea," he mumbled as he sucked at her nipple, turning it from pink to purple.

She grabbed his polo shirt until she wrestled it from his body. Curled, black hair dotted his chiseled chest. "What else do you have that's strong?" She licked along the waistband of his shorts.

He unzipped his shorts, and they fell to the floor. When she attempted to pull down his briefs, he stopped her. "Your turn."

She wrangled out of the soccer shorts, revealing a flawless peach, perfectly rounded behind clad in an antique white-and-pink lace thong.

"You have a beautiful ass." He walked his fingers down her curved buttocks.

"If you think that's something, wait until you taste it."

"I'll take that as an invitation." In one quick, powerful movement, Bertrand swung Caprice across the bed and parted her legs, each hand pushing her thighs into a split. He gently kissed those second lips, admiring how they turned from pink to red with each lick of his tongue. He could feel the ache in her body as she quivered, begging him for more. He resisted her grasp as she tried to guide his head between her legs.

No, baby, he thought. *If I'm going to jeopardize my job, then I control this ride.*

Her guttural moans told him, almost but not yet, *I can see what you mean. It is good. But this is good, too.*

He climbed on her, effortlessly inserting her like silk. He covered her mouth with his own. The echoes of her screams shook them both.

"I counted four. Is that right?" Bertrand nibbled the side of Caprice's neck.

"Really? I couldn't count at all."

CHAPTER THIRTY-THREE

"Lolly, your food's cold. I'll heat it up for you while you take the doctor to the guest room. It's quiet in there. Allow her to do some thinking. Come to the right conclusion."

Aspacio emptied the contents of the plastic bag onto a plate, nervously eyeing Naomi seated at the kitchen table. "Running is pretty futile. We know everybody around here. And everybody knows us."

"This is what's futile. I'm never going to change my mind. Extortion. Kidnapping. It won't work."

"Well, let's try it and see what happens. I want my way, and you want your way. There just doesn't seem to be any compromise. But after you spend a few nights in my guest room, I think we'll end up wanting the same things."

Lolly gestured for Naomi. "Come on, Doctor Lady. I'll show you to your room." He gripped her arm and pushed her in front of him, down the hall, and up a flight of stairs to what was clearly an addition. Then he opened the door to an all-white, well-appointed room. The bedding was startling white. There was a white alpaca rug, a white chest of drawers, and two white lacquered nightstands. The walls were all blinding white. Iron bars encased the skylight, the only source of natural light.

"What's this? Some kind of torture chamber?"

"Don't be silly. We don't need to torture you, Doctor Lady. You'll change your mind...all by yourself. After all, something is better than... nothing. And we're here until you do. Make yourself comfortable. I did pick you up some food. You want it now?" Lolly stood, blocking the door's threshold.

"I don't want anything from you but to let me the hell out of here."

"Well, I tried…if you change your mind, I'll save the food for you. Listen, I'll check on you in a few hours. I know the surroundings are new. You want to go home. But this is…your home away from home. And, Doctor Lady, we can last much longer than you can. You know what we want. And when you're ready to give it to us, the door will magically open." He smiled. "See, it's just that easy."

Lolly lingered at the door. "Oh, Doctor Lady? Don't get any funny ideas. It's soundproof in there…so screaming won't work, either."

The door clicked shut.

Naomi grabbed the doorknob and pulled hard with both hands. It was locked from the other side.

CHAPTER THIRTY-FOUR

"What are we going to do?" Caprice sighed, pulling her blush-pink silk T-shirt over her head. She stepped into her jeans, one leg at a time.

Bertrand walked out of the guest bathroom, a navy-blue towel wrapped securely around his waist, clearly lost in thought.

"I said, what are we going to do? He...they haven't called, and I'm worried about the Doc." Caprice brushed her hair. The strawberry-blonde curls fell around her shoulders. "Are you listening to me? Bertrand?" She scanned the room, but he was gone.

She walked barefoot from the guest bedroom and padded to the stairs leading to the master-bedroom suite. It was awash with the sun's early morning light. A large gold stripe circled two café au lait painted walls. His king-size bed with black coffee-colored linen lay undisturbed.

Caprice went to the closed door of the master bath and rapped on it. "Bertrand?" She pressed her ear against it, listening for movement. Hearing none, she pushed open the door and saw his damp bath towel limply hanging over the massive copper-colored, glass-encased shower. "Okay, big fella, where could you have gone so fast?" she muttered as she walked downstairs. The condominium was huge, but the expansive open floor plan made it impossible to hide.

She opened the unit's front door, peered down the empty hallway, and then ventured out onto the terrace, and followed the stone path that wrapped around the entire floor. No Bertrand. Caprice retreated inside and sat silently for a moment, enveloped in the large, worn, comfortable leather chair. She glanced around, finally focusing on the small glimmer of light emitting beneath a door at the far end of the condo. She went over and knocked softly on the door.

"In here, Caprice."

"I knew you had to be somewhere. After all you wouldn't just..." Caprice pushed the door open. Bertrand held his hand up silencing her. Then buried his head in his hands as he talked on the phone. "I know we have to find her. In the meantime, Dr. Van Stritton and Dr. Ellington will help you." He listened for a moment. "None? How can there be no dosages left? Well, can you break the bloody machine open?" He listened for a bit longer. "How many in their eighties? How many in their nineties?" He held the phone more firmly against his ear and wrote furiously on a pad. "Can't get them to Reversion? Shit. Tell their families we're looking into it. No, don't tell them that Dr. Morninglory is missing...no, don't close the Center. Better to let them in. Give as much information as you can without telling them anything. I don't know when I can get there. I have something to do first. No, not more important, Dr. Overbrook..."

Bertrand held the phone away and grimaced when he arched his back upward and stretched. Then he returned the phone to his ear. "Dr. Overbrook, we have to work together. You do want me to find Dr. Morninglory, right? I haven't seen the news." He aimed the remote control at the flat screen hanging on his wall. "It's on now."

"Patients and their families are flooding the Renew Your Youth Center. As of six a.m. this morning, there have been forty-seven deaths of patients in their eighties and nineties who were not able to get their youth-sustaining medication and accelerated to their real ages in a matter of hours. Shaneen, we have been unable to speak to anyone at the Center, but their spokesman issued a press release stating, and I quote, 'Though we are saddened by the recent deaths of patients at the Renew Your Youth Center, we also believe that the cause is due to normal age-related conditions. We sympathize with the families, because we consider our patients part of our Renew Your Youth family, and their well-being is of paramount importance to us.' I will keep you abreast of any developments. Live from the Renew Your Youth Center in Southeast Washington, I'm Petal Rodriguez. Back to you, Shaneen."

"Okay, I'll call you back when I know more." Bertrand rubbed his hands against the morning stubble of his salt-and-pepper beard. His eyes rimmed with worry.

"What's going on?" Caprice sat gingerly on the desk.

"The dosage delivery machines are locked. No one at the Center can open them. Patients are accelerating their reversion and getting sick. Our oldest patients—the ones in their eighties and nineties—are dying. Forty-seven so far. The government is trying to declare it a health emergency. I have to make some calls to prevent that."

"That's terrible. The Doc *said* this would happen."

"She said *what* would happen?"

"Dr. Morninglory is the only one who can open the dosage delivery machines."

"That's ridiculous. Other doctors open them all day long. That's part of our business—dispensing medicine." Bertrand drained the coffee from his cup. "Did you get some coffee?"

Caprice shook her head and eased further onto Bertrand's desk. "It makes perfect sense."

"What does?"

"Dr. Morninglory told me she was concerned that the other doctors were trying to pressure her...something about more patients. So, in order to keep the lions at bay, she had a chip installed in her hand. Every day, she goes to the Center and opens the dosage delivery machines with her chip. She said she never told anyone about the chip."

"When did she do *that* shit? Never mind...let me get this straight: unless we get Naomi back, thousands of people are going to get sicker, and the dying will just get worse? These people and their fucking power moves."

"Yes, that's why I promised her I would help her. That, and also because she said that is the only way I can keep my youth. I had to help her."

"Well, fuck...did she tell you how to open the machines?"

Caprice shook her head.

"Did she tell you whether she had a backup plan in case she wasn't available?"

"Let me think. Yes, she did."

"Well, what is it? Quickly..."

"She said her Chief Operating Officer had a chip. *You.* She said *you* have one."

"Me?" Bertrand thought about the myriad of ways Naomi could install a chip without him knowing. Maybe it was the previous fall, when the entire staff received mandatory flu vaccinations. At the time Bertrand thought it was Naomi being...Naomi. They argued, but he acquiesced when he decided there were other battles more important to fight. After his vaccination, he noticed a peculiar soreness in his right hand, but dismissed it as a strange aftereffect of the vaccination.

Bertrand raised his right hand in front of the window, turning the front of his hand and his palm. Nothing was unusual. "Okay, then, let's go. Since I can open the machines."

"No, wait. She said yours would only work if her pulse goes silent."

"Her *pulse* goes silent? In order for someone's pulse to go silent, that means they're—dead."

"Yes, that's what she said."

"Just like her. Damnit." He pounded on the wall of the light oak-paneled office. He looked at Caprice, and his anger slowly subsided. Embarrassment sprouted like a wild, untended vine as each of them remembered last night.

Caprice spoke first. "I want to thank you."

"Thank me? You have nothing to thank me for."

"Not true...I didn't know where you were this morning."

"I, uh, I had to take a call. Emergencies on a number of fronts."

"It's all right. But the reason I want to thank you is...when I was twenty-four, I blew up big in Hollywood. Guys were coming after me left and right. Some of them just wanted to be with me so that they could say they shagged Caprice Deveaux. Bragging rights, I suppose. Some wanted to be with me to see what shagging Caprice Deveaux could get them. Media coverage...a bigger part. Hollywood is funny like that. Some of them were A-list actors themselves. But you get even more publicity if you're with the latest, hottest star. I got bit a few times...maybe *more* than a few times before I figured out I couldn't trust them. Then Findlay came along. He was nothing to look at, but... his heart, man. He changed all that for me. I forgot what it was like. To be wanted just for yourself.

"So, *that's* why I want to thank you. For reminding me how empty those relationships were. I've been with Findlay for twenty-one years, since I was thirty-seven years old. And in all of those years, I never once had to look for him after sex."

"Caprice, I'm sorry. I don't know what happened last night. I only know it wasn't supposed to happen."

"Oh, I know what happened...too much wine." Caprice laughed. "Or maybe I wanted to see if I was attractive to someone I was attracted to. See if I still 'got it.'" She slid off of his desk and studied her folded hands. "Silly, huh?"

"Not silly at all. And, by the way, you still got it in spades, love."

She smiled and placed her hand on his shoulder. "You know, Handsome, yesterday, when you were talking about Dr. Morninglory, you should have seen your face. It was all lit up, like when you were watching those fireworks."

"That obvious, is it?"

"Only to a trained eye. That's why you got the spartan look going on here. Why you barely moved in, in three years. The right person, huh? Does she know?"

"She knows. But she doesn't want to know. She's stuck on this other chap."

"Haron Fitzgerald."

"You know about him?"

"I met him. Very impressive."

"Very married." Bertrand flopped back in his desk chair.

"Well, you know what I think, handsome? The Center should advertise you as part of their pain management package." She brushed her lips against his stubble. "If she knows what I know, she'll run, not walk, to you."

"Thank you, Mrs. Canary Diamond." Bertrand jerked Caprice away from him. "Your face is hot." He examined her eyes. "Your eyes are a little glassy...jaundiced. Your complexion is sallow. How are you feeling? When are you due for your next dosage?" He raised her up and eased her into his desk chair.

"Today. It's due today. If I don't get it today, I start reverting."

"It looks like you've already started. What time is the latest that your dosage could be due?"

She wilted in the chair, fighting the urge to faint. He gently shook her.

"Two p.m. Forty-eight hours will be two p.m."

Bertrand glanced at his watch. It was eight-thirty in the morning.

Caprice pushed her hair across her forehead, which was damp with perspiration. "If we're going to go and get the Doc, we better come up with a plan."

Bertrand slid his desk drawer open. "Do you know how to use a gun?"

CHAPTER THIRTY-FIVE

"Dad."

"So, your phone does work?"

"Yeah, it works."

"'Dad'? You haven't called me 'Dad'...come to think of it, you never called me 'Dad.' Just Aspacio, or Uncle Aspacio, but never 'Dad.'"

"I don't want to go into that. Not now."

"It sounds good coming out of your mouth, though."

Bertrand's voice lowered. "Dad, this...is between you and me. Let Naomi go so she can go handle her business. You've seen the news. People are dying. Let her go so that she can get back to the Center. Take care of her patients. If you don't let her go, many more people will die. I know you don't want that."

"It's been a long time. Too long. I miss you, Son."

Bertrand paced about the room, shifting the phone from his left ear to his right.

"Dad, let's you and me sit down. Let's talk about it before you do something you'll be sorry for later. Something you'll regret."

"Something I'll regret? Really? I have so much that I regret that I don't even know where to start. Anything else I do won't make any difference. No difference at all."

"It will to me."

"Think so?"

Words labored between the two halves of the same seed, struggling to push up through the hardened soil of unforgiveness.

"Son, I haven't seen you in a long time."

"I'll be there in an hour."

*　　*　　*　　*

"You alone?" Aspacio cracked the door, peering around the bushes and trees surrounding his Hillcrest Heights home.

"As alone as you are." Bertrand pushed the door open and walked into the house he had vacated more than twenty years ago.

"Hello, stranger. My son, the stranger. I haven't seen you in so long that I almost forgot what you looked like. I got to remind myself what you look like by reading magazines...searching the Internet. What you got going on that you can't visit me? Why can't you come see your own father?"

"I suggest you ask *yourself* that, Aspacio." Bertrand strode past Lolly, eyeing the younger man up and down, who stood erect as a sentinel beside Aspacio. Once he reached the living room, Bertrand threw a pillow from the sofa onto a facing chair and sat. "Where's Dr. Morninglory?"

"She's fine," Lolly answered. "She's safe. No reason for you to worry."

Bertrand focused his gaze on his father. "Let her go, Aspacio. She don't have nothing to do with this. Nothing to do with us."

"You didn't even ask me about how I'm doing. Did you know that I had a heart attack four years ago? I bet you didn't! I haven't heard from you in five years! Not one phone call in five years! Don't you think I deserve at least a phone call? All those years, I fed you, clothed you. And not even a single phone call. I'm an eighty-one-year-old man. Seems to me, a son ought to ask a father at the very least, 'How you doing?'"

Bertrand sighed. "Aspacio, where is she?"

"After I got better, I said to myself that I wanted to see my son. I didn't know where you lived. I didn't have your phone number. You just disappeared. I saw an advertisement on the television that you were giving a TED Talk in Beverly Hills, California, so I flew out there because I wanted to see my son. I saw you give that speech. I was so proud of you. And you...you were so excited and happy about this Renew Your Youth Center. A father likes to see his child happy. I set about making my son the head of this Center. Give it to you. So, I studied how I could get it for you. What were the weaknesses? It's damn near a fortress. But *Curtis* was the weakness. I set about getting close to him. Got him to owe me. Took almost three years, but eventually I got him to owe me, and that was my way in."

"Space, don't forget we—" Lolly interrupted. "I been working on getting an in, too. Don't forget about that other..." He shifted on his feet beside the older man, who glared at him.

"Shut up. It's not the time to go into all that." Aspacio returned to Bertrand and continued in a softer voice, "Then Curtis owed me all this money, and I told him to tell that doctor the only way to pay me back was with equity in the Center. She and I partners. But, by the way you're acting...charging in here all puffed up, it looks like it wasn't that Center you wanted, now, was it? I'm an old man, but I'm not *that* old." He grinned.

"Where is she, Aspacio?"

"What happened to 'Dad'?"

"Dad, where is she?"

"Come on in the kitchen and sit down. Talk to me, Son. I remember how much you liked Mandolin's baked chicken. I tried to make it like she did." Aspacio opened the oven, placing the golden-brown baked chicken on an eye of the stove to cool. "I got some potatoes cooking on the stove. I remembered you didn't like asparagus, so I made some broccoli. See, Son. Please just sit. Talk to me." He pulled out a chair from the kitchen table.

"Space, that smells good." Lolly removed the foil from the chicken.

"Tell me, where is she?" Bertrand leaned against the wall.

"This doesn't have to be a fight. We can work together on this. You and me."

"And me." Lolly stood closer to Aspacio.

"We want the same things. You want to run the Center, I want you to own the Center. Don't you see that? You got to think big. I can...I can make it happen for you." Aspacio's moist eyes widened.

"Dad, it's not going to work."

"Yes, it can work. We...we can make it work."

"And Naomi? What do you intend to do about her?"

"Okay, sit right here." Aspacio took a plate and spooned broccoli on it. He sliced the chicken. Juices spilled into the pan. Then he forked it onto the plate. "So, what I hear you saying is that, if I can get her on board, then *you'll* be on board?" He put the plate on the kitchen table. "I've got iced tea, lemonade, or, if you like something stronger, I can make you a drink. What would you like?"

"Aspacio, it *won't work*. This is Naomi's business. You can't just take it from her. This isn't like on the street." Bertrand sat in the chair, smoothed his hair with his hands, and exhaled deeply. He leaned toward his father, reached out, and surrounded the man's broad, wrinkled hands with his own. He examined the eyes of the older version of himself. In the five years since he had last seen his father, it seemed as if old age had crawled inside Aspacio and overtaken his face and body. His cheeks drooped, and small dark patches marked his temples. His eyes sunk into his dark-chocolate face.

"I'd like some lemonade, Space." Lolly placed a fully laden plate on the table.

"Lolly, Son, give me a little time. I have something I'd like to talk to my son about. Can you take your food into the other room? You don't mind, do you?"

Lolly licked his fingers. "I'll be right out here, if you need me."

Bertrand exhaled loudly. "Dad, thank you for making all of this. The food looks really good. It smells really good. You went to a lot of trouble, I can see that. It's just that I'm not really hungry right now."

"I don't know where I went wrong. But nothing in my whole life means as much to me as *you* do." Aspacio folded the dish towel in his lap.

Bertrand rose and hugged his father, massaging the older man's stooped back, racked with sobs.

"I did all of this for you."

"I know you did," Bertrand whispered hoarsely. "Aspacio, I don't want her business. I never wanted...how you live. You know that."

Aspacio sat heavily at the table, and Bertrand sat opposite him. "Remember when I was fifteen, and I asked you to give me money to buy a gift for that girl I wanted to take to the junior spring dance?"

"I remember. You had been living with us for about two years."

"I wanted to impress her. It was a little gold necklace with a pendant. Rhinestones shaped like a heart. You wouldn't give me the money, so I stole the necklace. It was a cheap little thing. And stupid me left my jacket in the kitchen, and you saw it dangling from my pocket and found it. Do you remember what you did?"

"Yes. I remember."

Bertrand placed his cheek against his father's. "What...what did you do?"

"I told you that if you couldn't pay for it, you couldn't have it. Stealing was wrong, and I wouldn't stand for it." Aspacio choked as he whispered each word.

"And..."

"I went with you and made you take it back to the store. I told you if they arrested you, then that was the consequence for your actions."

"The saleslady was so surprised."

"I remember the look on her face." Aspacio smiled. "She called Lost Prevention, and they took you in the back and dressed you down real good. They threatened that they were going to take you to juvie. Maybe even deport you back to the Bahamas." He seemed to relish the warmth of his son's cheek against his own.

"They didn't. Nothing came of it but a whole lot of embarrassment. But I learned my lesson, though. I never stole another thing." Bertrand pushed away from his father and laughed. "That's why, Dad. That's why when, later, you got into all that...I couldn't do it with you. Thieving, selling drugs. Why...why, I can't do this with you now. Because you taught me. You taught me right from wrong." Bertrand pounded his heart.

"It will be different if you come back, Son. You'll see. It can be *us* running things. A legitimate business. Father and son. I can be done with all the other...I'll change. I promise. I'll change. No more. I'm done with all of that."

"You still don't understand. I have no interest in what you're doing."

"Even if I change?"

"Change? Then start right now. Let Naomi go."

"I think what's important is...is...if we concentrate on the business. Once we get all the details worked out and put it in writing, then she's free to go."

"That's not changing, Aspacio. That's you still trying to control things. Control people. Control me."

"No, Son. That's not true. See this is a great opportunity. Something I can leave to you. I'm not going to live forever. I give this business to you, and then...then you can do whatever you want."

"Aspacio...I already do whatever I want. I don't need this. I don't want this."

"Well, what about what I need? What about what I want?" the older man yelled.

Bertrand gripped the side of the sink and closed his eyes. "I love you, Dad. You don't have to do this to get me to love you, because...I already do."

Aspacio twisted the dish towel into a tight coil. "You do?"

"Of course, I do. Now tell me...where is Naomi?"

"She's right here." Lolly presented Naomi in the living room in Bertrand's full view from the kitchen. His arm was firmly wrapped around her shoulder and his other hand was securely pressing a gun to her temple.

"Lolly, let her go. I don't think it matters anymore." Aspacio's voice trailed to nowhere in particular.

"It matters to me, Space. Hey, man, you said we were going to be like Bill Gates and shit. You said we were going to own everything in sight. You said she was the only thing standing in our way. Well, then, I'm ready. I'm ready to win the lottery."

Naomi hedged. "It's more complicated than that. If you kill me, then thousands of people may die. You don't want to be responsible for the death of thousands of people, do you?"

"What do I care if some rich motherfuckers I ain't never met die? I mean, really, who cares?"

"You should care, because they pay for the treatment. And if the brand is compromised by patient deaths, the company will lose its value. Quite simply, it won't be worth $73 billion. It won't be worth anything at all. Then you will have killed me, and you'll be responsible for the death of all of these innocent people and end up with nothing. Nothing at all. You were the one who said something is better than nothing. I can ensure that at least you leave with *something.*"

"Space, say something. Do something." Lolly nervously swayed, still holding Naomi.

Caprice suddenly staggered from the garage to the kitchen entryway, breathing heavily, brandishing a Glock. "Let me make it easy for you, Baby Boy. Let my doctor friend go, and I won't shoot you in the balls. I can't promise that I'm a great shot, but I can promise you that I will hit something really, really important."

Lolly dragged Naomi, jerking her in Caprice's direction. "Oh, no! You're the one that pushed me into the river! Hey, what are you doing here?"

"I got an awful lot invested in that doctor you're making really friendly with that gun. Where she goes, I go." Caprice steadied her knees, straining to remain standing. She hit the floor. Her gun scurried across the room.

"Lolly, let her go!" Bertrand demanded.

"Space is eighty-one years old. He may not even survive a trial. Me, I'll get tagged for what...extortion, kidnapping, even murder, because I'm the one that threw ol' dude out the window. I'm even looking at attempted murder because of this bitch. And those are just the charges I can think of off the top. Shit, I'll never take another breath of free air again. I don't have anything to lose by popping her."

"Dad, tell him to let her go!" Bertrand's voice cracked with fear.

Aspacio rose wearily from his chair, picked up Caprice's gun, and walked over to Lolly, placing his hands on the younger man's shoulders. "Lolly, don't make my mistakes yours. You're a young man. Just let it be."

"Let it be? Let it be? What about my money?" Lolly pushed Naomi arm's length of his loaded gun.

"Never mind that. You'll be well taken care of. Aren't you well taken care of now? Let's forget about this, and just let her go."

"No fucking way. What about my money?"

"I told you to let her go!"

"Space, no way, man. I got a big payday coming. I been waiting all this time for this. You promised me, man. Don't you remember?"

Aspacio pushed the Glock into the flesh of Lolly's belly. "Just let her go."

"Space, you wouldn't. Not after all I done for you. Who took care of you after your heart attack? I was here...every day." The corners of his mouth foamed. "Where was he? I was the one who bathed you, cleaned up your shit. I...I fed you because you couldn't even feed yourself. That was me. Don't you remember that? Space, it's been me. Me and you, all this time. And now he going to just roll up in here, and I don't exist for you no more." He wiped tears from his eyes.

"Of course I remember, but I'm tired now, Lolly. I don't want any more trouble."

"You think he going to stay? Do you? I'm the one you can count on. Me. Space, you said, I was like your son. Space...you called me...'Son.' He going to leave you again, Space."

"Let's just...let it be. Do what I say, hear? Let her go."

Lolly's breath slowed like a cornered wild animal concentrating on its exit. "You selfish, man. You got what you want. Your son is here. You promised me, man. I want my money."

Eyes loving and gentle, Aspacio approached Lolly and hugged the young man tightly. He fired a quick, loud shot. Lolly thumped to the floor. Naomi shrieked.

"Don't move!" Aspacio barked when Bertrand moved toward Naomi. "I'm sorry you had to see that, Dr. Morninglory. But he is right that I may not survive a trial. Very stressful, and I've had a heart condition. For almost forty years, I've managed to evade the law. I can't go to jail at this age, this stage."

Bertrand moved again toward Naomi.

"I said, don't move!" Aspacio jerked his gun up to Naomi's forehead.

"Dad, stop it. We'll figure something out. It'll be okay. Just put the gun down."

Aspacio rapidly blinked, glancing confusingly at Naomi, and then at Bertrand. He finally rested his eyes on his son. "I know you love her, Son. In my mind, I see this pretty picture, the two of you together, living life just like you want. Having children, being the family that I always wanted. I want you to be happy. I do. But I want to be happy, too. I don't want to be in some jail cell for the few years I have left on this earth. Life—it's funny—it just doesn't work out the way we want it to. The way we hope it does." His voice trailed off.

Bertrand crouched, stealthily moving closer to Naomi. "Dad, put the gun on the floor. We can make this work out for both of us this time. We can both be happy. A new life. A new start. Father and son. You'll see."

"Don't move, because I will shoot her. I will kill her. Don't try me, Son. I know if she dies those patients could die, but believe me...I care more about me than I do about them."

Naomi yelped and startled Aspacio. Bertrand leapt on his father, rolling with him along the floor. Two shots rang almost simultaneously. Naomi's scream pierced the eerie silence. She crawled to Bertrand lying on the floor and cradled his head in her arm. She pressed her other hand against the wound spurting blood from his chest.

He raised his head in Aspacio's direction.

"Bertrand, don't move. You're hurt. Let me look at it." Naomi cradled him while feverishly unbuttoning his blood-stained shirt.

"Let me go." He pushed away from her embrace. "Dad?" Bertrand crawled on his elbows toward the elder man sprawled near him. Aspacio breathed intermittently, lying in a pool of his blood.

Naomi ran into the living room and rifled among Aspacio's belongings to find her purse containing her phone.

"Why? Why'd you do it?" Bertrand rocked his father. His hot tears fell into Aspacio's left eye socket as it surged blood, seasoning the cauldron of generational soup.

Aspacio's face contorted, and he mouthed the words, "I love you, Son."

"I love you, Dad."

Aspacio stiffened in a spasm, shaking in Bertrand's arms. He then went limp.

CHAPTER THIRTY-SIX

"Where have you been?" Dr. Overbrook ran beside Naomi as she headed toward the dosage delivery machines. "We are swamped with patients needing their dosages. We don't have enough beds for the eighty- and ninety-year-olds who lay dying. We've been trying to keep them comfortable. Their families are yelling at every doctor they can find. This is going to be a legal nightmare that even your Bertrand can't solve."

"I don't have time to explain." Naomi brushed past Overbrook and reached for the laptop Astrid was handing her.

"Do you realize that forty-seven people have died because you chose this time to have some kind of personal crisis?"

"Oh, my God, that many?"

Astrid nodded gravely.

"You may not care about your professional reputation, Dr. Morninglory, but I care about mine. This is irresponsible, even for you."

"Excuse me, Dr. Overbrook, I don't have time to argue with you about this right now." She tapped the keyboard and quickly reviewed the patient chart. "Astrid, put the overflow patients in the consultation rooms. Tell Dr. Ellington that we won't be able to stagger the dosages. Tell her that we will administer full-strength dosages."

"I heard that." Ava came up behind Naomi. "I won't even ask where you've been. It's been a nightmare trying to mop up the mess around here."

Overbrook countered. "Full-strength dosages? Do we have time to accurately formulate them?"

Ava eyed Overbrook. "You worrying about full-strength dosages? I've seen it all."

"Look, staggering the dosages runs the risk that it won't be enough to stop sudden reversion and prevent the patients' bodies from going into shock. If it's a choice between full-strength or death, I choose full-strength."

"All right, all right, I'll alert my team. Morninglory, I'm sorry about that crack about Bertrand. I forgot. I didn't mean to mention Bertrand like that..." Overbrook dropped his head sheepishly.

"Any word about how he's doing?" Ava stood between Overbrook and Naomi.

"He's still in ICU." Tears welled in Naomi's eyes.

Astrid smiled and squeezed Naomi's hand. "He's going to be all right. It's just his way of seeking attention. You know how dramatic he is."

Naomi quickly wiped her eyes. "He's at Johns Hopkins, getting the best care. Let's focus on our own patients in crisis. Do you have a list of the priorities?"

"I do." Ava tapped at her keyboard.

"Yeah." Overbrook glanced at his laptop.

"Then distribute the list with instructions to your teams. Let's get busy."

Overbrook scampered down the hall, followed by a squadron of nurses. Ava proceeded in the opposite direction trailed by two nurses.

Naomi turned to Astrid. "We do have the staff capacity to deliver the dosages to everyone here at once?"

"I'll round up the other doctors and nurses. Between them and the techs, we should be able to cover everyone that's here. The techs will have to work overtime to get the dosages ready for those patients we turned away." Astrid paged through her laptop. "I'll have staff call those patients and schedule their appointments to return. We will be crowded and have to schedule appointments all night."

"At this point, we'll have to do what we have to do to get everyone serviced as soon as possible."

"Okay, Doc. I'll distribute this list and be right back."

CHAPTER THIRTY-EIGHT

Mildred Baker-Jones blanketed the sanctuary with her lilting alto rendition of "Precious Lord," temporarily diffusing the hostility that festered on each of the pews of the First Baptist Church of Hillcrest Heights. Reverend Kilgore Wood nodded approvingly at Mrs. Baker-Jones when she concluded and squeezed into her seat in the empty choir loft. Rev. Wood was grateful that Mrs. Baker-Jones, the only one from his thirty-five-member choir, elbowed her way through the crowd of angry protesters gathered noisily on the sidewalk in front of his church.

Rev. Wood had spent so much of the last forty years in the chancel that its magnificent angles were etched into the folds of his ginger-brown face. His eyes were weak and weary from the too many funerals that always happened after the annual Fourth of July neighborhood revelry. But now, his eyes burned with fatigue from arguing until four o'clock this morning with the trustee board and the deacons. They refused to budge, and so did he. They were at an impasse, but in the end, it was his church. They would have to live with the fact that he refused to find another location for the funeral of Aspacio Aranha.

The trustee board and the deacons pressured Rev. Wood, but he declined to vilify someone who tried as hard as Aspacio Aranha to work out his salvation. The neighborhood youth lobbied to canonize Aranha, but Rev. Wood also declined to do that. So, Rev. Wood stood between the two feuding camps, fueled with viciously opposite opinions about Aranha, and he unsuccessfully tried to broker understanding. Maybe the reason he couldn't get the camps to reconcile was because of his own ambivalence about Aranha. Yet, still, everyone deserved a funeral, if they wanted one.

Rev. Wood stroked his silver-white goatee and scanned the camps as they filed into the pews. Aimless, he thought, categorizing the trail of young men with multidirectional afros and slouchy jeans that displayed their underwear as they ambled down the aisles, sliding into the first three rows of the pews. Aspacio could have set them on a good path—guided them in the right direction instead of them dragging him into the wrong one. Aspacio, at his age, should have known better.

The arrival of the assortment of young men clad in black T-shirts stenciled with the wording "Space in Time" and a picture of a smiling Aspacio drew scorn from the congregation who filled the remaining pews—the other camp. Rev. Wood bristled. At least they're here, he thought as he remembered the absent deacons, the trustees, and all of the choir members.

He shielded himself behind the pulpit, wiped his brow, and mulled what to say about Aspacio Aranha. He hadn't had much time to prepare a eulogy since he had been up all night arguing. He searched the expansive sanctuary for inspiration, but his mind kept wandering. *A shame about Aranha's son, Bertrand.* Funerals were always for the living. Rev. Wood closed his eyes and prayed for words to sear the hearts of the camps as each member watched his every move.

He wiped his forehead again and locked eyes with Naomi Morninglory, who was sitting in the front pew. He recognized her from all of the pictures he had seen of her in the news. A well-heeled woman with flowing blonde hair sat next to her. He surmised that the elegantly dressed man and the woman with the wiry hair on the other side of Dr. Morninglory worked with Bertrand at that Center. They had a medical air about them. Such a tangle, this business of restoring youth. *Such a tangle when man tries to interfere with what only God can do.* Yes, funerals were always for the living.

The rousing organ solo finished. It was time. Rev. Wood rose to the glass pulpit, laid his handkerchief in front of him, and clasped his hands. He inhaled deeply, summoning strength from his higher power with each breath: "I am not deaf. I hear as well as the best of you. I hear what those protesters outside are saying. I even heard what those inside these doors said, too. I was up to the wee hours of this morning with them. They have their opinions. I have mine.

"You know, I listen to the news reports. I read the newspapers. I even read what they put on the Internet. If the reports are to be believed, this man is a deadly arsonist, setting fire to whole communities. If the reports are to be believed, this man sold drugs to our children and committed murder, and many other despicable and heinous acts. And if the so-called eyewitnesses are to be believed, nothing is beneath what this man was willing to do—even shooting his only son.

"Some preachers find it difficult when faced with eulogizing someone like Aspacio Aranha. I've had conversations with many of my peers—other pastors and clergy—where they have said to me, 'What do you say about someone whose havoc inside his soul seeps out and breeds chaos in the lives around him?' Me, I believe in sending someone home to the best of my ability. You see, the word of God says, 'Judge not, for the same measure you use to judge will be used against you.' You see, the word of God says, 'All have fallen short of the Glory of God.' You see, I know I am a sinner, too. I rely on the grace of God each day...to cover me. I leave it to the Judge to judge His creatures. He knows all-omniscient. Only He can examine the crevices of a man's heart. Listen to me well, there is a time when all of us, the so-called saints and the so-called sinners, will meet their Creator. That time has come for Brother Aspacio."

Rev. Wood moved from behind the pulpit and stoically inched down the marble steps, stopping at the glossy black-and-silver casket. "You say, 'Well, Reverend Wood'—or to some of you who choose to be more familiar, Kilgore—'those are just flat, small words on thin pages of a rather thick book.' But those words govern my life. They are my law, my statutes. As for me and my house, we will serve the Lord. So, I leave it to the protesters outside and to those sitting here in this congregation looking at these young people with derision. I leave it to you, those of you who think they know so much about the comings and goings of Aspacio Aranha. I leave it to you to be the judge and jury about this man's life."

Rev. Wood squinted into the casket and laid his hand gently on Aspacio's still chest. "Frankly, I don't know what Aspacio Aranha did. I wasn't there. I didn't see it. He didn't tell me, and I didn't ask. I can only speak from what I do know. I know that Aspacio Aranha was a deeply devoted husband to Mandolin, and he loved her. Yes, they divorced, but their love endured all of her life and all of his. I know he loved his homeland, the Bahamas, and never failed to tell anyone crossing his path about its beauty. He was a tireless civil servant for thirty-five years. And yes, yes, despite all we've heard, all we've read, he loved his son, Bertrand.

"I know that Aspacio served as a deacon for many years. Since his training was as an accountant, he assisted with the church books until he retired. Then he just stopped. Stopped coming to church services. Told me that God left him. I told him on many occasions 'Aspacio, God will never leave you or forsake you.' I said, 'Aspacio, don't let the world break your heart. Keep going. Keep coming. God loves you.' But he closed his ears. Closed his heart. When a man becomes despondent to his God, well, no telling what he will do. But even though he felt that way, Aspacio hung around the edges of the church. I'd look up, and there he was, painting my office, cleaning out the lost-and-found closets, mowing the lawn, scrubbing the refrigerator in the All Saints breakroom. You know, the stuff y'all sitting here wouldn't do.

"I know that Brother Aranha, every Christmas that I've been here—and that has been forty years and counting—made a donation to the church to ensure that all of the children in the neighborhood had a present to open Christmas morning. And not just any present. Somehow, he'd slip in the shadows and find out just what the youngsters wanted.

"You may say, 'Well, that's nice, but that doesn't make up for all of the other...' Maybe. But let me tell you what he did for me personally. As some of you know, I had a heart attack last year. Brother Aranha had a heart attack about four years ago. I was right out there on Pennsylvania Avenue, and my tire blew. Pouring down sleet and rain. Lightning. Thundering. A cold rain on a winter day. I called AAA, and they said, at the earliest, it would be two hours before they could get anybody to me, which would make me late to perform a wedding. I couldn't change the tire myself—too weak to lift it. Doctor told me not to do any heavy lifting, because it could cause another heart attack. Aspacio was driving by and saw me. That man knew I had a weak heart. Don't you know he changed my tire in the pouring sleet? That man was frozen and drenched. I didn't have to get out of my car, so not one drop of rain fell on me. And you know what else? I was not late to that wedding, either. I'll never forget that.

"So, you say what you want about him. But I tell you what I've learned. I know that people can be complicated. I choose to focus on whatever is true, whatever is noble, whatever is right, whatever is pure, whatever is lovely, whatever is admirable, whatever is praiseworthy...all that other stuff, I leave that to you."

Rev. Wood squinted into the casket again. "Sometimes, it takes a lifetime for a person to find peace. Brother Aranha, what you did not find in this life, may you find it in the next. To God be the Glory."

CHAPTER THIRTY-NINE

"You didn't have to come to the funeral. I know you weren't feeling well, and it was a strain." Naomi perused the pages of Caprice's chart on her computer.

"If you were going...I was going." Caprice adjusted herself on the examination table.

"Loyal to the end. And how are you feeling today?"

Caprice smiled her megawatt smile at Naomi. "Like I survived being run over by a cargo truck. But better than yesterday, now that Findlay's here."

The small squat man nuzzled Caprice's neck. "I love you, baby. Glad to meet you, Dr. Morninglory. You have my girl looking fantastic. She raves about you."

Findlay held out his hand and Naomi shook it.

"Isn't he delicious? My own personal slice of angel food cake."

Findlay blushed.

Naomi smiled. "From her chart, her vitals are looking fantastic, too. No permanent organ damage and minimal reversals from waiting for her dosage. I just wanted to check you out myself. Make sure everything is progressing as it should."

"Thanks, Doc." Caprice hesitated. "Doc, it's not that I don't trust you or that the staff here hasn't been great, but...Findlay and I have been talking." She clasped Findlay's hand. "I'm...I'm not going to continue with the therapy, anymore. I want to be my age. I've been twenty-four. Now that I look twenty-four again, it's no fun having a husband who is sixty-three. Every time we go out, everyone thinks he's my father, for heaven's sake! You should see the scoffs we get. Besides, my life is in Cali with Findlay. We have so many places we want to go and see and things we want to do. With this regeneration therapy, I have to be on a plane every week. I admit it's liberating to be twenty-four years old again, doing all the stuff I used to, looking like I used to, but this maintenance bit is too limiting. I'm tied to this Center. I guess I'm not explaining it very well. Do you know what I mean?"

"You want to start the reversion process?"

"I...yeah, I want to start the reversion process."

"If that's what you want, I understand. I'll note that on your chart and alert Dr. Cyril Macintosh that you will be starting the reversion process, and he'll enter you into the program. When did you want that to begin?" Naomi tapped the notes on Caprice's file on her computer.

"Well, we haven't decided the time just yet." Caprice drew Findlay's hand close and held it in the softness of her cleavage. "Maybe after *Water in the Wilderness*, the picture I'm shooting with Ryan Gosling. I'm not his love interest, but at least I'm not his mother, either. I play this...very flawed woman with a big heart."

"Congratulations. It sounds perfect for you." Naomi smiled.

"But she is going to—revert—soon?" Findlay smoothed Caprice's hair.

Caprice pulled Findlay's face to hers and kissed him. "Yes, dear. Soon. Very soon."

Naomi backed into the examination room door, holding it ajar. "Ok, just let us know when you want that to start. Oh, Caprice?"

"Yeah, Doc?"

"Thank you for everything you did for me. I couldn't have gotten through all of that without you."

"Oh, I don't know about that, Doc. From what I know about you, you're a pretty tough cookie."

Naomi smiled. "Well, in any event, it was good to have you with me. Thank you."

"Any time. But really, seriously, let's not do that again. Let's do lunch or dinner or something less stressful. Doc, any news about Bertrand?"

CHAPTER FORTY

Naomi trudged through the mud on the field toward the flurry of excited little girls hopping in the center of tires. "Where's your coach?"

"Mr. Bertrand?"

"Yes."

"Oh, he over there." Dekka, out of breath, pointed across the field to a tall figure with his arm in a sling handing water bottles to a group of girls.

"Hi."

"Hey...." Bertrand looked up, surprised to see Naomi. "Hey, you girls start your laps around the field. I've marked your bottles. They'll be here for you when you finish." Bertrand gathered the bottles from the girls, laid them on the grass beside a cooler. "I see you found me."

"I went to the hospital. They said you wouldn't stay and checked yourself out. Then I went to your condominium."

"Ah, Percy told you where I was."

"No, he didn't."

"He didn't? Then how'd you find me?"

"You weren't too hard to find. You're pretty predictable, too."

Bertrand smiled and started slowly walking down the field. He rubbed the sling-clad arm. He stepped on a stone and, with his free arm, threw it into the woods that rimmed the field.

Naomi kicked a stone from her path. "You know, you're supposed to be home resting. A ten-day recovery after a gunshot wound as severe as yours is just not enough. You're quite a lucky fellow. The doctor told me it just missed your left lung and was inches above your heart. You really should be home."

"Careful, Dr. Morninglory. Someone might mistake you for

someone who actually cares."

"Bertrand...I don't deserve that."

"You're right. I'm sorry. I didn't mean to be short. It's just that I have a treating physician. I don't need another one." He kept walking.

"I went to your dad's funeral. You were missed."

"I'm not a funeral person. I said my goodbyes." His voice lowered as he kicked another stone in his path.

"Well, you missed quite a spectacle. People inside the church jeered. There were protesters outside the church. Some were protesting that the church even held the funeral. Reverend Wood even mentioned it in the eulogy."

"Sounds like quite a circus."

"People were saying that they were glad Aspacio was dead."

"Yeah, well, what ain't caught you, ain't past you."

"What?"

"Just something my Bahamian grandma used to say." He picked up another stone and flung it toward the woods. "Roughly translated, 'Don't revel in the misfortune of others, because...you never know when...when misfortune will befall you.'"

"I see." Naomi was baffled by the moodiness that had crept between them. "Other than that, Reverend Wood did his best to give Aspacio a good funeral. I think you would have been pleased."

Bertrand glanced sideways at her and quickened his pace.

"Well, we miss you at the Center. Overbrook and Ellington asked about you. We all want to know, when are you coming back to work?"

"I've been thinking about that. You know, Aspacio was wrong about a lot of things. But I think there was one thing he was right about."

"What was that?"

"Growing up, he used to drill into me don't stir your pecker at the job."

"You know it was more than that. Much more..."

"Yeah...well...maybe...I don't know."

"This isn't still about Haron, is it? It's over between him and me."

The two continued to traverse the field until Naomi broke their silence. "In fact, if I remember correctly, there was a marriage proposal on the table." She playfully rubbed up against Bertrand.

He chafed, and then protectively stroked his swathed arm. "Over there! I see you!" he shouted to a straggling trio of girls whose strides had slowed to a walk. "This is no time to stop! You all have two more laps! Don't think I'm distracted and not counting! I'll make you do another one if you don't pick up the pace!"

By now, Bertrand and Naomi had circled the field, ending where their walk had begun. "That seems so long ago." He straightened his folding chair and retrieved more bottled waters from the cooler.

"It was just a few weeks ago. What's wrong, Bertrand?"

"It's not just Haron. It's not just Aspacio. It's not just the Center. I don't know, Naomi. Maybe it's all of these things...maybe it's none of these things."

Sheila led two small girls onto the field. "Hi, Mr. Bertrand, I'm so sorry we're late. I had to wait for this to cool." She handed him a pan of warm, late-summer-peach country cobbler. "I heard about your daddy. I'm sorry for your loss. Shequi told me about your...accident. This is guaranteed to help you heal."

"Thank you. It wasn't necessary." He lifted the foil from the pan and inhaled.

"I asked her to, Mr. Bertrand. I'm so glad you didn't get killed...like my daddy." Shequi mashed her toes clad in neon-pink sneakers into the muddy field.

"My brother got killed," N'dreishia muttered into the collar of her purple jersey. The girls ringed their arms around Bertrand, burying their small heads in his waist.

"Hey...hey, I'm glad I didn't die, too. I'm going to be fine."

Shequi wiped her eyes with the back of her hand. Sheila handed N'dreishia a tissue when she wiped her nose on her jersey and lifted a few beaded braids from inside the girl's shirt. "You see how much you mean to them."

"Well, yeah, we already did the warm-up, so you two find Dekka and do what her group is doing. Practice will be over soon."

"Okay. Oh, look, Mr. Bertrand, we friends again." Shequi

laughingly pushed her friend in front of her as she and N'dreishia ran toward Dekka and the other girls.

"Good. I want to see more of that. Now, get a move on it," he bellowed.

"I hope you enjoy it." Sheila straightened the foil around the pan. "Since practice is going to be over soon, I don't want to go home and then come right back. It seems like a waste of gas. Is it okay if I just sit right here and wait for practice to be over?"

"Sure. By all means." Bertrand removed a towel from the seat of the chair.

Naomi scrutinized Sheila as she took a seat and saw her cross legs so pretty that she should never wear trousers. Sheila settled in the folding chair, looked up at Naomi, and smiled.

"Naomi Morninglory." She held out her hand for Sheila to shake.

"Nice to meet you. I'm Sheila."

About the Author

Caryn Hines is a second-generation Washingtonian born to an accountant father with a passion for sketching and a housewife mother, who blazed her stamp on design and décor. Both Caryn and her older brother—a finance-trained artist/actor—inherited their parents' bursting creativity.

As a child, Caryn drew weekly comic strips, published monthly magazines, and splashed the walls of their family home with her reflections of the issues of the day. A vivid storyteller, her characters have always populated her dreams, and yes, to her...they are real. She fashions stories that reimagine the world by answering the question, "What if?"

When not writing, Caryn practices law, is an arbitrator, and is a professor. She lives in the Washington area with her husband.

carynlhines@gmail.com
www.thepilltrilogy.com